# the
# Way Girls

4/07

# Around the Way Girls

## Angel Hunter
## LaJill Hunt
## Dwayne S. Joseph

URBAN BOOKS LLC
www.urbanbooks.net

FIC

Urban Books LLC  342-4739
10 Brennan Place
Deer Park, NY 11729

ISBN-13: 978-1-893196-80-3
ISBN-10: 1-893196-80-1

First Mass Market Paperback printing: March 2007
10  9  8  7  6  5

*This is a work of fiction. Any references or similarities to actual events, real people, living or dead, or to real locales are intended to give the novel a sense of reality. Any similarity in other names, characters, places, and incidents is entirely coincidental.*

Submit wholesale orders to:
Kensington Publishing Corp.
c/o Penguin Group (USA) Inc.
Attention: Order Processing
405 Murray Hill Parkway
East Rutherford, NJ 07073-2316
Phone: 1-800-526-0275
Fax: 1-800-227-9604

Printed in the United States of America

# Acknowledgments

## Angel Hunter

My first acknowledgement goes to my Savior, Strength, Friend, Provider, and Advisor . . . the ALMIGHTY GOD. There is none greater.

I'd like to thank my partner and other half, Tony Irby, for the inspiration of Grape (always having my back), my niece Jasmine G. for her input "on the train", my cuz Quass for making me keep it ghetto, and my "around the way girls". To those I miss, I may have forgot you, but you're not forgotten. For your belief in me: DaNeen, Shana, Kretia. For your words of wisdom: Trina, Kelly, Angel E. For your support: Tina, Aisha, Stephanie, Tonya, Tavia, Cassandra, Gail, Lekenta. To the elder around the way girls: Barbara Jean, Norma Jean, Cora Lee and Marian LaJean.

I want to thank Carl Weber for opening the door and letting me in, for guiding the way and including me in the big things that lay ahead. You are appreciated.

I'd also like to thank my writing partners, Dwayne S. Joseph and LaJill Hunt. Together and apart, we can conquer the world. Our belief in one another and ourselves is what will keep us going.

Please note that this story is dedicated to the ex hookers, proper hoes, business women and semi-pros, ladies working to achieve more, females letting HOPE in their door; dedicated to my sisters in spirit, sisters in soul, sisters bonding, becoming whole.

To my readers . . . contact me at msangelhunter@aol. com or selfofessence@aol.com and check out my website: WWW. MSANGELHUNTER.COM

# Acknowledgments

## LaJill Hunt

I would like to thank God for His continuous mercy and favor throughout this entire process. You have opened doors for me that I never even imagined were there to be opened and I praise You for Your unconditional love.

To my husband and daughters for sacrificing the family time and understanding that to whom much is given, much is required.

To my family for all of their assistance and giving of their time as I pursue my dream.

To my friends who have always been there for me—you know who you are and what you bring to my life. I told each of you, but again, thank you.

To Pastor Kim Brown and the MLBC family—there are no words to express the appreciation I have for you.

Wherever I go, I tell people there's no place like The Mount! You are the true epitome of a church home.

To Yvette and Robilyn, you all have been my right and left hand even before *Drama Queen* dropped. I love you, I thank you, I appreciate you.

To my godson, Darius—you make me proud and are the son I always wanted. To Cheryl Pleasant for always stepping up and being there even when I needed you at the last minute. Know that your genuine love for my daughters and my family will always be treasured.

To Keith and Tasha Price, thank you for the love. Ours is a unique relationship that I don't even try to understand, just enjoy.

To my uncle and aunt, Roy and Kim Hunt, who were not mentioned in *Drama Queen*—I love you! Told you I got you in this one. Oh, Ashley Scott and Corey Hunt, I got you this time, too, lol.

To my co-authors, Angel and Dwayne, you have always been there for me. Your continual support and encouragement means so much to me. I love you.

To my editor, Martha Weber, know that you have taught me so much and it is because of your talent and skill that *Drama Queen* is the success that it is. To the beginning of a wonderful friendship! Thank you for everything—as I always tell you, you are Da Bomb!

To the talented writers that I have met over the past few months, thanks for welcoming me to your world. Shout outs especially to my friend Nikki Turner.

To the readers who have given me much love for *Drama Queen* and *A Dollar and a Dream,* thank you for the e-mails, letters and personal thoughts and letting me know that you enjoyed my writing.

Finally, to my brother, Carl Weber, for making me laugh when I wanted to cry and guiding me along the road, even when it got rocky. Know that my success is a reflection of you. I love you.

# Acknowledgments

## Dwayne S. Joseph

I would first like to thank God for giving me the gift of storytelling. It is a blessing to be able to do what I do, and I will forever be grateful.

Next, I would like to thank my beautiful wife, Wendy and my little princesses, Tatiana and Natalia. You three inspire me to make this happen. Wendy, it wouldn't be the same without you.

I would next like to thank my family: Mom, Dad, Daren, Teens & Vaughan, Granny, Grandmother. Thank you for believing and supporting. I love you guys! My in-laws Lourdes and Russell: the best! Grace, Ivan, Prianna, and Leila: much love to you all. Kirt, Mike, Aleah, Greg, Tre, Dahlia, and the rest of my cousins, aunts, uncles: thank you.

To my friends, Chris, Lisa, Jessie and Jasmine, Gregg and Kristy, Tho, Carlos, Micah and Tiffany, Mariana, Julian,

James Scott, Mike Howell, Adeena, Brian Keister and Mia, Joy Young, Julie May, Brandee Izquierdo, Sabrina Riley, Quaasmirah: thank you all for the friendship and support.

I have to give a special shout out to Heather Seegal: Heather, you showed up when others didn't, you read when you didn't have to. I am thankful and blessed to know you, Ms. Reader Extraordinaire!

Portia! Are you ready? I am. Let's do it! Thank you for EVERYTHING! Martha, you are the woman!! Thank you for helping me blow the stories up! Charles, big ups to the site. Keith, thanks for the banging cover. Yasmin Coleman from *APOOO*, Gwenn from *Cushcity.com*, Robilyn Heath (I'm ready . . . Bring it!)

To the writers who have become my close friends: Carl Weber (Inspiration extraordinaire!), La Jill Hunt (Twin and great friend), Angel Hunter (Ms. Inspirational story-teller you!), Suzette D. Harrison (Those e-mails mean a whole lot), Eric E. Pete (We've got to do one, man). To the writers I've met and who inspire me: Marcus Major (Sharing that panel was an honor), Darrren Coleman (Thanks for the advice.), RM Johnson, Karen Quinones Miller, Travis Hunter, Roy Glenn, Marc Anthony, Anthony Whyte, Eric Jerome Dickey. Thank you all for inspiring a brotha to work toward being at the top of his game.

Finally, to the book clubs and readers of my previous novel *The Choices Men Make*, and my story *One Night, Six Dreams in A Dollar And A Dream*: I hope you all enjoy this story as much as you did the others. But hold tight, because *The Womanizers* is coming to blow you all away!

And that's real! Thank you all for the e-mails and reviews. Don't stop. Keep them coming! E-mail a brotha anytime.

Djoseph21044 @yahoo.com
And check the site: www.DwayneSJoseph.com

Lastly, to the New York Giants: We have a new coach! It's time! Let's do this. And Michael Strahan: Thanks for signing my jersey!!!

Dwayne S. Joseph 12/19/03

# Busted and Disgusted

## by Angel M. Hunter

# 1

Cream was lying in the bed massaging the inside of her legs. It'd been so long since she'd had an orgasm and she felt long overdue. It was time to have a release of some sort, and what better way than sexually? Now, the sensible thing would have been to call up her man, Wise, and have him come over and scratch her itch, but his ass was missing in action. So the next best thing was the power of the hand.

Closing her eyes, she let her mind wander, trying to decide on who would be the star of her fantasy today. She'd been doing a lot of fantasizing lately. It was all good though, because more often than not, her fantasies were better than what was taking place in real life. Her man wasn't hitting it or licking it right. They were going to have a discussion about it; at least when she worked up the nerve they would.

Cream settled on Ving Rhames to be her man

tonight. She liked those big, manly men; the protection that she felt they offered. They were like a safety kit, a security blanket, better than a weapon. She thought about his broad back and how her breasts would feel pressed up against his hardened chest. Her hands would roam down the length and across the width of his muscularity, cupping that nice, round ass. She'd stand on her toes to kiss him; she'd close her eyes and get lost in the sensuality of his tongue. He would wrap his hands around her waist and pull her closer to him, pressing his manhood into her. She'd step back and place her hands on his chest, while thinking, *damn, this man has muscles in all the right places*. Moving her hands further down, she would grab his dick, a little rough, and ask him, "What would you like me to do?"

As Cream got deeper into her fantasy she relaxed her body and started to squeeze her nipples with one hand while rubbing her clitoris with her other. She rubbed and dipped her finger into her pussy, rub and dip, rub and dip, causing her vaginal walls to contract.

*Damn, this feels good,* she thought to herself.

By now, she was on her knees licking the head of Ving's dick, teasing him. She cupped his balls in her hand, rolling them around while she lowered her mouth onto him.

Cream could feel her juices flowing. It wouldn't be long before her hips were in the air and she was calling out. She could feel the pressure building up and the pace of her fingers quickened.

"Shit," she said. It took all her concentration, but when the point of no return came, it came hard and fast, causing her to call out and cover her pussy with her whole hand and squeeze.

"Ahhhh." She moaned, pleased with the outcome and with herself. Before she could get up the phone rang. She didn't want to answer it, but thought it might be Wise.

"Hello."

"Hello."

"Yes."

"This is Doctor Markus."

"Oh, hi." Cream's heart started racing. Why would he be calling her? Dr. Markus was her gynecologist.

"I have the results of your pregnancy test. You're pregnant! You're pregnant! You're pregnant!" Although he didn't say it that many times, that's how she heard it, with an echo effect.

Cream couldn't believe what she'd heard. If she was a child, she would have covered her ears to replace the words with something other than what the doctor was saying.

Shit! How could this be happening? How could she have been so stupid? Why was she so stupid as to let that no-dick-having, no stamina, can't-fuck-me-right-anymore, won't-kiss-the-pussy-unless-I-beg-and-plead, ex- (or so he claimed) drug dealer impregnate her? Was it because she thought she was still in love with him? Was it because she was still with him out of habit, comfort and security? The one night she believed she might have gotten pregnant was the night the sex was better than it had been in a long time. She could kick herself in the ass.

Wise just wasn't there for her like he used to be.

For one, she believed something was going on with him. She believed he'd been lying to her. About what, she wasn't sure. When she asked him he didn't admit to anything; not that he would, because there was no real evidence, so why tell on himself? All she had was hearsay and someone constantly calling her phone and hanging up. That shit was getting on her last nerve.

First thing tomorrow morning she would call the phone company and get caller ID. It was a damn shame that she even had to go that route. Whoever was calling would disguise their voice and say "Bitch" or "Whore." The caller sometimes wouldn't say anything, just breathe into the phone. This only happened when she answered. When her son, Shacquille, or Shala, her cousin who she was caring for answered, the caller would hang up. So she knew it was personal. Something was going on and she was determined to get to the bottom of it.

Irritated, pissed off and horny was not the combination to be. Horny because lately Wise hadn't been hitting it right, if at all. The last time, his dick didn't even stay hard. What the hell was that about? Just the sight of her naked used to turn him on. Irritated because she didn't want to be pregnant; she already had a six-year-old. Another child this late in the game would be out of the question and just not something she planned on. That's why she should have gotten her damn tubes tied. Pissed off because Wise was nowhere to be found when she needed him. His ass was always running off, talking about he's taking care of business. He'd better be out there looking for a job and not standing on the corner selling that cocaine shit.

\* \* \*

Cream's body was tight, not an ounce of fat on her. It was all due to genetics. She was one of the top strippers at High Rollers gentlemen's club. She could shake it, shiver it, move it and groove it with the best of them. Niggas requested her when she wasn't there; they would ask for her the second they walked in the door. She made the most in tips, and in all actuality she didn't have to work as hard as the other girls to get them. Lapdancing? Oh hell, no. She definitely wasn't doing that. Little did she know that was part of her appeal. They liked that whole hands-off mystique: you can look but you can't touch. She wasn't raunchy. She was sexy, and the men picked up on that shit. They knew who to fuck with and disrespect and who to treat like a lady.

Cream was hands-off for two reasons. One was her man, Wise Allah. No one fucked with him or his property. That's how women in the ghetto were viewed—as some man's property. The men in the club knew that if they violated this rule they might catch a bullet or two. They also knew that Grape, the bouncer at the door, was protective when it came to Cream.

One time, a customer who was new in town went a little too far. After Cream finished dancing, he cornered her and started groping. Before she could let out a sound, he was picked up by his throat and thrown out of the club, never to be seen again. Normally Grape would step in, make a threat and then proceed with violence if the rules were broken again, but for Cream he went straight to violence. The other dancers noticed this inequality but didn't say a word. High Rollers was an exclusive club and they knew that there weren't many options out there that provided rich men and a clean environment.

Cream White was her real name and Shacquille was the son of Wise. They'd been together now for seven years, since she was seventeen and spotted him in a picture.

Thinking back, she laughed and went to her dresser, pulling out the picture that had caught her eye. It was old as hell and he was looking like a don, wearing a Gucci leather suit and tons of gold around his neck. It was taken in the eighties. Today he wouldn't have gotten away with wearing it without being considered country. But back then, it gave him that gangsta thug look. It appealed to her immediately.

He was standing next to a red Jeep Cherokee with the doors off and the top down, one foot up on the ledge. He even had a joint in his hands. His hair was in waves that were thick and noticeable. He sported a goatee. His expression said, "I'm the motherfucking man, and who are you?" He knew that it was all about him, and Cream knew it too. That's why she asked Tina, the girl who had the picture, "Who is that?"

"Girl, that's my cousin, Wise." Laughing, she touched the picture and said, "He thinks he's something, doesn't he?"

*He is,* Cream thought to herself. To Tina she said, "You didn't tell me you had a fine ass cousin."

"That's because you never asked me."

"When are you gonna see him again?"

Hearing the curiosity in Cream's voice, Tina looked at her and asked, "Why?"

"Because."

"Because what?" Tina liked Cream but wasn't sure she was girlfriend material for a family member. She didn't really know much about her.

"Well, I'd like to meet him."

"Well," Tina started. She was thinking that maybe Cream couldn't be all that bad. Heck, she couldn't be any worse than the knuckleheads Wise was usually bringing around now. "We're having a cookout Sunday. You can come if you want to and I'll introduce you to him. That's all I'm gonna do; introduce you. You're on your own after that."

"Bet." Cream thanked her, and in her mind she started planning what she would wear.

That Sunday took long as hell to arrive and Cream made sure she looked her best. She knew that Wise belonged to the Five-Percent Nation, so he considered women to be queens. With that in mind, she set aside the hoochie outfit and replaced it with something more befitting a respectable queen. She wore a long, white, form-fitting jean skirt that skimmed her ankles, and a white tank top that accentuated her 34C's without looking cheap. *Please, don't let me spill anything on myself,* she silently prayed. She also had on white, flat sandals. Her hair was out and curled, flowing down her shoulders. Instead of wearing the bright red lipstick she loved to wear, she put on lip-gloss.

During the days leading up to the barbecue, she'd done some investigating and found out that Wise was five years older than her and one of the most popular drug dealers in the area. He had a couple of women, but no one he considered his main girl. Cream would make it her business to change that, and she did it well. Now it was seven years after that first meeting, and they had a six-year-old son together and possibly another on the way. Now ain't that some shit.

Why wasn't she sure she wanted to carry this child to term? Well, for one, Wise already had three kids besides Shacquille—two before his birth and one after. He had gotten someone pregnant while he and Cream were together. That was someplace she didn't want her mind to travel. She'd made her choice to forgive and stay with him when she found out. Now, don't get it twisted. She caused a scene, kicked his ass, put the pussy on lock down. Staying with him was easier said than done, but she did it. Devastated and all, she did it.

Sometimes she regretted being so crazy and in love. That was another reason she wasn't sure about keeping this baby. She wasn't in love with Wise anymore, not the way she used to be. That love that will make you do crazy things—stay up all night and wait on a nigga; that love that will have you in tears and going against yourself; that love that steals your soul and leaves it out to play. Shit, that was the love that had allowed her to accept his betrayal. Now, she loved her baby's daddy, but she just wasn't in love with him anymore. She loved him the day she met him and would always love him, but like Tina Turner says, what's love got to do with it? Cream knew the answer: Not a damn thing.

How would Wise react to her being pregnant? Cream recalled one night they were laying up in the bed talking and he said something to the effect that he didn't think he wanted any more children. That four was enough.

"Then get a vasectomy," Cream told him.

"Why don't you get your tubes tied?"

Cream looked at him like he'd lost all of his mind.

"Why are you looking at me like that? How are you gonna stand there and act like you want more kids? You told me you didn't."

"Well, I might have changed my mind."

"Anyway," he said, "Shacquille is six. The way I figure it, if you were going to have more, you would have done it by now."

Cream ignored him because she didn't know whether she wanted more or not. What if they broke up and she found another who loved her deeply and she loved just as much and he wanted kids? If she got her tubes tied that couldn't happen.

There were many cons to this whole pregnancy thing. She'd yet to think of the pros. Would she continue stripping? Cream had seen some girls stripping right up until the sixth month with their bellies protruding. She knew that would not be the case with her. That was straight up trifling. But once she stopped, how would she pay for Shacquille's private school? She and Wise had some money stashed, but how long would that last? Would he resort to selling drugs again? That is, if he wasn't still selling them now.

Damn, shit was all fucked up, or at least it was about to be. Putting on her black leather trench coat and matching hat, she took a quick look in the mirror. She liked what she saw; a five foot, four-inch, 120-pound woman who still had a glow to her. There was one thing the ghetto didn't take from her and that was her looks. She had watched her mother go to waste and was extra careful not to let that happen to her. Grabbing her bag filled with stripper gear, she walked out of the rented house. *One day I'll have my own,* she'd tell herself each month when the rent was due. She was tired of letting her money go to waste.

Glancing at her watch, she was glad she would be getting to the club a little early. Her fifteen-year-old cousin Shala had said she was going to a girlfriend's and Shacquille was staying the night with one of his classmates, so Cream would hang out a little while with Grape at the club. It was Thursday. Thursday was moneymaking night. All the ballers, white and black, came out.

# 2

Cream pulled up in front of High Rollers. She was driving a silver Lexus coupe. It was a damn shame it wasn't hot enough to have the top down, but Fall was coming to an end. There weren't any parking spots in front so she drove to the lot behind, grabbing her signature lightly tinted Versace glasses. She strutted inside with her head up and her shoulders back, adapting her club persona, her I'm-the-baddest-bitch-don't-fuck-with-me-or-you-will-get-fucked attitude. No, she wasn't being aggressive with her shit. She just liked to let everyone know that she was 100% woman. Actually, those that were close to her knew she was just the opposite. She was the sweetest one in the club with the biggest heart and the kindest personality. If one of the other strippers barely made enough to feed her kids then she would hit them off with a few dollars. She was always baking and bringing desserts in for

Grape. That was her way of thanking him. If she had to, she'd work the bar and watch the door. Everyone called her the manager of the joint. It was an unofficial position. That was also one of the reasons she got away with not doing lap dances.

All kind of deals went down in the club—drug deals, gambling deals, but mostly sex deals. Sex for money, money for sex, oral, vaginal, sometimes even anal. It was a well-known secret which girls would do what in the back rooms. As long as it stayed a secret. It was like the motto at AA and NA meetings: What's said in this room stays in this room. It helped that some of the best customers were cops also, so if there were going to be a bust the club owners would get a warning and shit would be correct for a week or two: no sex in the building.

It was so easy to get caught up in that lifestyle. Too easy. Once a girl got a hold of the dough, she'd spend it and want more and more. It was a never-ending cycle. That was one of the reasons Cream was in the game for so long. But she was starting to realize that money wasn't always gonna make her happy. She wanted out now.

Thankfully, she'd never turned tricks. She'd seen too many girls get caught up. They'd get hooked on a man, hooked on drugs and hooked on crime, on a man's time and making that dime. Some were hurt mentally, some physically, a lot spiritually, and she refused to be one of those. She wasn't trying to take a chance. She had a son to take care of. Her little man meant the world to her and she wanted the best for him. On the few occasions when she did let her mind roam, wondering what it would be like to live the life of a true hustler and not just an around the way girl, she thought of her son.

*Boom!* Her eyes would open real quick at that thought. *Does Shacquille know what his mommy does?* She told him she worked at a bar. It wasn't the whole truth but it wasn't a full lie either. Did it really matter if she planned on quitting sooner rather than later? She wanted to in the worst way and as the days, weeks and months passed she envisioned it. She wanted to go back to school, get her GED, possibly become a nurse, maybe even a teacher. She wasn't sure what just yet. Whatever it was, she knew it would service the people.

How did she get into the strip game in the first place? How did her man allow it? Life threw her some mean curves, for one thing, and for another, it wasn't up to no man. It was up to her. Cream did what she had to do in order to survive. She wasn't left with many options. In this life, sometimes you're not. Sometimes you have to step outside of yourself and play the by-any-means-necessary game. That's just what she did when her mother died.

Cream's mother died of AIDS when she was thirty-one and Cream was sixteen. She caught it from her long-term boyfriend. Cream never knew her daddy. All she knew was that his name was Lewis. That wasn't unusual, at least not in her Brooklyn neighborhood, which was full of on-welfare, drug-infested, single family homes and babies raising babies. Hell, here nothing came as a surprise. She grew up used to seeing all kinds of things.

When her mother died, there was no one to step up to the plate to raise Cream or her cousin Shala, who was living with them. Shala's mom was in jail for armed robbery. The rest of the family lived down South. Being sixteen and streetwise, there was no way Cream was going down there. She didn't even know those people and she doubted they wanted to know her. Hell, no one even showed up for her mother's cremation, although they sent a little—a very little—money. It was devastating. There stood Cream, Shala, and a couple of people from the church her mother had joined shortly before her death. Not one additional family member in sight. It would have been embarrassing had it not been for the pain.

The realization that her mother was dead tore Cream apart. They had been close; they could talk about everything from the weather to boys. They were poor in cash but rich in love. When her mother died, it left a void in her life. She often thought she would fall through it. So many nights she just wanted to give up.

But Cream knew she had to make a decision for herself and Shala, who was still a toddler. It was either be on their own or go to foster care, and that she didn't want to do. She could just imagine her and Shala being separated and sent to abusive families. So many bad things could happen in the system, and she didn't want to find out.

So she did what she had to do and went to one of the local strip joints to see if she'd qualify for a job. She'd overheard some girls on the train talking about how much money they made from stripping.

"Girl, I made over two hundred dollars in three hours."

"Shit, that ain't nothing. Come to LaLa's and you can double that, especially on a Friday night."

Cream made plans to check out this place called LaLa's on the upcoming Friday. Running low on funds, she had to do what she had to do. After begging the neighbor to watch Shala, Cream put on the hoochiest outfit she could find: a black mini-skirt that barely reached past her ass, a too-tight T-shirt and a pair of her mother's heels. Looking in the mirror, she thought she looked like a slut and almost changed her mind. Then she remembered that the alternative was foster care so she headed out the door.

When she walked in the club, she freaked out. It was a straight up nasty dive. It even possessed a rancid odor. It was dark and there were drunken men everywhere. They were staring so hard at her that she felt frightened. Gathering her strength, she refused to leave. This wasn't about ego and pride, it was about having a roof over her and Shala's head. It was about having food to eat.

"Yo, can I get you a drink?" a strange man asked with liquor on his breath.

Knowing she should say no, she said yes, thinking it would loosen her up some. She ordered a shot of Stoli. She'd remembered her mother saying that's what her father drank. The burning sensation almost caused her to throw up.

Watching one of the dancers on stage, Cream thought to herself, *I have a better body than her, and look at these nasty ass men giving up all the money. I could make a killing.* She watched the girl's every move, trying to memorize each one.

"So, you dance here?" asked the man who bought her the drink.

"No."

"You should, 'cause you're one hot mama." Spit was spraying out of his mouth.

Moving back, Cream asked, "Do you know where the manager is?"

He pointed toward the back of the room and said, "You see the little nigger, the one with the Lakers cap? That's him."

Looking in the direction he had pointed, Cream spotted a Gary Coleman lookalike.

"Excuse me." She climbed off her seat. The man had the nerve to try to touch her ass. She caught his hand just in time.

After introducing herself to the manager and putting up with his stinking breath, they agreed that she would try out the following week. Of course he made her turn around and bend over, shake her ass and show him her breasts. By the time she was done she wanted to burst into tears, but she knew this was no time for crying. She needed to get home and practice her moves. She did this every day for a week.

The following week when she went to try out, the second she climbed on stage and one man touched her, she burst into tears.

"If you can't take it, honey, you need to get to stepping."

"What are you, a punk?"

"Come on! Show us your pussy. Don't be scared."

"Let me dry those tears for you, baby. I'll take care of you if you suck my dick."

The comments were ruthless. Cream knew there was no way in hell she could go through with it. She was just going to have to turn herself in to Social Services. She was running out of money and needed to do something quick.

Later that night in bed, she thought about Boss, one of the local drug dealers. He also owned a restaurant that she used to frequent with her mother. He was always checking her out. Whenever he saw her he'd pull over and ask her if he could take her out to dinner or to a concert. She always told him no because he was at least twenty-eight and that was too old. She was also scared of him. It was rumored that he was a killer. Whether it was true or not didn't matter. The thought alone frightened her.

After her mother passed she still went to his restaurant and he still tried to get with her. His woman Chris, knowing Cream was on her own, would only charge her if there were other customers around. So here was this lady being all sweet to her, and Chris' man was trying to get with her. There was no way Cream could disrespect Chris like that.

At least that's what she thought. When she started owing on the rent, the respect issue went out the window. Knowing that stripping just wasn't for her, Cream quit school and started working at Denny's. To make ends meet, she moved with Shala into an efficiency apartment where the rent was lower. It was heartbreaking to leave the place she grew up in. And on top of everything else, she had to sell some of her mother's jewelry and clothing. If something didn't happen soon, she didn't know what she would do. Struggling at the age of sixteen was one thing, but struggling with a toddler was something else all together.

Well, her prayers were answered. One morning Boss came into Denny's. He'd spotted her walking in and decided that he wanted to pursue her actively. The second he walked in the door he asked to be seated at one of her tables.

"Hey, sexy," he greeted.

"Hey there." Cream wondered why he was eating at a place other than his own.

"So this is why I haven't seen you around my restaurant."

"Yep, this is it. Do you want to place an order?"

"No, all I want is you."

Cream was about to walk away when she thought about her near-poverty state and decided to go for it. Even though he was older, it wasn't by much. Girls her age in the neighborhood were dealing with men in their late twenties and early thirties every day.

"Listen, I've got to finish working. How about you pick me up from work around five and we talk?"

"I can do that. Take my pager number and page me when you're ready." He stood.

"Wait. Don't you want to place an order?"

"No. I just came in here to see you." He pulled a wad of money out of his pocket and peeled a fifty off the roll. "This should cover the meal and your tip."

He placed the money on the table and walked

away. Cream looked at the money then back at him and knew that by taking the money she was sealing the deal. She picked it up and placed it in her pocket.

That's how their affair began. That evening he picked her up. While they were driving around she decided to ask him about Chris.

"Why you wanna know about her? She's my lady."

"If she's your lady, why are you tryin'a take me out?"

At this point, he pulled over and faced her. "Listen, Cream. You know that I've been watching you for some time and you also know my game. You know what I do. You know I can take care of you. I know you're on your own and you have a child."

"That's my cousin."

"Whatever. I know you're struggling. I'm in a position to help you out. Let me."

Cream was a virgin, and she knew that if she accepted his proposition then she wouldn't be for long. Still, she accepted it. The night she lost her virginity was the night she attended her first concert. Boss took her to see Rob Base and Doug E. Fresh. She had the time of her life.

"It takes two to make a thing go right." She was singing in the car, laughing, joking and just having a good time. The first she'd had since her mother's death.

Looking over at her, Boss made his decision to take her to the Sheraton. He'd been spending his money on her, supporting her and her cousin for over a month, and still hadn't gotten the pussy. He was tired of being patient. He had a surprise for her, too. He'd gotten her an apartment and would give her the keys in the parking lot. That way she'd feel obligated to give up the pussy.

"You had a good time tonight?" Boss asked while pulling into the parking lot of the Sheraton.

Cream noticed where they were, but decided not to comment on it. She knew this day would be coming soon enough. He'd been paying the rent on their efficiency and had gotten her a babysitter for Shala on numerous occasions. "Isn't it obvious?" she answered.

"Yeah. I'm glad. Now we're going to have a better time."

Cream's heart was in her throat. She'd never been this scared in her life. She didn't have many friends, at least not since her mom passed, and the only person she really associated with was Tina, one of the other waitresses in Denny's. They didn't talk about sex much, so she didn't know what to expect. Would it be painful? Would it be pleasurable? Would she see fireworks? Would she cry? Should she tell him that she was a virgin? Maybe then he would decide to wait. Yeah, that was the way to go.

No such luck.

Taking Boss' hand, Cream looked him in the eyes and said, "I need to tell you something before we go inside."

"Wait. Before you tell me anything, I have a surprise for you." He reached into his pocket and pulled out a set of keys.

"What's this for?"

"I've set you up in an apartment."

Cream was stunned. The only words she could manage were "Thank you."

"Now, what is it you have to tell me?" He wished she'd hurry up and spit it out. He'd waited too long and couldn't wait to get in her drawers.

Clearing her throat, she told him, "I'm a virgin."

This shocked the shit out of him. After all, he thought she was at least nineteen. He'd never bothered to ask her age. "You're a what?" He couldn't believe his luck. There were no virgins in this day and age, at least none in the hood above the age of thirteen.

"A virgin," she repeated.

Pulling his hand away, he asked, "How old are you?"

She almost told him the truth, that she was sixteen, but she didn't want to turn him completely away. She still needed what he was offering—support and cash. "I'm seventeen and a half."

"Seventeen and a half," he repeated. "When will you be eighteen?"

"Next month." That was almost true. Her birthday was coming up. She'd just be turning seventeen.

Boss had to think. She wasn't eighteen yet. Not quite. But she was on her own, practically a woman, taking care of a child. And still a virgin. He couldn't decide if it was worth it. He believed that once a girl lost her virginity to a man, she would become his stalker, and if Chris got wind of Cream, all hell would break loose. At the same time, he was feeling Cream. She made him feel like a man, like the king. She listened to what he said, she didn't go out, she either went to work or stayed home. He didn't have to question her. She was sexy as hell, always looked and smelled good. Fuck it. He didn't plan on using her or discarding her. He planned for Cream to be his for a long time.

"For some reason I thought you were older and more experienced."

"I'm not."

What's a guy to do? Unlocking the car doors, he said, "It'll be alright. I promise to be gentle."

*Shit.* She really thought she was going to get out of that one. Opening the door, she climbed out of the seat and met him behind the car. "I'm scared."

"Don't be. Haven't I taken care of you for the past month or so?"

They were walking side by side. "Yes."

"And I'll take care of you tonight." Just the thought of getting this virgin pussy was making his dick harder and harder. It took everything in his power to contain himself and not grab his dick while they were walking.

Once inside the room, Cream tried to act nonchalant. She sat on the bed and he sat next to her. They started kissing, slow and gentle at first, the way they'd been doing since the beginning. They'd gone as far as to caress each other through their clothes, but that was all. He'd always wondered why she made excuses when it came down to the nitty gritty. Excuses like, "My period is on." That one lasted a week. "I'm sore," or, "I think I have a yeast infection." Now he knew what all the excuses were about. He hadn't tried to pressure her and he was glad now.

As he reached up to unbutton her shirt, she put her hands on his and said, "I need to shower first."

He knew she was procrastinating, but he let her. "Okay. I'll take it with you."

"No, I want to take it by myself. You can go after me."

"Fine," he told her, even though it wasn't. He would wait however long he had to for her to get comfortable, as long as it was tonight that it happened.

In the bathroom, Cream turned on the shower and leaned over the sink, looking in the mirror. She said to herself, "I will no longer be a virgin after tonight." She took a deep breath and tried to collect her thoughts. She wasn't saving herself for any particular reason; she just hadn't had that many boyfriends. Besides, watching her mother grow ill with a sexually transmitted disease was enough to turn her off. Plus, everywhere she looked, girls her age were having babies and she didn't want to be like them.

Opening the bathroom door, she yelled out, "Do you have condoms?"

*Do I have condoms?* Boss couldn't believe she was asking him that. He wasn't wearing no fucking condom. He wanted to feel that tight pussy raw. "No. What we need condoms for? You're a virgin."

"Yeah, but you're not." She decided at that moment: no condom, no sex. And she meant it. If she had to run out of the hotel room kicking and screaming she would do so. "I'm not having sex without one."

He couldn't believe her. He was about to protest when he remembered that her mother had died of AIDS. *Damn it!* Getting up off the bed he yelled, "I'll be right back." He went downstairs to the store in the hotel and bought the thinnest condoms he could find.

When he returned she was just getting out of the shower. She walked into the bedroom with a towel wrapped around her and sat on the bed. "Your turn to shower."

Cream's first time was not what she thought it would be. First of all, once Boss saw her naked, extensive foreplay went out the window. He must have kissed her for all of five minutes before he put the condom on, climbed on top of her and pushed her legs open. She wasn't even that wet when he tried to put it in.

"Wait, wait. What are you doing?"

"I'm trying to make love to you."

"No, you're rushing me, Boss. Slow down." She started crying. "It hurts."

Ignoring the tears, he told her, "Come on, baby, it's your first time. It's supposed to hurt." On that note he pushed himself inside her.

Crying, she lay there and let him do his thing for all of five minutes. It hurt like hell. She was bleeding and he was coming.

When he was done, he said to her, "You're mine now."

After that fiasco, she didn't plan on being his for much longer. There was no way in hell she wanted to endure this so-called lovemaking. Unfortunately, it was a harder challenge to leave him than she thought because of what he offered her.

The sex between them didn't get any better. She refused to suck his dick, which pissed him off. And he was always rough with her. She wondered what made women chase after him, why Chris and the other female he was seeing—whom he didn't know Cream knew about—saw in him. It had to be the money and the status that came with being his girl. Cream didn't care for the status because she was supposed to be a secret anyway, but each time she let him invade her, he would give her a large sum of money. He was still paying her bills and had even purchased her a little Toyota. She was practically selling the pussy and she knew it.

What brought them to an end was fate. He got locked up. Feeling obligated, she went to the jail to visit him, only to be confronted by Chris. They actually had a full fledged, fist-throwing fight in the parking lot, and when Boss learned of it, he didn't even take up for her. That was the breaking point. It wasn't the bad sex, it wasn't his getting locked up. It was the fact that when she almost got her ass whipped, he didn't handle it.

Instead, his response was: "Well, what do you want me to say? You knew about her. I told you we had to be undercover. Chris is my main bitch. She's been with me through thick and thin."

Cream couldn't believe what she was hearing; he was saying it like it shouldn't be a big deal, like she was just supposed to put up with the nonsense. He thought that just because she'd given up her virginity to him that she was going to take his trash. Well, he had another think coming. First of all, she had a little money saved. Each time he gave her money, she would put the majority of it in the bank. Also, she had kept her job at the restaurant. Each time he had tried to get her to quit, she'd refused. She made plans to move out of his apartment so she wouldn't owe him anything anymore. It was shortly afterward that she met Wise.

# 3

It was a Thursday night, busy as usual, and Grape was standing by the bar. He spotted his Cream the second she walked in. That's just what he called her, My Cream. He loved that girl; he was very protective of her. It wasn't a sisterly love, either. He wanted her to be his woman but settled on being her friend.

They'd tried the boyfriend/girlfriend, let's-be-intimate thing once when Cream and Wise had broken up, but it didn't work out. They didn't have that chemistry together. He had it for her; she just didn't reciprocate the way he would have liked. Maybe under different circumstances they may have been more, but she still had Wise in her system. He tried everything in his power to get Wise out of her memory but to no avail. She had his son, and once a woman has a man's child, it's hard for any other person who comes along. He knew this and accepted it.

The way he saw it, Wise would eventually mess up again. He was an asshole who took advantage of Cream. Grape would wait his turn. It was bound to happen. Cream would someday see him for what he was. She was getting older and her needs would change. When that happened, Grape would be right there to pick up the pieces.

"Hey, sweetheart." Cream greeted him with a hug and kiss on the cheek. "What's up?"

Grape put in a little squeeze and held her for a second longer than he should have. "Nothing."

She didn't mind. She was aware of how he felt and he never disrespected her or tried anything. He was there for her when she needed an ear and a shoulder, and he would have to be there for her tonight. She definitely needed someone to talk to.

"It's crowded as usual and your man is in the back." He wanted to add that she needed to go see what his shifty ass was doing. There was something up with him. Grape didn't know what it was. He couldn't pinpoint it, but he would find out, and then expose him when he did. Then Cream could be his.

Grape had been in love with Cream from day one, the minute he met her. That was at LaLa's. He was there the day she auditioned. When he saw her bust out in tears during her audition, he knew that she didn't belong. He wanted to help her out in any way he could. Working in LaLa's was beneath her. He never met her that day, but he never forgot her.

When Cream told Tina that she was thinking of quitting the restaurant to start stripping, Tina tried to talk her out of it.

"Girl, you ain't working in that hell hole."

"How do you know about it?"

"One of my boys work at a couple of spots. LaLa's is one of them. Maybe he can get you someplace better. That place ain't safe. You ain't hear about that girl getting gang banged in the bathroom?"

"I did hear about it."

"Well, you need to rethink that shit. My boy's name is Grape. I'll introduce you to him."

When Tina bought Cream to Grape, he recognized her immediately. He'd already checked out her size 8, curvy, no stretch marks, no scars or signs of abuse body. So he became her manager of sorts. He knew she was a potential moneymaker and he wanted to get to know her. "Listen, I work at different clubs. Most are exclusive, meaning upscale. Where I go, I'll take you with me. How's that?"

At first Cream was a little suspicious. Why was this brother being so nice to her? What did he want from her? Probably some pussy. Instead of second-guessing, she asked him, "And what do I have to give you in return? I'm not fucking you."

Grape laughed at her bluntness and he told her, "I'm not asking you to fuck me, although it would be nice. I like you. You're a friend of Tina's and well, she doesn't recommend just anybody to me."

So their friendship began. When she hooked up with Wise, Grape was devastated but held it in and continued to be her friend, listening when she needed an ear.

The first time they made love, he felt a little guilty. It was when she found out that Wise had gotten someone else pregnant and he took advantage of her vulnerability. Actually, the first time they made love, it was strictly for her. He tried to eat her pussy dry, licking the walls and putting his tongue as far up in her as he could. He knew he was doing a hell of a job, too, because soon her tears and heartache turned into, "Dell, oh, Dell." That was his real name and only a few people were privileged enough to know it.

Grape was the owner of High Rollers. Working in strip clubs for a number of years as a bouncer, a bartender, and the manager, he had learned a thing or two. When he had enough money saved he opened his own spot. No one knew he was the owner, and that was just the way he wanted to keep it. That way people would do things in front of him they normally wouldn't, would say things and try to handle business in front of him, and he would know who to let in and who not to let in.

"Who's in the back with Wise?" Cream asked Grape.

"Amber."

"Oh, okay." Amber was her girl. She didn't have anything to worry about. But let it have been another bitch and she would have been speedwalking toward them.

Cream walked through the crowd, past the bar and dance floor, which was surrounded by lights and filled with dancers.

"Hey, girl."

"What's up, sexy?"

"You dancing tonight?"

"Let me buy you a drink."

Several people greeted Cream, and although it felt good to be one of the most popular dancers, she knew she had to get out of this hustle. She was getting too old for this shit, too old to keep lying to her child. She was also setting a bad example for Shala.

Shala knew what Cream was doing for a living. Cream had tried to keep it a secret, but in the hood, nothing is a secret. They were sitting at the kitchen table when Shala told Cream she knew what was up. "I know you're a stripper," she blurted out.

"What are you talking about?" Cream wasn't ready to 'fess up to it.

"I've known for some time. How come you kept lying to me instead of just telling me? I'm a teenager now. I'm not dumb."

Cream didn't even try to play it off. She told Shala, "I never said you were. I just didn't think it was any of your concern."

That hurt Shala's feelings and she let Cream know. She also reminded her that Cream always said they were a team and a team stuck together and shared the game plan. Shala wanted to know how Cream could try to teach her about respecting her body when she wasn't doing it.

Cream knew that Shala was right, so she had to come up with a plan fast. Moving toward the back, past the pinball machines and pool tables, she opened the door to the VIP room. Wise was there, talking to Amber. Cream stood back for a few seconds and just watched their interaction. Something didn't feel right. Glancing around the room, she saw three other people in there. One man was getting a lap dance and one of the bouncers was smoking weed. They weren't paying Amber and Wise any mind.

Cream looked at them and noticed they were sitting too close. Every time Wise would say something, Amber would laugh and touch his arm, laugh and touch his leg. It seemed a little too intimate. Cream couldn't help wondering what the hell that was all about. *Nah, I'm just tripping,* Cream told herself, but when Amber's hand went a little too high up Wise's leg, she stepped in the room.

"What the fuck is this?"

They both jumped.

"What the fuck is what?" Amber asked.

"Your hand was almost on his dick," Cream accused.

"Girl, please. I know you ain't standing there accusing me of anything."

Cream looked at Wise and waited for him to say something. "What, you ain't got nothing to say?"

"No," Wise answered her. "Other than you must be seeing things. The girl just touched my leg."

Looking at Amber she said, "Well, her hands really shouldn't be on your body. How she like it if I was all up on her man? Oops, she doesn't have a man."

"You know what?" Amber started. "I'm gonna leave you two alone. Maybe y'all need to talk. Cream, you should know that I wouldn't try to press up on your man, so you need to take it down a notch or two. If you're having a bad day, then you're having a bad day. Why you got to take the shit out on me?"

Cream didn't respond. She just watched Amber leave the room and then she tore into Wise. "Why are you always up in Amber's face? Are you fucking her or something?"

"Whoa, whoa. Why I got to be fucking somebody? We were just talking."

"I'm not stupid. It looked like more."

"Well, it wasn't. Amber's your girl. I'm your man. We wouldn't do that to you."

Cream looked him in the face. She wanted so bad to believe what he was saying. Maybe her emotions were getting the best of her. Amber was cool. She never even commented on Wise like the other girls who said things like, "You've got a fine ass man, girl. You better watch him."

Cream wanted so bad to tell him that she was pregnant. She had to first make the decision about what she wanted to do. Could she go through with an abortion? She wasn't too sure. She'd had one two years before and it was the worst experience of her life. She still felt guilty about it. Of course Wise didn't know. The only person who knew was Grape. He went with her and stayed by her side. Damn, he was a good friend. She wanted to tell him about this pregnancy as well, but she felt stupid for letting it happen again. He'd probably think she was careless. Cream knew he didn't care for Wise. She could see it in his eyes when he was watching them. Hell, she didn't have to see it in his eyes.

"You could do so much better than that knucklehead," he always told her. "What do you see in him anyway? He should have married you by now."

Cream knew he was right, but she had his son and she never thought she would be without the father of her child. She didn't want to go out like her mother and have her child be without his father. She knew how she felt growing up: like a part of her was missing, like she didn't totally belong. She'd tried to get her mother to talk to her about her father, but other than his name, she wouldn't give up any information. She didn't want that for her son, so no matter how much drama Wise brought to her life, she was determined to try to stay with him.

**4**

A few minutes before the time Cream was to appear on stage, she felt the urge to vomit. She ran into the bathroom. Thankfully no one was in there, which in itself was a rare occurrence. She went into the stall, closed the door and started to throw up. It was a good thing she always carried a small toothbrush.

"Who's in there?" someone called out.

Taking some tissue and wiping her mouth, Cream called out, "It's me." She stepped out of the stall and saw Amber.

"Oh, girl, are you okay?"

"Did I sound okay?" Cream was still pissed with Amber for being all close up on Wise.

Amber put her hands on her hips and said, "You know what, Cream? You really need to take it down. I don't know what your problem is, but you've been snappy for the past week and you're taking it out on the wrong person. So instead of being an ass, you need to know that I'm here for you. I'm your friend and whatever is bothering you, whatever has you bugging, I just might be able to help you out with it."

Amber was straight lying. She didn't want to help anyone out. She was for self all the time. Amber was from the poorest projects. Her grandmother, a stone cold alcoholic, raised her. Amber couldn't remember a time when she didn't see her with a drink in her hand or smelling like liquor. Amber used to be so embarrassed when she had company and her grandmother would come in the room. She'd start singing and dancing, cutting up a storm, stumbling and not making any sense.

Amber had three sisters and she was the youngest. They moved out as soon as they were able to, so she always felt alone. Even when they lived together, her sisters stayed gone. Amber had to learn to look out for self. She was smart in school and capable of college. She just wasn't encouraged, so she chose the fast life, the money life. A quick dollar is what she wanted and she would make it however she could.

If it meant sleeping with Tom, Dick and Harry, then she would. If it meant making up some kind of scam or being a part of one, then she would. Amber knew how to separate the pussy from the heart.

She didn't have many friends and cared for very few people unless they could look out or do something substantial for her. Her friendship with Cream was because Cream had something she didn't, something she wanted. It was respect, an aura and an innocence. Cream had that "It" quality. When she walked into a room, all heads turned. Amber noticed it the first time they met. She noticed it when they went places together. When she was traveling solo, she might get a glance or two, but when she was with Cream, niggas would step up to the plate and offer all kinds of gifts.

Amber wanted to have that rub off on her. She made friends with Cream hoping to gain her trust and learn her secret. She didn't realize that it wasn't a secret. It was just who Cream was. It was a part of her being.

When Amber walked into the bathroom and heard someone throwing up, she knew it was Cream. She had spotted her shoes under the door. All week, Cream had been acting like a bitch. What Amber really wanted to do was punch her in the face and tell her to get a fucking grip, that she wasn't the only one in the world with problems. She restrained herself because she knew that would be foul. Besides, she knew that if she fought Cream, Wise would kick her ass.

She couldn't have that, because she wanted Wise to keep giving her the dick as often as possible. And even that wasn't often enough.

"Are you pregnant or something?" Amber asked Cream.

This caught Cream off guard. How could she possibly know? "What are you talking about?" She started brushing her teeth.

"You've been moody, treating me like a stepchild

instead of a friend, you're in here throwing up, you haven't had a drink yet. I know you, Cream. Usually by now you've had at least one drink."

"Just because I'm not drinking doesn't mean I'm pregnant."

Amber knew she was onto something because of the look on Cream's face. She had three sisters. She knew the symptoms. She also knew the look of a liar, since she was such a good one. "You can tell me. I'm not going to say anything."

Rinsing her mouth out and popping a mint in her mouth, Cream told Amber, "We'll talk later. I have a show to do." She walked out, leaving Amber standing there.

Cream knew she had a decision to make. She also knew she couldn't wait long, because if she decided to keep the baby, she would have to tell Wise. If she decided to abort it, she would have to do it as soon as possible. She also knew the longer she waited, the less likely she was to go through with it.

After work she was going to talk to Grape. She needed to talk to someone, and although Amber kept saying, "Come to me. You can talk to me," there was something about her that Cream didn't trust. That was messed up, because it wasn't always like that. There was a time, up until about a month ago, that she thought Amber was her girl, her partner, but Amber had been acting real shady lately.

Cream hung around until closing time, something she rarely did. She wanted some time alone with Grape. They were sitting in his office with the door closed.

"What's up, baby girl? Is everything okay?"

She didn't want to tell him, but she knew that he would make some sense out of this.

"I'm pregnant again," she blurted out. She didn't mean to say *again,* but figured she would rather say it than have him say it.

"Damn," was his reply. He didn't know what else to say. They'd just been through this two years ago when he went with her to have an abortion. He could recall how devastated she was and didn't think she'd want to go through that again. "Damn," he repeated.

"I don't know what to do about it. I don't think I can I go through another abortion, but I don't know how much longer me and Wise are going to be together."

This shocked Grape. "I don't know what to respond to first. You saying you're pregnant, or you saying you don't know if you and Wise are gonna stick it through."

"I'm facing reality here. I want more than what he's giving me. I want a real family, not some ghettofied version of a family."

*I can give you that,* Grape wanted to say, but kept the thought to himself. "I thought you were on birth control."

"I was. I mean I am. I don't know what happened."

Before they could go on, there was knock on the door. "Who is it?" Grape yelled out.

"It's Amber."

Cream rolled her eyes. "Listen, I'll call you tomorrow." Cream stood up and walked toward the door.

Standing up, Grape asked her not to leave. "We're not done talking."

"I'll figure it out on my own. I'm always asking for your help and I know it's not fair, especially with how you feel for me." Cream opened the door before he could say anything. "I'll call you."


"You know your girl is pregnant, right?"

"What?"

"Cream. She's pregnant."

"What the hell are you talking about? Did she tell you this?"

Amber and Wise were sitting in the kitchen. He'd just finished cutting up his package of cocaine and was waiting on his boys to come by and pick it up. He was doing this at Amber's place because he'd told Cream that he was no longer in the business, that he was going to try to go legit. He'd meant it when he said it, even went so far as to go fill out applications at FedEx and UPS. But in the back of his mind he doubted that he was employable. Who would want to hire someone with a prison record?

Besides, Wise wanted to make money fast. His plan was to make as much money as possible and move down South: Charlotte, Atlanta, someplace where Blacks had it going on. He would take Cream, Shacquille and his other kids, if their mothers allowed him to. The only way he was going to make enough to move was selling drugs. Selling drugs was all he knew, all he could do, all he'd ever done. Hell, his father was a drug dealer and his grandfather was a numbers runner. His mother knew it and luxuriated in the money. She enjoyed the lifestyle until his pops was killed.

Wise knew that eventually he would have to discontinue his hustle, especially if he wanted to keep Cream. But there was just too much money to be made; Crack, cocaine, weed, dope. You name it, he'd sell it, especially if it meant being back on top, at least for a little while. He just had to be careful Cream didn't know about it.

"If you want to be together, you have to stop. I can't picture my life with a drug dealer forever; wondering if you're going to go to jail or not; wondering how long you're going be alive; wondering if one of your enemies will try and kill you; wondering if your runners will turn against you. Look at what happened to your father. Do you want that to happen to you?" Cream had said to him when he came out of prison the first time.

"I'm tired of living this way. I'm tired, Wise. We've been together too long to still be living here in the hood. All the money you done made, we should have a big ass fucking house with a yard and a pool by now. But no, you want to buy cars, clothes and jewelry. I don't understand that."

When Cream went off into one of her fits, Wise really didn't know what to say, much less what to do. His best bet was to sit, listen, and yes her to death. He could only hope she believed him. Shit, he believed himself when he said it.

Now here was Amber telling him that she was pregnant.

"She's not sure if she wants the baby." Amber

knew she was dead wrong. Cream didn't tell her she was pregnant. She'd caught the tail end of the conversation between Cream and Grape. She didn't have to do that to figure the shit out, though. It was obvious Cream was pregnant.

Amber was tired of Wise acting like Cream's shit didn't stink. When they were together, he managed to work her into almost every conversation, as if to remind Amber that he was taken. She knew he was taken just like she knew that he was against abortion. The way she figured it, if Wise knew Cream was thinking of killing his child, he might be pissed enough to leave her, and the second he did, she'd step up to the plate.

Amber had been checking Wise for as long as she could remember, but he didn't pay her any mind. At least not until the night Cream and Wise had a big blowup over some bullshit. One of Wise's baby mamas, Trina, stopped by their house unexpectedly and overstayed her welcome. Wise lost track of time and was just kicking it with her. After all, they were on good terms. According to Wise, it was no more than conversation. Anyway, Trina heard the key being turned in the lock. Figuring that it was Cream and wanting to start some drama, she waited until she thought Cream would be walking into the living room then leaned over and forced a kiss on Wise.

"What the fuck!" Cream yelled out.

Pushing Trina away, Wise looked at her and asked, "What the hell are you doing?"

"You know you wanted to kiss me," Trina said.

"You trippin'," Wise protested.

Cream, believing her eyes and not her ears, walked out. She and Wise had just been through some drama a couple of months before over some he-say-she-say, and she wasn't going through it again.

Wise ran after her. "Wait, wait! She was kissing me." Cream ignored him. Realizing that she wasn't going to come back inside, he went in the house and gave Trina the riot act.

Later that night when Cream hadn't arrived home, Wise went out to look for her. He rode around looking for her car and when he didn't find it, he went to Amber's.

"Do you know where Cream is?" he asked the second she opened the door.

"No."

"She didn't come by here or call you?"

Figuring something was up, Amber asked, "What happened?" She opened the door wider and walked away, hoping he'd follow her in. He did, all the while eyeing her ass, which was peeking beneath the T-shirt she sported.

Wise told her what had happened, and Amber being the opportunist that she was, told him, "She's probably with that nigga Grape. You know she claims that's her best friend." She put an emphasis on the word *claim*.

"What do you mean *claim*?" Wise picked up on it.

"I'm just saying, everyone knows he attracted to her. Just ask your cousin Tina. That's her boy. She'd know. I even think they dated a couple of times when you and her broke up."

This was all news to Wise. "What the fuck you mean, they dated? Cream ain't never told me that."

Raising her finely arched eyebrows, Amber asked, "Do you tell Cream everything?"

"You have a point," Wise told her. He was pissed now because Amber had him thinking all kinds of shit and wondering what else Cream hadn't told him.

"You want a drink? Who knows? Maybe she'll show up or call."

He accepted.

"You got any coke with you?" Amber asked.

"Yeah." He reached into his pocket and pulled it out.

After having a couple of drinks and doing some lines together, Amber decided to put it down. Moving closer to Wise, she told him, "You know I suck a mean dick."

*Damn,* Wise thought, *why did she have to go there?* He was high. That made him horny, and here she was talking about sucking dick. "Yeah?"

"Yeah. Want me to show you?"

"Nah, girl. Come on. You're my woman's friend." He tried to resist, at least verbally, but when her hand started massaging his dick through his pants, he didn't try to stop her. When she started unzipping his pants, he didn't try to stop her. When she pulled his dick out of pants and said, "I'm going to suck the skin off your dick," he didn't stop her. And definitely when she said, "I swallow," there was no way he was going to stop her.

That was over six months ago, and since then they'd had sex at least four times a month. Wise knew it was wrong and wanted to put a stop to it, but the way Amber gave head had him coming back for more and more. He was afraid that her feelings were getting involved, but when he'd discussed it with her she said, "Nigga, please. It's just sex."

Well, she'd lied.

# 5

The next day, instead of holding it in, Cream decided to talk to Amber about her suspicions. She pulled up in front of Amber's house. Hearing the car door slam, Amber looked out the window. Damn! Wise had just left. A part of her wanted to get busted. She was tired of all this sneaking. She wanted Cream to catch them, not find out through word of mouth or by her revealing it. Seeing is believing in the hood. This was why she allowed his boys to pick up their packages from her house. She figured by now word would have gotten back to Cream. How it hadn't, she didn't know. Normally, even in Brooklyn, word got around quick. So if you were screwing someone else's man, word would spread like wildfire. Amber didn't know that Wise had threatened his boys. He told them that if they said a word they should fear for their lives.

Glancing around the house Amber looked to see

if Wise had left anything. He had—his T-shirt. She went to pick it up but changed her mind. She recalled that he took if off when he was fucking her from behind. He almost always did. This time he'd taken off his sweatshirt and his black DMX T-shirt. Obviously when he got dressed to leave, he'd forgotten the T-shirt.

"Damn baby, this pussy feels good," he'd told her while he was banging it up.

She'd messed it all up when she asked, "Does it feel as good as Cream's pussy?"

This didn't make him go soft. It just made him go harder and faster so he could get his shit off and leave. This time she'd taken it too far. Occasionally she would say little things and make little comments about Cream and he either ignored her or pretended that he didn't hear. This time he was more upset than usual.

Pulling out, taking off his condom and walking toward the bathroom he told Amber, "We can't do this anymore. It's not right."

"I've heard that before," Amber said, not believing him.

"Yeah, but this time I mean it."

"I know you ain't having a conscience attack. You've been fucking me for six months and all of a sudden you're serious about breaking it off?"

"Yeah," Wise answered. With Cream thinking about aborting his seed and Amber acting like she was proud to let him know it, he was feeling bad. He'd figured out what Amber was up to. He could feel it happening and knew that now was the time to just cut all ties before this got ugly.

"Well then step, motherfucker! Don't come back! Get the fuck out of my house!"

He didn't say a word. He just zipped up his pants and threw on his sweatshirt. He walked out the house, leaving Amber sitting on the couch. Now she smiled at his T-shirt still lying there for Cream to see.


Cream rang the doorbell. When she walked in she told Amber, "I ain't seen Wise's ass all day and today was the day I planned on telling him I'm pregnant." She had decided to tell Amber since she would learn of the news anyway.

"Oh, damn," Amber responded. "I knew you was pregnant! Why didn't you tell me the other day?"

"I wasn't sure what I was gonna do."

"So now you sure?"

"Yeah. I'm gonna keep the baby," Cream answered. She sat on the couch and spotted the T-shirt before Amber could respond. "Wise has that exact same T-shirt."

"Oh yeah, that's my new man's T-shirt." Amber tried to hide the smirk on her face.

"So who you fucking now?" Cream asked.

Amber wanted so bad to say, "Your man, bitch." But she didn't. She knew it had to come out another way. "What do you mean by that?" she asked. "Are you calling me a ho?"

"Damn, you're sensitive today. What's that about?"

"I'm just tired of your little innuendoes."

"I'm sorry. I'm just saying. You know we joke like that."

"Well, I don't wanna joke like that no more," Amber said.

"Amber, even you talk about all the men you have. How you have this one paying for this and that one paying for that. How the hell am I supposed to know when to say something and when not to?"

Amber knew she was right. She was just in a bad space. "Well, the truth of the matter is, I've met someone. Someone I think I could fall in love and settle down with."

"Get the fuck out of here. How come you haven't said anything about it?"

"Because you've had your head up your ass for the past couple of weeks."

"Who is he?"

"I don't want to say yet."

To be honest, Cream couldn't care less. She'd learned from experience that a man only meant one thing to Amber: a means to an end. Plus, Cream wanted to discuss her issue, not Amber's new man. This pregnancy thing was bugging her out and driving her over the edge.

"Look, Amber, I apologize. I'm just stressed. I can't believe I let myself get caught up out there like that. I'm careful, I'm responsible, I'm on birth control, but I let this shit happen again. I must be straight retarded, crazy *and* ghetto. I should know better. I promised my mother that I wouldn't have a whole bunch of babies, and look what's happening."

Amber thought Cream was being a little melodramatic. She couldn't help but wonder what

Cream meant by the word "again". The way Cream said it implied that she'd been pregnant before, and it sounded like recently. Amber figured that shit couldn't be true because there was no way Wise would have let her have an abortion. No way in hell, especially being a Five Percenter.

Laughing to herself, Amber recalled an incident when she was younger and her sister was dating a Five Percenter. She thought it meant he was five percent of a man and couldn't understand why her sister wanted to deal with someone who was only five percent of a man.

"No," her sister told her when she questioned her. "Five Percenters believe that only five percent of people are aware of and teach the truth, and they hold the exclusive divinity of Black men."

That was more information than her young mind could handle. Getting hyped, her sister went on to explain, "The Five Percenters believe that the Black man is God. They believe everything that you do is because you have total control over your destiny, and when you die you go back to the earth."

Even as an adult, Amber wondered about this. How could they believe they were God and act righteous when a large majority of them were selling drugs and doing other negative things? The reality was that most of the Five Percenters that she knew had three, four, five kids by different women. Come to think of it, Wise did also.

Leaving that train of thought Amber said to herself, *Hold up, hold up. Wait a minute. Maybe she didn't have an abortion. Maybe she lost the baby.*

Instead of trying to guess at it, Amber asked her, "What do you mean, again?"

"What are you talking about?"

"You said this couldn't be happening to you again, like you were pregnant before. What? You had an abortion, you lost it?"

Cream was looking at Amber like she was out of her damn mind. On one hand, she couldn't believe she'd let the word slip, and on the other hand, instead of acting like a friend and trying to console and advise her, Amber was acting like a gossip who just wanted to know her business. The intensity on Amber's face and the seriousness of her tone bugged Cream out. She wondered why Amber wanted to know so badly. Why, out of all the shit she'd said, did Amber focus on the word 'again'? This was not the kind of support she needed after the difficult night she'd had making the decision to keep this child.

Cream had been going back and forth all night about the decision. Now was not the time to have another baby. Not now, when she'd made the decision to register for school, to get out of Brooklyn, to better her life.

Cream was feeling like shit, not only about her life, but about the quality of time she was spending with her son. Feeling down and confused about her life and her relationship was emotionally draining, and it was making her unavailable. She knew she was neglecting her baby and cutting short the time they normally spent together, reading, watching movies and just talking.

He knew it too, in his childlike way. He was getting some attention by coming into her bedroom at night. When she and Wise would wake up, Shacquille would be balled up at the foot of their bed.

She didn't mind. It warmed her heart because she understood that was his way of saying he missed her. Wise, on the other hand, did mind.

"You need to put that sleeping in our bed shit to an end."

"Why, Wise? He's our son. Besides, he's not in the bed with us. He makes a pallet on the floor."

"What do you mean, why? He's acting like a punk, like a mama's boy."

"And? You have a problem with that? Maybe if you spent more time with him then he wouldn't be a mama's boy. Plus, it's his way of showing us he loves us. You should be glad your child wants to be in your presence. Most kids can't stand being around their parents."

"He can tell us he love us." The reality was that Wise was jealous that Shacquille preferred Cream to him.

"He tells me all the time. Maybe he doesn't tell your sorry ass because you're always in the street trying to make a dollar, trying to hustle and fuck with your boys instead of spending time with your family."

"Your ass didn't mind me hustling when I was bringin' home the money and passing it off to you. Your ass didn't mind when you were buying the hottest shit on the market and your ass didn't mind when we'd go to the mall and buy whatever he wanted."

"You know what? You're right, but you need to understand that money don't buy love."

"What the hell is this? What are you talking about, money don't buy love? What kind of sad song are you singing?"

"What I'm saying is you're right, Wise. I was happy with the money, but you have to understand that I was also young and dumb. I thought being fly in all the gold, having the hottest gear and being covered from head to toe in name brand gear was important. I thought that you buying me whatever I wanted, whenever I wanted, was love. I didn't realize that I was alone a lot; that most of the times we were together it was just for fucking; that I was letting you get away with giving me no real affection and attention. But not anymore. Hell, no. I'm older and that material, buy-my-love, buy-my-forgiveness mind game just don't work no more. I want love. I want passion. I want a real relationship, not a relationship for show. I want a house in the suburbs, in New Jersey. I want to see more, do more, be more."

"Girl, you're bugging."

"I ain't bugging. What's wrong with what I want? Why can't you want a better life for your family too? Why can't you understand?"

This discussion with Wise wasn't a one-time thing. It had been happening more and more often, and that was why Cream wasn't one hundred percent sure she wanted to have this baby. That was why she was over here seeking advice from Amber, who was acting like a bitch and not a real friend. That was why her eyes started watering up, and that was why she was about to go off. But she decided to calm down. It could just be her nerves.

Taking a couple of deep breaths, Cream looked at Amber and said, "I didn't mean anything by saying 'again', plus whether I was pregnant recently isn't any of your business. I came over here for help from my friend, not to be questioned with the third degree."

Amber was surprised at the little speech Cream had made. She had to watch her tone and her questions. She wanted Cream to believe she was still one of her closest confidantes.

Cream was looking at Amber trying to read her. Amber was starting to feel a little uncomfortable. Cream wondered what happened to their friendship. She wouldn't go so far as to say they were best friends, but they were pretty close for a while. Close enough to be able to turn to each other and pour out their hearts and souls. Close enough to hang out and get drunk and feel safe. Close enough for Amber to baby-sit once in a blue moon.

It wasn't an overnight friendship, either. It took some time to develop. Cream thought it would be a lifetime friendship. She was thinking now that might not be the case. If it lasted for another year, that in itself would be a miracle.

They'd met at a club called Exclusively Yours. It was one step below High Rollers, meaning the clientele's money was more illegal than legal. Neither of them worked there for long, especially after "the incident."

That's what they called it, Amber's near drug overdose. Had Cream not come in when she did, Amber might not even be alive. Amber, being the money hungry person that she was, had spotted Duke, one of Brooklyn's top drug dealers, the moment he walked in the door. For him to the come to the club was a rare event. He usually kept a low profile. The second he sat down, she staked claim by out-dancing all the women around him. Knowing it was against the club policy, she even went so far as to flash her clean shaven pussy a couple of times.

Duke didn't miss a move. He wondered what she was about and if her pussy felt as good as it looked. He motioned for the manager, Palmer.

"What's up with this bitch?" That's what all women were to him except his wife. He had no respect for them because they were always throwing themselves at him. Of course, he rarely turned them down.

"What do you mean, what's up with her?"

"She keeps flashing her pussy at me. I thought you didn't allow that."

"I don't. She knows better. I can't control these hoes every second, and obviously she wants something from you."

"She gets high?"

"All of them get high. You want her?"

"Yeah."

Palmer, knowing that Duke might become a frequent customer if Amber did her thing right, told Duke, "Look, there's a room in the back that's for special customers, and I consider you one. Take this key." He pulled the key out of his pocket and handed it over to Duke. "And fuck the shit out of her."

Cream was standing not too far away and heard the exchange. She knew Palmer was an ass but now she could add disrespectful and ignorant to the list. Cream couldn't stand Duke and was thinking of making this her last night. As a matter of fact, she hated him. When she was going with Boss, Duke worked for him and would often come to the hotel to pick up packages of cocaine. He always made Cream uneasy.

"I don't like him," she'd told Boss one time.

"Why not? You don't even know him."

"I don't need to. There's something about him that rubs me the wrong way. Call it woman's intuition, call it what you may, but I don't want him around me."

"You know what, Cream? You have nothing to do with my business. So what are you saying?"

Cream was right not to trust his ass, because one night she was at her and Boss' meeting place when she heard a knock at the door.

"Who is it?" Cream called out. Boss would have a key and she had not called room service.

"It's me. Duke!"

What the hell was he doing here? "Boss isn't here."

"I know. He told me to meet him here."

He told him what? He knew she didn't like Duke, didn't trust him. And he told him to meet him here? "Hold up!" she yelled through the door.

Cream threw a robe over her nightgown and called Boss.

"What's up, baby? I'm on my way."

She tore into him. "Why would you tell Duke to meet you here when you know how I feel about him?"

"Girl, please. That nigga ain't gonna do nothing to you. Just let him in."

Cream didn't want to let him in but she couldn't disobey Boss. She just knew that if Duke made one move she would break his neck. "Alright."

After slamming the phone down, she opened the door. She told Duke to have a seat.

He did, but not before saying, "Damn, girl. For a minute there I didn't think you were gonna let me in."

"I wasn't," she replied, letting him know she couldn't stand him.

He sat on the chair in the corner and she sat as far away as possible.

"So, you and Boss serious?"

"What do you think?"

"I don't know, being that you're not his only woman."

Cream didn't satisfy him with a response.

Duke stood up and walked over to where she sat.

Standing up, Cream asked, "What do you think you're doing?"

Duke grabbed her face and tried to ram his tongue down her throat. She pushed him away with enough strength to knock him on the floor.

"I think you need to go wait in the hall," she told him.

He stood and laughed. "Come on, girl. You know you want me. I've seen you checking me out."

Cream stared at him in disbelief. "You must be losing your fucking mind. Get out of my room right now and wait in the hall. And don't think I'm not telling Boss."

Duke started laughing. "Bitch, please. We share girls all the time. He ain't gonna do nothing about it."

And he was right. Boss didn't do anything about it, at least not as far as Cream knew. He should have fucked Duke up, put a hurting on him, but instead he just told her, "I'll take care of it." How he took care of it, she wanted to know, because Duke not coming around her wasn't enough. He was still walking around with two arms and legs, and that should not have been the case.

Cream didn't see Duke again until she started working at Exclusively Yours. Duke recognized her immediately. He also recognized the fact that she was Grape's protégée. He knew that Grape was one nigga not to mess with, so he never tried to make a move. All he did was look her up and down and say, "Damn, you're all grown up now. Just know I'm here if you want me." She just looked at him and replied, "I'm sure I won't."

Cream knew about the back room where Palmer told Duke to go with Amber. She knew it was used for sex and drugs, but only to the highest bidder. It was also a known fact that Duke liked to beat on women while they were having sex. That night, she found herself watching his every move.

As the night progressed, he appeared to get more intoxicated. Amber was all over him, whispering in his ear, kissing his neck, putting on a show. When they finally stood up to go to the back room, Cream felt an unease wash over her.

*Damn, let it go,* she kept telling herself. *Don't get involved. It's not any of your business.*

About thirty minutes had passed when Cream saw Duke leave the back room in a hurry. He didn't stop at the bar or say "Peace" to any of his boys. In fact, he practically ran out. Ten more minutes passed and Cream didn't see Amber come out of the back room.

Growing concerned, Cream made her way back there. Amber lay passed out on the floor.

"Oh shit!" she yelled. Running to the door, she called out for Grape. Hearing the panicked state in her voice, he ran to see what was going on. When he got to the room, Cream was pouring a bucket of ice on Amber.

Amber and Duke had been in the back room doing coke. She must have snorted too much or the supply was bad. Either way, they took her to hospital and told the emergency doctor what they believed had transpired. Amber wouldn't give any information. She just kept saying someone must have slipped something in her drink.

From that day on Amber and Cream were friends, or something like it. For a while, Amber was grateful that Cream had basically saved her life, but that didn't last long. As with everything else, Amber was only interested in self.


"Listen, I'm sorry if it seems like I haven't been a good friend. It's just that I want to make changes in my life, too, and it's been consuming me."

Cream didn't say a word. She didn't believe Amber.

"So," Amber started. She was hesitant about what she was going to reveal to Cream, but she needed a second person to pull off her plan. "I have an idea. A way to get out of this life, out of this area. A way to make some serious cash, quick cash."

This got Cream's attention. "Go on."

"Okay, you know how we have that window in the

dressing room that lets us look out into the parking lot?"

"Yeah. That's how we tell which customers have money and which ones don't, by the cars they drive."

"Yeah."

"You also know that I'm always on it and how I usually ask them what type of business they're in?"

"I thought you were just being nosey or trying to find the money-makers."

"You're right. Well, come to find out we have one guy that comes in on an irregular basis and sometimes he has business meetings and clients with him. He owns a law firm and drives a big silver Benz."

"And you tell me this because?"

"That's the one that's gonna get us paid."

"How are you gonna get him to come up off some money?

"Just listen. I'm gonna get him to invite me to a hotel."

"How do you know he's going to fall for that?"

"Because, girl, he's propositioned me before. That time he came in with those Chinese dudes. He must have spent over five grand that night."

"Go on."

"I'm going to slip something in his drink and put him in a compromising position and you're going to take pictures."

"I don't know about all this."

"You're the one that's saying you want a better life for your son."

Taking a deep breath, Cream told her to continue.

"So, we have the pictures developed immediately at a one hour spot, then we'll call him and threaten to tell his wife."

"But how do you know he's married?"

"The ring, bitch. On his finger. Damn, don't you be paying any attention to these assholes?"

"Just finish with what you're saying."

"Alright. We'll bribe him with the pictures, tell him we'll give them to him along with the negatives for ten thousand."

This is what got Cream's attention. "Do you think we could get that much?"

"Hell, yeah. We should ask for more, but better safe than sorry. That's five thousand a piece, minus what we pay my cousin to go with us to meet him. That way it's guaranteed he won't try any funny shit."

Cream wasn't sure they could pull this off, but she needed that money in the worst way. And it did sound easy. Going against her head, she said, "Alright. I'm down. I just hope Grape doesn't find out."

"Why should he? I ain't gonna say nothing and you shouldn't either. I figure if we do this twice, that's ten thousand each. Enough to relocate."

"We don't know when he's coming again."

"I do. Next Thursday. Plus I heard him telling someone he was heading out of town and would see them Friday. So it's perfect. We'll get him the night before he's leaving."

They had a plan. Now they just had to follow it through.

# 6

Cream and Wise lay in bed. She'd finally told him that she was pregnant, and he pretended like he was surprised. It had been a week since Amber had spilled the beans and it had taken everything in Wise not to say anything. He'd wondered why she hadn't said anything yet, and if she was seriously considering aborting his seed.

"How long have you known?" he asked her, wondering if she was going to tell him the truth.

Surprising him, she was honest. "For a couple of weeks."

"Why did you wait so long to tell me?"

"Because I wasn't sure what I wanted to do about it."

"What you mean? You were thinking about having an abortion and not telling me?"

Cream didn't answer him.

"What? You were just going to deprive me of a

child, kill my seed?" Even he had to admit he'd gone a little too far with that one. Cream sat up and faced him. He knew this meant they were about to have another discussion.

"Let's be honest with one another for a change," Cream said.

For a second there, Wise thought he was about to be busted for all his wrongdoings, seeing Amber and selling drugs again. As recently as last week, he told Cream he was looking for a job.

"First of all, you told me a while ago that you didn't want any more children."

"I've changed my mind."

"Also, I don't understand how you always have money if you're not working or selling."

"You know I had money stashed. I still have a little left."

Cream didn't have any choice but to believe him, or at least she wanted to believe him. Even though he was a spender, Wise always had money stashed in jars, in sneakers, under the mattress, so it could be true.

Wise was tired of trying to fake it, though. He wanted to say to Cream: "Listen. I'm a drug dealer. You knew it when we met, when we had our son and when we moved in together. This is what I do and will continue to do until I have what I consider the right amount that will allow me to stop. Either you take it or you leave it."

"Alright, let's do that. Let's be honest with one another," Wise said.

The way he said it almost made Cream reconsider having a talk. The last time they had a let's-be-honest talk it had caused so much tension that they broke up. They were a little too honest, especially Wise, who was fucking like a rabbit. Cream was having a phone affair, too afraid to make it physical, but that was bad enough. She never thought she'd live that one down.

Never again, they'd both declared. The more Wise thought about it, the more he wondered if the reason Cream was bugging was because she was seeing someone.

"Are you fucking around on me?" he blurted out.

Cream looked at Wise and said, "I know you're not asking me that. I should be questioning your ass."

"Then what do you want to he truthful about?"

"You and your getting angry with me for thinking about having an abortion."

He was a little relieved. "It's my child too, and I have a right to be upset."

"Wise, you're not exactly there now for Shacquille and any of your other children. So for you to act like you're Father of the Year, it doesn't make sense."

"I know you didn't just sit here in my face and tell me I'm a bad father."

"You're not the Father of the Year."

"Fuck you." Wise slipped up and totally disrespected Cream.

"I know you didn't just say that to me." She was fuming.

"I know you didn't just sit here and say I'm not a father to my children." The real reason Wise was getting angry was because he knew she spoke the truth.

Cream climbed out of the bed and went toward the bathroom.

"Where are you going?" Wise asked.

"Out."

"But I thought you wanted to have this truthful conversation."

"I did until I realized what a jackass you've become."

"Well, you're the one who's putting a brotha down."

"No, I'm just being honest. Calling it as I see it. I don't even feel like talking about it now."

"We need to. This isn't something we can not discuss. It's a baby."

Plopping down on the bed, Cream said, "Listen, I'm only six weeks. I have a few more weeks before I make a decision."

Wise was looking at her like she was crazy or something. "You mean to tell me you're really thinking about not having it?"

"That's what I'm telling you, Wise. I don't know if I want another child with you."

He caught the 'with you' part. "I'm letting you know right now. If you decide to abort this baby, that just may be the end of us."

"Is that a threat or a promise?" Cream wanted to be clear.

"'Is that a threat or a promise?' I know you're bugging now. Maybe you should just go on and do whatever you were about to do, because both of us are likely to say something we'll regret."

"I think you already did."

Wise didn't reply. He just turned over and covered himself up with the blanket.

* * *

Later that night, Cream and Amber were sitting in front of the club. Amber was psyched, adrenaline racing. The only thing she could think about was the money that would soon be in her pocket.

"I know it's the perfect plan," she told Cream.

"I hope so, because I'm nervous about the whole thing."

"Ain't nothing to be nervous about. If you do everything exactly as I said then it's all good."

"What if Grape finds out?" That was the one thing that had Cream on edge. She was putting him in jeopardy. Not physically, but his livelihood, his place of business. She'd thought about whether or not she wanted to take part in this scam for the past week, and went back and forth with it. She was going to go through with it, she wasn't, she was, she wasn't.

But after this morning, when Wise said "Fuck you" and then threatened to leave her, she knew it was something she had to do. Especially when he said aborting the baby would be the end of them. She had felt nothing, not an ounce of sadness or heartbreak when he said that. She knew she had to do this for the cash because she'd leave him first.

"The only way Grape is going to find out is if you tell him."

"I'm not. I just don't want it to backfire."

"Will you stop being so pessimistic about it? I told you this dude is perfect. He's white, he has money, he's going out of town. I even did some research on his firm and believe me, he would not want to be found out."

Cream's stomach was turning in knots. The shit hadn't even gone down yet and she was on the verge of a panic attack.

"Listen, stop worrying. I've got it all under control. We're going to dance together for him in VIP."

"Wait, hold up. You ain't say nothing about that earlier." There was no way Cream was going to dance for him. He might put the shit together and know they'd planned the whole thing. One of the reasons she even agreed was because she thought all she would be doing was taking the pictures.

"How else do you think we're going to get to the hotel with him?"

"I thought you were going to handle all that and I was just taking the pictures."

"For five thousand dollars? You must be out of your mind."

"What all do I have to do?"

"We're going to make him think he's getting with both of us, that we're having a threesome. All men like that shit. You know it and I know it. I'll tell him he can get both of us. Because we're strippers, he'll think it's something we do on the regular." Looking at Cream, Amber could see that if one thing went wrong she would back out. "Remember, Cream, you're not doing this for you. You're doing it for your son."

"I know. I know. Come on, let's just go inside."

A couple hours passed by and the man still hadn't come to the club. Cream was feeling a bit relieved, thinking they'd gotten out of doing it. Just when she was getting over the loss of the money, Amber rushed up to her.

"He's here. He's here. Are you ready?"

"No."

"Well, get ready." Amber walked away. Cream followed her. "Come in the back with us. This is my friend I was telling you about."

Their target looked Cream up and down, liking what he saw. "Better yet," he said, "let's meet at the Hilton downtown in one hour."

Amber was shocked. She didn't think things would move this fast or that he would initiate them. Cream was relieved because she could have sworn she'd seen Grape looking their way.

"Give me your card with your cell number on it and I'll call you when we're on our way."

Pulling a card out of the pocket of his Versace suit, he handed it to her and said, "I'm looking forward to both of you." Of course he put an emphasis on the word *both*.

Cream took a look at the card and read his name: Jim Wilson. She was taking in everything about him. He wasn't a bad looking white dude; a little on the nerdish side, but she wasn't sleeping with him, so it didn't matter. She wondered how far she and Amber would have to go to make this whole thing believable. Would they have to kiss? She certainly hoped not, because that was something she wasn't down with. There was no way she was going to do the lesbian thing. She wasn't into women at all and didn't know if she could pretend that she was.

* * *

One hour passed like lightening. Amber came up to Cream and said, "He wants us to follow him."

"I thought we were meeting him there."

"Well, I don't know what to tell you. He said he wants us to follow him."

Cream was driving. The whole time they were following Jim he was on his cell phone.

"Who do you think he's talking to?" Amber asked.

"I don't know. Maybe he's getting his lie together for his wife."

"Do you have the pill?" Cream asked.

Amber knew she was talking about the drug they were going to slip into his drink to knock his ass out. "Yeah, I have it. Just be ready."

"We in this together. I've got your back and you've got my back, right?"

"Yes, Cream." Amber was getting tired of Cream acting like she had never done anything wrong or illegal before.

They parked the car in the parking lot and met up with Jim at the door. "Here goes," Amber said.

"Walk behind me at a distance. Don't make it obvious we're together," he told them.

It was getting creepier and creepier to Cream. Her intuition was working overtime, warning, "Leave. Run. Don't look back." Of course, she didn't listen. The money was calling her.

Jim didn't bother to stop by the front desk as they followed behind him. Amber started up a fake ass conversation. Cream was talking back, but had no idea what she was saying because she was in a zone. They walked onto the elevator together in silence.

The second they got on, Amber asked Jim, "What? You didn't have to sign in?"

"Nah, they know me here. I called them ahead of time."

Amber was impressed. Cream was not.

When they were headed toward the room, Amber looked at Cream and whispered, "Remember to follow my lead."

Cream, too nervous to respond, just nodded her head and said a silent prayer. *Lord, forgive me for what I'm about to do.*

Jim put the key into the door and pushed it open. They walked in and glanced around. There, sitting on the couch, was another man. Amber and Cream didn't even take in the fact that they were in one of the top suites.

"Oh, hell no," Cream said out loud.

Amber looked at her and said to Jim, "Do you mind if we go into the ladies' room to freshen up?"

"No, I don't mind at all. We'll be out here waiting."

They went into the bathroom and closed the door behind them. Before Cream could start going off, Amber shushed her and turned the faucet on to drown out their conversation.

"What the fuck is going on? You didn't say anything about another man."

"I didn't know about another man. I don't know what's going on."

"Then let's step."

"We can't do that."

"Why not?

"We just can't. I'm looking forward to this money. We've come this far."

"I'm not trying to fuck anyone. I thought I made that clear."

"I'm not fucking anyone either. We'll go out and have a drink. I'll dance real sexy like and you'll slip the pill in their drinks while you're making them." She went into her purse and pulled two pills out of a bag that contained about ten of them.

"What are you, a walking pharmacy?" Cream asked, wondering why she had so many.

Amber rolled her eyes.

"All I have to say is this better work," Cream stated.

"It'll work. Shit. We can get money from both of them."

Turning off the water, they both took a quick look in the mirror and took deep breaths.

"Gentlemen," Amber said, entering the room. "Let the party begin."

Cream, trying to play along, went and sat on the couch next to the other man. "You're a surprise," she told him. "We weren't expecting another guest."

"That's Michael," Jim told them. "He's my partner."

Amber's eyes went straight to Michael's ring finger. He wore a wedding ring. Dollar signs started appearing right before her eyes. She looked at Cream, who could read her mind by the sparkle in her eyes.

Looking around, Amber noticed the bar across the room. It was in a perfect location. They wouldn't be able to see what Cream was up to.

"Turn some music on," Amber told Jim. "Cream,

make us some drinks." She was ready to get the ball rolling.

Standing up, Cream walked over to the bar and asked the men what were they drinking. They didn't know.

"How about some champagne?" Cream suggested, thinking the bubbles would camouflage the taste of the pills.

Jim had the music playing by now and Amber was in front of them doing an enticing dance.

"Yeah."

"That's good."

Neither of them were looking her way so Cream slipped the pills into the glass and poured the drinks. She carried the drinks over to them.

"Aren't you two lovely ladies going to join us?" they asked.

Amber pulled Cream by the arm and said, "Yes, but we want you to watch us first."

This was the shit Cream didn't want. She wouldn't even dance with the other women at the club, and she knew that was a sure winner as far as tips were concerned.

Amber knew this. She also knew that Cream wasn't really into women, so she decided to fuck with her and tease her a little. Whatever consequences she had to deal with when it was over, she'd deal with.

Cream was standing in front of Amber, who wrapped her hands around Cream's waist and pulled her toward her, pelvises touching.

"What are you doing?" Cream whispered.

"Relax. We're putting on a show." Amber ran her hands up Cream's back. The men were all eyes, watching and sipping on their drinks.

Amber moved her hand down the dress to Cream's ass. Cream took Amber's hands and placed them gently by her side then turned around so her back was to Amber. She decided to play along, but on her terms. When this was over and done with, she was going to curse Amber out.

With her back to Amber, Cream placed her hands in the air and started swaying her body from side to side. Amber followed her movements, then decided to run her hands up and down Cream's body.

"Yeah, baby," Michael said. "That's how you do it. Touch her breasts."

Amber obliged and started to caress Cream's breasts through her dress. Cream moved away from Amber and stood directly in front of Michael, whose dick was rock hard and about to come through his pants.

"What's that?" Cream teased, touching his dick with the tip of her finger while trying to figure out what to do next.

Amber moved toward Jim and straddled him. "Want a lap dance? A special lap dance?" She knew that the pill would start taking effect within five minutes. They needed to milk that time for everything it was worth. "Why don't we each give them a lap dance?"

Michael and Jim leaned back against the couch and finished the last of their drinks.

Cream didn't want to face Michael so she turned away from him and slid her body down between his legs. She came back up slowly, feeling his penis against her ass. She was disgusted with herself at this point.

Amber was also in a dress, but hers was pulled up to her hips. Underneath she wore a thong. Cream wondered why she was going all out. *Let this be over soon,* she thought.

Turning to face Michael, she saw that his eyes were closed. Amber had noticed it as well because Jim was dozing in and out.

"What's wrong, sweetie? I know you're not going to fall asleep on me."

"No, no. I'm just feeling the champa—" Before Jim could finish the sentence he was out cold.

In less than two seconds, Michael was out as well.

"Oh, shit." Cream was excited. "It worked."

They climbed off the men.

"Come on. Let's get them undressed."

They tried to work as fast as possible, but it was harder than they thought. So they just took off their shoes, pulled down their pants and underwear.

"I know just what to do," Amber said, pleased with herself for her twisted mind. She took Jim's hand and placed it on Michael's dick. She positioned it so that it looked like he was giving him a hand job.

"What are you doing?" Cream asked.

"I've got one better." Amber pushed Jim's head down in Michael's lap and stepped up on the couch. "Go get the camera."

All Cream could think was that Amber was sick in the head, but she went and got the camera out of her purse.

Amber was standing up on the couch with her dress pulled up, straddling Michael's face. "Take the picture. Just don't get my face."

Cream started snapping away while Amber did a number of poses. After about ten shots, they grabbed their bags, fixed their clothes, sat Jim back up and left the room.

Once in the car, Amber started cracking up. "We did it! We did it!"

Cream didn't think it was amusing, so she didn't join in the laughter. She just sat there and asked, "Now what?"

"Photo Moto to get the film developed. My cousin works there. He's the one who's gonna go with us to get the money. Just take snapshots of whatever to use up the rest of the film."

One hour later Cream had the photos. Amber wanted to keep them but Cream refused. She wasn't letting her hard work out of her sight.

"Fuck it, then. You keep it. Just be at my house first thing in the morning so we can make the phone call and take care of everything else."

Cream agreed to do just that. Amber started to get out of the car but Cream stopped her.

"What?"

"I didn't appreciate all that funny shit you tried to pull in the hotel."

"What funny shit?"

"Touching my ass and feeling on my titties."

"Girl, please. Don't nobody want you. I was just doing it for show." On that note, Amber walked into her house with a smile on her face, wondering if she'd turned Cream out.

When Cream arrived home, she left the pictures locked in the glove compartment. Once in the house she checked on Shala and Shacquille. They were both sound asleep. She went into the bedroom and was surprised to find Wise stretched across the bed.

Closing the door, she went into the bathroom and took a shower, trying to wash off the scent of betrayal and guilt she felt.

## 7

Cream fell asleep with money on her mind and woke up with it in her sight. Lying on the dresser was a pile of money. She walked over to it and counted over eight hundred dollars. She looked at Wise, who was snoring, stood over him and debated whether she should wake him or not. She wasn't stupid. She had a feeling he was on the streets selling that shit again.

Turning over, Wise opened his eyes to see Cream looking at him with a frown. *What now?* he thought to himself. I'm *tired of the talks.* Sitting up and letting the blankets fall to his waist, he rubbed his eyes and asked, "Why didn't you wake me when you got home last night?"

"I don't wake you up any other time."

"Damn, girl, must you have so much attitude this time of the morning?"

Cream just looked at him.

"Oh, oh, I know what this is about. You're still upset about yesterday."

"You damn right I am. Did you hear what you said to me, the mother of your son? You said, 'Fuck you.' I would never disrespect you like that."

"Yeah, but you disrespect me in other ways.

"Like what?"

"Like telling me that I'm not a . . . You know what? Never mind. I don't even feel like getting into it this early. Why don't you go ahead and take the kids to school and leave me to rest?"

"Why don't you take them to school?"

"What do you mean, why don't I take them to school? That's not my job."

Cream huffed and told Wise, "You are such an asshole." She left the room and went to wake Shala. Her door was locked. This was a new thing. Cream didn't know whether she wanted to allow it or not.

Knocking on the door, she yelled, "Come on, Shala. I know I heard your alarm go off. What's the hold up?"

"I'm up," Shala yelled back. Cream could have sworn she heard her say 'Damn' under her breath.

She went into Shacquille's room, which really was the dining room. She sat on the bed and rubbed his back. "Come on, sweetie. You have to go to school."

Lifting his head up, he looked at his mother and whined, "Do I have to? Can't I stay home today?"

"Not." Cream started tickling him. She knew this would get him up.

An hour later, Wise was still in the bed. Everyone else was dressed and ready to go. After dropping

Shacquille off, she took Shala to school. As Shala was climbing out of the car, Cream was surprised to see Shala was wearing a thong.

"Where did you get those panties from? I didn't get them for you."

Shala just looked at her.

"Well?"

"I bought them with my babysitting money." Shala tried to walk away.

"I'm not done. Come here."

Shala plopped back down in the seat.

Cream's instinct was telling her to just go with what she wanted to say. "You bought some thongs?"

"I'm wearing them, right?"

Cream wanted to pop her in the mouth.

"Come on, now. Everybody's wearing them."

"What else is everybody doing?" Cream asked.

"What are you talking about?"

"If everybody else is having sex, are you going to do that too?"

"Why are we having this conversation?"

"Because you're wearing a thong and that represents sexiness, and if you're thinking about being sexy, what else could you possibly be thinking about?"

"I need to go in the school or I'm gonna be late."

"This is more important." Cream hesitated before moving on. "Are you thinking about sex?"

Shala didn't answer her.

"I'm asking you a question. Are you thinking about sex?"

"No, alright? No."

"Because if you are, you need to know that you

can come to me. I love you and I'm here for you. I
don't want you going to your friends for advice on
something so serious."

Trying to hurry her along, Shala said, "Yeah,
okay. Whatever."

"Don't yeah, yeah me. Listen to what I'm saying.
I'm here for you."

Shala got eerily quiet.

"Why are you being so quiet? Is there something
you want to say to me?"

"No," she said in a whisper.

Cream thought she was lying, so she asked her
again. "Is there anything you want to talk about?"

"I said no. Dag."

Taking a deep breath, Cream said, "Alright, you
can go."

Shala jumped out of the seat and ran into the
school without looking back. Cream just shook her
head and drove away.


When Cream pulled up to Amber's house, she
saw Amber looking out the window. Throwing the
door open, Amber asked, "What took you so long?"

"I had to take the kids to school. I told you that. I
got here as soon as possible."

"You ready to make that call?"

Cream followed Amber into the house. "No, I'm
not ready. Are you ready?"

"I'm ready to get paid. Did you do what I asked?"

"Yes, Amber, I had the pictures taken by a mes-
senger to his office, along with a note that said—"

Before she could finish, Amber's cell phone
started ringing.

"Aren't you going to answer that?" Cream asked.

"No. We have more important business to attend to."

"What if it's Jim?"

Amber looked at Cream with tight eyes and a bit of nervousness. "What do you mean, what if it's Jim?"

"Well, if you had let me finish, I told you I sent the package and I put in the letter for him to call you on your cell."

"You told him to what?"

"To call you on your cell when he received the package."

"Why would you do something like that? Now he'll have my number and can have it traced."

"Girl, get a new number. What's the big deal?"

"What's the big deal? What's the big deal?" Amber was getting agitated and Cream was loving it.

Laughing, Cream said, "It's about time. I've finally gotten some kind of emotion out of you."

"What? Is that all you have to say?"

"Girl, I'm playing with you. You've been all calm, cool and collected through the whole thing. Here I am on edge like a motherfucker and you're acting all it-ain't-nothing."

"You think that's funny? That shit ain't funny."

"Do you really think I would be stupid enough to give him your number? Not!"

Amber wanted to smack Cream upside the head, but decided it was best to keep her cool. "What did the letter say?"

"Basically to expect a phone call around nine thirty a.m."

"Cool. By then he should have gotten in touch with Michael. Shit, girl, we got two for one."

"How much are we gonna ask them for?" Cream was finally getting excited.

"Ten thousand a piece."

"You think we'll get away with it?"

"I'm certain. I told you I did some research on the Internet and found out about their firm. They can't afford bad publicity. Believe me."

"I'll take your word for it," Cream answered.

Glancing at her watch, Amber said, "Let's go get a cup of coffee or something to waste time before we hit a phone booth."

"Cool."

They went to a local diner and sat in silence, willing the time to go by. The half-hour they waited seemed like an eternity. Looking at the clock on the wall, Amber said, "It's time."

They got up and walked to the phone booth near the ladies' room. Amber pulled Jim's card out of her pocket and dialed the number. Cream noticed her hands were shaking. The phone was answered on the first ring.

"Hello." It was Jim.

"Hello, Jim. Do you have Michael with you?" Amber got right to the point.

"What the fuck do you want?" he asked angrily.

"Cash."

"What did you put in our drinks? I don't remember doing anything in those pictures."

Amber could hear someone in the background saying, "Give me the phone. Give me the phone."

"You can give him the phone, but it won't make a

bit of difference. We have copies. And don't worry about how the pictures were taken, just worry about how it would look if they become public."

"What makes you think I care?" Jim asked.

Amber frowned, which caused Cream to ask, "What's he saying? What's he saying?"

"Shhh," Amber said while covering up the mouth-piece on the phone. "He asked me what makes us think he cares."

Cream was feeling bold. She snatched the phone and said, "I'm sure your wife and your clients would care about you sucking another man's dick, and I'm sure Michael's family would care that he's eating the shit out of a black woman's pussy."

Amber looked at Cream with surprise.

"Hold on," Jim said.

Cream could hear him whispering.

"Alright, alright. What do you want and where do you want to meet?" Jim asked.

"We want ten grand from each of you."

"Ten thousand dollars?" Jim's voice was disbelieving.

"That's right; not a penny less," Cream insisted.

Covering up the phone and moving it away from her mouth, Cream told Amber, "He wants to know where we want to meet."

Taking the phone from her, Amber said, "Meet us at the Denny's around the corner from your office. And Jim, don't try any funny shit, because I'll have someone watching."

This surprised Cream. When they hung up she asked Amber, "What were you talking about? You said someone will be watching."

"Girl, I ain't stupid. You never know what the

White man will try. My cousin Duran and his boy are going to meet up with us. Just in case."

"You told him what we did?"

"No. I told him someone owes us money for a bachelor party and they've been acting funny, so we may need him."

"Does he know how much we're getting?"

"You must really think I'm retarded. Hell no. We have to pay them a hundred a piece."

Just thinking about the ten thousand they would be receiving made Cream smile. She didn't mind giving up a hundred for protection.

They decided to go and wait at Denny's. An hour later Amber spotted Jim's car. "There he is, and Michael's with him." She stood up and went to the door so he could see her.

When she sat back down, Cream asked her, "Where is Duran and his boy?"

"Across the street."

Cream looked, and there they were, standing against the pole, looking like gangsters. "Can they be more obvious?"

"That's the point. That way Jim and his boy won't try to fuck us over."

Jim and Michael entered the restaurant looking nervous as hell. They sat down next to the women.

Jim said in a whisper, "You know you could go to jail for this shit."

Amber responded by saying, "Just like you know you could lose your reputation. Don't worry about us. Just pass the dough."

Nodding his head toward the window, Michael asked, "Are those your thug friends?"

"Glad you noticed them," Amber said as she took the envelope off the table where Jim had placed it.

"Tell me this one thing," Jim said. "What did you do to us? I know I wouldn't suck another man's dick."

Amber didn't answer him. She just stood up and Cream followed her lead. "Don't worry. You won't be hearing from us again."

On that note they walked away, each trying to contain themselves. They went across the street and met up with Duran and his boy.

"Did they pay you?" Duran wanted to know. He was looking for trouble.

"Yeah, they know the deal," Amber said.

Looking at Cream with lust, Duran said, "What's up? You still with that nigga Wise?"

"Yeah," Cream told him.

"Well, when you find out what his sorry ass is about, you know how to find me."

Cream didn't feel a need to respond.

Amber went into her purse and pulled out an envelope. "Here's your money."

"Bet," Duran said. "Call me if you need me to do anything else."

Amber kissed him on the cheek and winked at his boy. "Peace, y'all."


Once in the car, Cream asked her, "My part of his money was in the envelope you gave him?"

"Yeah, I didn't want him to see the fat ass envelope we got." She pulled it out. "Can you believe it went so smooth?"

"No, it's almost too good to be true."

"I know." Counting the money out, Amber said, "I should get a little more. After all, it was my idea."

Cream looked at her like she'd lost her mind. "I don't think so. We both put ourselves on the line."

"I know, I know. I was just playing with you."

"No, I think what you were trying to do was play me."

"Here." Amber passed her the money.

Cream counted it, put it in an envelope she'd stashed over her visor, stuck the envelope in her purse and started the car. "Are you going home?" she asked Amber.

"Damn, I thought we could go shopping and celebrate."

"I'm not trying to shop. I needed this money for other reasons."

Amber looked at her and shook her head. "You need to loosen up."

# 8

The second Cream walked through the door, Wise attacked her verbally. "I thought you told me you took the test already."

Startled, Amber asked, "What are you talking about?"

"You know what the fuck I'm talking about." He pulled the pregnancy test from behind his back. "This is what I'm talking about."

Cream stood there looking at the empty box. She could have sworn she threw the box away a long time ago.

"Where did you find that?"

"Double-wrapped in a plastic bag in the kitchen, like it was supposed to be hidden or something."

"Double-wrapped . . ." Cream couldn't even finish her sentence once she realized that the box Wise was holding wasn't the brand she used.

"Oh, shit. That's not mine." Cream knew the only other person it could belong to was Shala.

"What?"

Putting her purse on the counter, Cream slumped down in the chair. "This cannot be happening."

"What can't be happening?" Wise was getting confused.

"Wise, that's not my pregnancy test. The only other female in this house is Shala. It must belong to her."

"Who, your cousin?"

"What other Shala would I be talking about?"

He was stunned. "Damn, I ain't even know she was fucking."

Irritated and upset, Cream rolled her eyes at him and said, "You could be a little more sensitive."

"Well shit, what you want me to say? I didn't know she was fucking and obviously you didn't know it either. Well, I guess you've got to handle it."

Listening to the insensitivity in his voice, Cream remembered the nine thousand nine hundred dollars that was in her purse: her escape money. She knew she would be leaving Wise. She just wasn't sure when. The only thing she was one hundred percent sure about was that she was tired of being disrespected and talked to any kind of way. Looking at the pregnancy test that was still in Wise's hand, she took it and turned to walk out the door.

"Where are you going? You just got here."

"I'm going to Shala's school. I need to talk to her."

"Why can't you just deal with it when she comes home from school?"

"Because, Wise, she's like a daughter to me and I need to take care of it right now."

"You don't even know if it came out positive."

"I don't care if it came out positive. The point is that she had to take one." On that note, Cream walked out the door, slamming it behind her.

She was thinking of what she would say to Shala once she saw her. She recalled the talk they'd had in the car. The conversation she'd forced on Shala. She wondered what had given her the initiative to discuss it. Maybe it was her mother's spirit.

When Cream parked her car at the school, she reached for her purse and realized with a panic that she'd left it on the counter at home.

"Damn." All she could do was hope Wise hadn't looked in it. If he had, there would be too many questions. She decided she'd just sign Shala out and rush home.

When Cream first walked into the school, she thought she would be able to remain calm. Instead, she was furious, especially when she saw Shala walking down the hall with the thong showing past her hips. She wanted to smack her, but instead she grabbed her arm and said, "Come on, let's go."

Walking to the car, Shala kept asking, "What's up? Why did you sign me out?"

Cream was too upset to talk. All she could say was, "Wait until we get into the car."

When they got in the car, Cream didn't hesitate. She asked, "Why didn't you come to me?"

"Come to you for what?"

Reaching under her seat, she pulled the pregnancy test box out and shoved it in her face.

There was nothing Shala could say or do because she knew she was busted. She started crying.

"What are you crying for? Are they tears of shame?"

Shala continued to cry.

"Well?" Cream was waiting to hear if she was pregnant or not.

"Well what?"

"Come on now, Shala. Are you pregnant or not?"

"It came out negative."

Cream breathed a sigh of relief, but then she thought about teenagers she'd heard about who try to hide their pregnancies and then flush their babies down the toilet. Who was to say Shala was not lying? "We're going to make a doctor's appointment and go together. You're getting on birth control, and I want to know who you're having sex with so I can talk to him and his parents."

Shala looked at her like she was crazy.

"Can I go back to school now, or do I have to come home?"

Cream, wanting to return home to her purse, let her return to school.


For the second time that day Wise tore into her the minute she walked in the door. Holding the envelope with the money in it, he demanded, "What is this?"

Trying to play it cool, she said, "Money."

"I know it's money, Cream. It's almost ten thousand dollars. Now tell me, where would my woman get ten thousand dollars from?"

"Why don't you tell me what you were doing in my purse?"

He ignored her.

For a second there, Cream thought about lying

and saying she'd saved it, but then why would she be carrying around so much money? She decided to tell him the truth.

"Me and Amber pulled a scam together."

Wise felt his heart beating through his chest. "A scam?"

"Yes."

"What kind of scam?"

"Um, we, um—"

"Out with it, Cream. Did you fuck someone?" he asked, knowing he'd fuck everyone up if she did.

"Hell, no."

"Did you suck somebody's dick?"

"Wise, you are seriously bugging."

"Well, you need to tell me what kind of scam y'all pulled that would pull this much cash."

Cream decided to be truthful and told him what they had done, leaving out the part about the lap dance and ending with, "All I did was take the pictures."

"Where are the pictures?"

Cream left the kitchen and returned with the copies she kept. Wise looked through the pictures and became infuriated.

"You actually went through with this stupid ass plan? Don't you know you could have gotten hurt or killed? Who's to say they won't come after you two?"

"Cream had her cousin Duran and his boy come with us to pick up the money."

"So, you're telling me some niggas knew about this and I didn't?"

"No, I'm not telling you that. Amber made up

some lie about why we were picking up the money. You know what? Never mind. Just give me my money."

Wise threw it on the floor and Cream picked it up. He was shaking his head. "I don't know, Cream. Something about this just doesn't feel right. I find it very hard to believe that nothing happened."

"You know what, Wise? Think what you want to think. Either you're going to believe me or you're not."

Wise was real quiet. Cream started to walk away but turned around when he asked, "So Amber got you mixed up in this, huh?"

"She didn't have to hold a gun to my head."

"No, but it was her idea."

"And?"

"This is just one of the reasons I didn't like you stripping."

That was a comment that threw Cream off.

"What are you talking about, the reason you didn't like me stripping? You never asked me to stop."

"What does that look like? Me telling you what to do and what not to do. I didn't want to get cursed out."

"You try to tell me what to do any other time. Wise, I would have stopped for you a long time ago. All you had to do was say the word. But no, you liked showing me off, showing your homeboys your fine ass woman with the tight body. I've heard you say it on more than one occasion, so don't stand there and give me that bullshit about wanting me to stop."

Wise didn't respond. He just stood there looking at her because he was still in shock over what she'd done. He was also a bit jealous that she had access to so much cash. He wanted to go to Amber's and whip her ass. He couldn't believe she would do this and get Cream involved without telling him. What was she up to? What was she trying to prove?

"You know what? I'm out." Wise turned to leave.

"Where are you going?"

"To handle some business."

"What kind of business?" Cream wanted to know.

Looking her square in the eye, Wise said, "You know what kind of business."

He left Cream standing in the middle of the floor.

# 9

Wise pulled up in front of Amber's house. He didn't bother knocking. He just walked through the front door. "Amber!"

She appeared from the back. "Damn, nigga, you can't knock?"

"What's up with you getting my girl involved in some bullshit plan?"

Amber, knowing her cousin Duran was in the back room, decided not to back down from his anger. "She did what she wanted to do. I didn't hold a gun to her head."

"No, but you initiated it."

"Yeah, and she could have said no."

Wise started pacing back and forth. "You're a fucking trip, you know that? What are you trying to prove?"

"I'm not trying to prove a damn thing. I'm just

trying to make a dollar, and ain't nothing wrong with that."

Wise stood in front of her and shook his head. "You are so sorry, Amber. Do you know that?"

"If I'm so sorry then why the fuck are you fucking me?"

"I keep asking myself the same question."

Thrown off by his answer, Amber walked up to him and pressed her body against his. "You know why. Because you can't get enough of this sweet pussy."

Wise pushed her away and she stumbled. "You don't have to worry about me fucking with you again. You best believe that."

He turned and started to leave. Amber jumped up and yelled, "Wait, Wise. Let's talk."

"I don't want to talk. I don't even want to see you again, and you better believe I mean it this time."

"You know what? Fuck you, Wise. Fuck you!" Amber was losing it.

Wise just walked out and Duran walked into the living room. "Was that Wise?"

"Yeah." Amber was still looking at the door.

"You're messing with your friend's man?" Duran asked in disbelief.

"I'm my only friend."

"Yeah, okay. He seemed pretty upset. I was almost ready to come out here with my nine." He pulled a gun from underneath his shirt.

Amber looked at the gun then at him and shook her head. "Nigga, you're crazy."

"Nah, I'm just looking out for my family, because I will put a cap in his ass and take his woman."

"That's all right. I got it under control."

"You're sure?"

"Yeah. Listen, I'm tired. I need to take a nap before I go to work tonight. You coming by the club?"

"Nah, but I might stop by later. I need a place to crash."

Amber left the room and returned with a key. "Here, take my extra key in case I'm not here when you come."

"Alright."

"And don't be bringin' no bitches up in my crib either."

Duran responded with a laugh.


Walking into the club, Cream looked around for Grape. With the emotional day that she'd been experiencing, she realized what was missing in her life. One of the things was a true friend and true support. She missed Grape's friendship. She missed him being there and she missed being able to open up without being judged or criticized. He'd been her protector for so long and he had this ability to make her feel safe all the time. She knew she'd been shutting him out.

Cream thought back to when they tried to have a relationship, if that's what you wanted to call it. She should have known better than to get involved with him, especially when her heart belonged to Wise. It didn't matter that they were broken up. Her emotions and energy had still been with him.

Grape offered her a shoulder to cry on and so much more. She knew she had taken advantage of him, not in a financial way, but in other ways. For one, she didn't have to work as hard as the other dancers. But she did try to balance it by helping him with his books. He paid her every week. This was their little secret.

Cream sat at the bar and was lost in thought when Grape came from the back with a worried look on his face. He had been watching her from the camera that was placed in the corner of the room. The second she walked in the bar, no makeup, wearing jeans and a baby tee, he thought, *Damn, she's beautiful.* He could also tell something was bothering her.

He startled her out of her thoughts. Cream turned around and immediately started crying. They were tears of frustration over the day's events, tears of guilt over what she'd done with Amber, but most of all tears of relief to see someone who loved her unconditionally.

Grape reached his arms out and Cream fell into them. Grape didn't say a word. He just held her. After she had composed herself, he spoke.

"What's wrong? Did something happen? Did Wise do something?" He hoped so, because he was looking for a reason to bust Wise's ass.

Cream looked into his eyes and told him, "Grape, I'm getting out."

"Out? Out of what?"

Waving her arms around, she said, "This. This life. Dancing, the hood, Wise. Everything. I feel like I'm about to have a nervous breakdown. I'm disgusted with myself. What kind of example am I setting for Shala? I don't have a high school diploma, yet I expect her to go to college. How much longer can I keep what I do from my son? I'm tired of pretending to be happy. I want to go back to school. I want more out of life. I want to be more than an around the way girl."

"You are more than an around the way girl. You're special, Cream. I've always told you that. You just never listened. You're beautiful, you're sexy, and you can do anything and be anything you put your mind to. Only you are limiting yourself."

Looking into his eyes and seeing the love, Cream felt a warm sensation run through her body. Cream asked him, "What would your girl LaLa have to say about all you said?"

"It doesn't matter what she would have to say. You're my number one girl."

Cream knew he meant it, too. "And little do you know, you're my number one guy."

Cream loved Grape in her own way and truth be told, she always thought he would be there for her on the back burner until he met this LaLa chick. Grape's new girl. She was one of the reasons they'd stopped spending so much time together. Call it women's intuition or whatever, LaLa knew something was either going on or had gone on between the two of them, and she let Grape know it. She also approached Cream, not with an attitude, but with a question: "What if this was your man who had another female for a best friend?" Cream had understood her point and tried to keep her distance out of respect.

"Am I?" Grape asked.

"Are you what?"

"Your number one guy."

Cream knew he was talking about more than friendship so she chose to leave it alone. Taking his hand, she said, "Come on. Let's go do your paper-work."

Grape let her change the subject but not before asking, "Are you dancing tonight?"

"No," Cream told him. "I won't be dancing ever again."


Cream left the club early that night and went home to find Wise sitting on the couch.

Surprised, she asked, "What are you doing here?"

"I live here," he told her.

"Yeah, but you're always out when I get home this early."

"I wanted to spend time with our son," he told her.

Cream wanted to say, "Well, it's about time." Instead, she decided it was best to leave it alone. "Well, where is he?" she asked.

" 'Sleep. I wore his little butt out."

"Where is Shala?"

"She's staying the night at a friend's."

Cream made a mental note to make a call to ver-ify that later.

She plopped down next to Wise.

Turning to face her, Wise said, "Cream, I've been thinking a lot about us and I don't want to lose you. I promise to make more of an effort. I know you're thinking about leaving me and I don't want you to, so please let's give us another chance."

Cream had heard it all before. She was tired of going back and forth with it. "I need time to think, Wise."

"What's there to think about? Either you want to be with me or you don't."

"It's not that easy."

Standing up, Wise told her he was going to take a shower. Before he was out of the room, Cream told him, "I quit the club."

This stopped him. "You what?"

"I quit dancing. As a matter of fact, I didn't even dance tonight."

Wise didn't know what to say.

Cream, seeing that he was at a loss for words, told him, "Go ahead and take your shower. We'll talk tomorrow."

Meanwhile, across town, Duran was arriving at Amber's house. He saw her car in the driveway and couldn't wait to get inside. He had some shit to tell her about one of her old men. Using the extra key she gave him, he walked in and yelled out her name. "Amber!" There was no answer. He knew she was home because he could hear the television in her room. He figured she was asleep and he felt no qualms about waking her. "Yo, Amber, let me tell you about Keith."

Her bedroom door was slightly ajar and before he even opened it, Duran got a sick feeling in the pit of his stomach. Something wasn't right. He was afraid to open the door because his street sense was telling him not to.

He thought, *Please let everything be okay.* Duran loved his cousin even though she could be a bitch at times. She let him stay with her without any questions when he needed a place to crash and she often threw a couple of dollars his way.

Opening the door, his worst fears were confirmed. Amber lay on the floor, face swollen and bleeding. She'd been beat down and didn't appear to be moving. Her eyes were open and pleading with him for help.

"What the fuck?" He rushed toward her and picked her up slowly. "Who did this to you? Amber, talk to me. Who did this to you?" He was ready to wreck shop.

Amber kept trying to say something, but she was in too much pain.

"I don't know what you're saying. Who did this to you?"

"911 . . . over some bullshit . . . 911," she kept repeating and pointing to her dresser. "Call him, call him." Then she passed out.

"Oh shit, oh shit." Duran started pacing back and forth, trying to collect his thoughts. He checked to see if she had a pulse and found one. Picking up the phone, he dialed 911 and said, "Get here fast. My cousin is unconscious." He gave the address. The operator tried to keep him on the phone but he hung up on her. He walked over to the dresser and saw some pictures.

"Oh, hell no. He will not get away with this." Putting the phone on the floor, he waited until he heard sirens and quickly left, unseen and unheard.


After Wise finished taking his shower, he and Cream were dozing on the couch. The sound of someone banging on the door woke them.

"Who the hell is that?" Cream asked.

"How the hell should I know? Maybe it's one of your friends."

"I don't have any friends that'll drop by unannounced at this time of the night. It's probably one of your drug dealing buddies."

"Now, why they got to be all that?"

"Just answer the door," Cream told him, standing up and heading toward the bedroom. "And you make sure to tell whoever it is not to come knocking on the door this time of the night again."

"How you know it's for me?"

"It's for you," Cream said and stepped into the bedroom.

Wise went to the door and peeked through the peephole. "What the hell is this nigga doing at my door this time of the night?" They were cool, but they weren't that cool. Cracking the door, Wise asked, "Yo man, do you know what time it is?"

Ignoring the question, Duran said, "I need to talk to you."

"About what? We don't have any business together." Wise was about to close the door.

Duran put his foot in the door. "Your family here?"

"Why?"

"Is your girl home?"

"Why you want to know if my girl is home? What the fuck is this all about?"

Duran pulled two pictures out of his pocket. One was of Wise chilling in Amber's house, on the couch smoking some weed, looking way too relaxed. Another was him sleeping naked on her bed.

"What the . . . ?" Wise stepped out of the front door.

The second he did, Duran jumped on him and punched him in the face. Caught off guard, Wise stumbled back, looking confused. "What the fuck?"

Before he could finish his thoughts, Duran threw another punch. "You hurt my cousin. I'm gonna hurt you."

"What are you talking about?" Wise knew that Duran was Amber's cousin, but he had no idea why this was happening. Getting his balance and throwing a punch, he said, "I don't know what you're talking about."

They continued to wrestle. "You know what I'm talking about. I was there when you blacked out on her this afternoon. Then you went back and beat her up."

"I don't know what you're talking about, man."

The words were spoken in between punches. By now they were banging against the door and Cream came running to see what was going on. When she saw, she ran back into the house and grabbed Wise's gun. She pointed it at Duran. "Get off him! Get off him now!"

Duran stepped back and looked from one to the other. "You're protecting this asshole?"

"What's going on? What are you doing here?"

Duran pointed to the pictures that were on the ground. Snatching them up, he handed them to Cream. Cream glanced at the pictures. She looked at them and at Wise, who was holding his head down, busted.

She looked at Duran. "Are you here over these pictures?"

"No, I'm here because Wise beat Amber's ass and now she's on the way to the hospital."

Cream looked at Wise in disbelief. "What is he talking about?"

Wise shook his head, "I don't know. I've been here all day. Ask Shala. Ask Shacquille."

"Why would he make something like this up?"

Interrupting, Duran said, "Yeah, why would I make this up?"

"Maybe it was those white boys they pulled that scam on."

Duran was lost. He didn't know about a scam. He thought the women had been collecting money from a bachelor party when they were at Denny's with those white boys.

"What the fuck are you talking about?"

"What do you think I'm talking about?" Wise said. "Didn't you go with them to pick up the money?"

"Yeah, but I'm sure ain't no white boys gonna do this shit over a few hundred dollars."

When he said that, Wise started laughing. "A few hundred dollars? Is that what you think? Try almost ten grand."

Duran was shocked. Not even waiting for him to say anything, Cream said, "Wise, I want you to leave."

"What?"

"You heard me. I want you to get the fuck out of my house."

Looking around to see if any of the neighbors were listening, Wise said, "Listen, you go back inside and we'll talk about his when I come inside."

Cream looked at Duran and asked, "Where's Amber now?"

"At the hospital. I called 911 before I came here."

"Why don't you go to the hospital and check on her? I'll be there shortly. I need to handle something." She looked at Wise. "You need to pack up your shit and step."

"What we need to be doing is looking for some white boys," Wise said.

"Duran, please just go. I'll talk to you at the hospital."

Duran turned around and walked away, leaving Cream and Wise standing at the door.

"You might as well go inside," Cream told Wise.

Wise walked in and Cream, tired, hurt, disappointed and disgusted asked, "How long have you and Amber been fucking?"

"Ain't nobody fucking that girl," Wise said.

"Wise, please don't lie to me. I have the proof right here in my hands." She flung the pictures at him.

He didn't answer.

"So what? You can't talk now?"

"Listen, it was a long time ago," Wise lied.

Cream couldn't even bring herself to cry. She was numb. "I don't care if it was five years ago. She was supposed to be my friend and you knew this."

There was really nothing he could say.

"Leave, Wise. Just leave."

"Baby." Wise started to beg.

"Don't baby me. I want you to leave."

He didn't budge.

"Now!" she yelled, on the verge of hysterics, waving the gun.

Wise looked at Cream and looked at the gun and decided it was best that he did leave. "Let me grab my shoes and a T-shirt."

Cream followed him into the room and watched his every move. She followed him to the front door and opened it. "Goodbye, Wise."

Wise didn't like the finality in the way she said it. "We'll talk later."

Cream pushed him out the door and closed it, locking it behind her. Walking over to the phone, she placed a call to Grape.

"Hello." He answered in a sleepy tone.

"Grape, it's Cream. We need to talk."

"Can't it wait until later?"

"No, it's an emergency. I'm afraid someone is after me, Amber is fucking Wise, I'm home alone, and I'm scared."

"I'm on my way," Grape told her.

"Okay, I'll see you when you get here. Just ring the phone once and let me know when you're outside."

Cream sat on the couch in one spot until Grape arrived. When he entered he looked around and saw the gun, the pictures of Amber and Wise, and the state that Cream was in. He asked her, "What's up?"

Cream decided to tell him everything that had transpired—the setup and the scam. She gave him Jim's business cards, then went and got the pictures she'd hidden. She told him Amber had been beaten up, then told him about how Duran came to the door and how she put Wise out. Grape listened in silence until she was done.

"I don't know what to do. I don't know who to turn to. What if they come after me?"

Grape stood up and asked, "Where are the kids?"

"Asleep."

"Listen, I want you to get some rest as well. I'm gonna take care of everything."

"But how? Aren't you angry at me?"

"I'm more disappointed than anything, but we'll deal with that later. What we have to work on right now is solving this potential problem." Looking at the card with Jim's business address in his hand, he told her, "I'm gonna take care of this first and we'll talk about us later."

"Us?"

"Yes, us."

Grape stood up and Cream pulled him back down. "Please. Will you stay with me until morning? I don't want to be alone."

"I'll stay," he told her.

Cream just looked at Grape and knew everything would turn out all right. For her, that is. Not for Jim and his boy Michael.

# 10

The following day turned out to be an event in itself. Amber survived and Cream went to visit her at the hospital. She wasn't sure why she even cared, but she did. She also needed to understand why. Why would Amber sleep with her man? Why would she betray her?

"You have two men who love you, Cream—Wise and Grape. I have no one."

"That's your reason? That's your excuse?" Instead of going off in the hospital, Cream ended up feeling sorry for her. "You know what? You can have Wise. You two are made for each other."

When she left the hospital Grape was waiting at her house. "I took care of everything. Believe me, you won't be hearing from those white boys. They're gonna regret the thought of even putting you in danger's way."

Nervous, Cream asked him, "What did you do?"

"Don't worry about it. What you don't know won't hurt you. But in the meantime, I want you and the kids to stay at one of my houses in Jersey."

"One of your houses in Jersey? What are you talking about?"

"I own property, Cream. I thought I told you that."

Cream couldn't even respond.

"Will you do that for me?"

She started crying.

"Why are you crying?"

"Because, because. I've always wanted to live in Jersey."

"Are you gonna tell Wise where you're staying?"

"No, not right away."

"Is it really over between you two?"

"Yes."

"Good, because you know I love you, right?"

"I've always known."

Holding her close, Grape asked, "What are you gonna do about the baby?"

"I'm not going to have it. There's just no way."

"Well, just know I'll be there, whatever your decision."

"So are you saying this is the beginning of us?"

"Yes, the ending to an old way of life and beginning of a new way of life."

# Southern Comfort

# by LaJill Hunt

# 1

*I hate this place. I hate these wannabe thug ass niggas, I hate these wannabe fly, ghetto ass girls. I hate this cold ass weather. Everybody wanna be somebody important and really ain't shit. I hate New York and I just wanna go home. I wanna go back to Atlanta, where people are courteous enough to speak and man enough to look you in the motherfuckin' eye. Where you don't gotta have the same blood running through your veins to be considered family, just being true to who you wit' makes you a member. I wanna go where it's hot in the summer and winter. I wanna go home.*

Sydni looked at the words she had written in her journal a little over five years ago. She was only fifteen years old then and she had been miserable. Her mother had decided to move back to Brooklyn after Nana Brown, Sydni's great-grandmother, had passed away. Her mom sold Nana Brown's house, packed Sydni, her twelve-year-old sister, Miriam, and her sixteen-year-old brother, Aaron, and they relocated. Sydni's father was from New York and even though he was long gone, Sydni felt that her mother thought she had a chance of running into that sorry bastard if they headed up to Brooklyn. So far, they hadn't. The move didn't really bother Miriam, who they called Magic, or Aaron as much as it did Sydni. They both seemed as comfortable in the Big Apple as they were in the Peach State. Aaron excelled in sports and Miriam in socializing, so neither had a problem fitting in. But Sydni was shy. She kept people at a distance and made no effort to befriend anyone, even though people often commented on her beauty. She was continually mistaken for Puerto Rican, and she hated that fact too.

" 'Sup, mami? Tu eres ta belle!" one guy yelled from the passenger side of a car as she walked home from school one afternoon. She tried to ignore him, but he was persistent.

"What?" She turned to face him.

"I'm sayin', yo. What a brother gotta do to get wit' a fly mami like you?"

"I don't have any kids, so I'm not anybody's mommy, yo!" She rolled her eyes and kept going. Suddenly, the guy jumped out of the car and ran to catch up with her.

"I'm sorry. I thought all of you Hispanic chicks liked to be called mami."

"Well, guess what, stupid? I'm not Hispanic. Everyone with light skin and long hair ain't from Puerto Rico, so I don't speak Spanish. Now if you'll excuse me, I have a life to get on with." She eyed him from head to toe and brushed past him again.

"Damn. If that accent wasn't so sexy, I would be

pissed at you and your bitch ass attitude. But I guess a brotha gotta take the good with the bad. What's your name, shorty?" He was walking next to her at this point, matching her swift stride. She tried to speed up but he stayed right next to her.

"What do you want? Can't you see I got some-where to go?" she asked without looking at him.

"Come on, D, let's roll. Leave that trick alone!" The driver pulled beside them and yelled out of the window. Sydni rolled her eyes at him and bit her tongue instead of cussing him out. *No home training. None of these niggas got home training.*

"I'm saying, yo. I just wanna know your name." The guy, whose name she assumed was D, contin-ued.

"Just leave me alone. I ain't bothering you, so you don't have to bother me." They got to the corner and to her disappointment, they had to stop for traffic. She was two blocks from her house and she was not trying to put up with D's company the re-mainder of the way. She pushed the button on the light pole several times, hoping the WALK signal would light up so she could keep moving.

"That ain't gonna help. You still gotta stay here with me a few more minutes," the tall, lanky figure said sarcastically. Sydni turned to face him, prepar-ing to cuss him out, but as she looked at him, she paused. He was dark, and his skin was smooth as silk. Sydni was almost attracted to him, but then he continued to be harassing as hell and anything she remotely felt about him diminished instantly. He was a typical broken English, every-female-wanna-get-wit'-me, I'm-hard-cuz-I'm-from-New-York-and-that-makes-me-a-gangsta hoodlum.

"Look, I ain't playing wit' you. Leave me alone, or else!" she yelled as the light changed and she crossed the street. Her anger seemed to excite him.

"Or else what?" He laughed.

"Or else you gonna have to deal wit' me. Now leave her alone!" The voice came from behind them. Sydni turned and was secretly relieved to see Aaron standing in the middle of the sidewalk. He approached and stood beside her like he was her bodyguard.

"Who the hell are you?" Sydni's follower squared his shoulders and asked Aaron.

"None of your business. Now leave her alone."

"Nigga, fuck you. I don't have to do shit. I was just asking your girl what her name was. She the one that got a bitch ass attitude."

"Then leave her the fuck alone and you don't have to worry about what kind of attitude she has." Aaron took a step toward him. Sydni put her hand on Aaron's shoulder in order to stop him.

"Forget him, Aaron. Let's just go."

"'Aaron'? Aaron Johnson?" The follower blinked.

"Yeah, that's me," Aaron answered, ready to rumble in case something jumped off.

"Man, Coach Sheppard been talking mad shit about you. He said you got hella game. You supposed to be trying out for the team, right?"

"Yeah." Aaron relaxed a bit and soon the two boys were talking about basketball as if nothing had ever happened.

"Hey, this is my sister Sydni." Aaron pulled Sydni by the arm and she jerked away. She was undoubtedly pissed. Here Aaron was supposed to be knocking this nigga out for harassing her, but he was acting like they were boys from way back.

"This your sister, for real?" He looked from Aaron, tall and darker than him, to Sydni, short and as light as any mixed chick that he had ever dated.

"I get my color from my dad," Aaron told him.

"I see, but y'all do look alike once you get past the color. What's up, Sydni? I'm Darrius." He held his hand out for her to shake, but she looked at it as she turned to walk away. "She like that all the time?"

"Yep. Sometimes worse," Aaron told him.

"I can't imagine." Darrius watched the beautiful girl storm off and could not help picking with her some more.

"It was a pleasure walking with you, mami. Yo quiero ser tu hombre."

"That will never happen, pendejo," she turned and yelled back at him.

That was the beginning of Aaron and Darrius' friendship, and now, five years later, Sydni still hated Darrius. She had never liked him, especially today, at this moment. She loathed Darrius and the friendship he had with Aaron. If they had never been friends, this day would not be happening. She closed her old journal and picked up her latest one, turning to the next blank page. She wrote the date at the top and began her entry.

*Today, we are burying my brother.*

# 2

"Syd, can I come in?" she heard the soft voice ask. Sydni had just changed out of her navy blue suit and was pulling on a pair of sweatpants when she heard the knocking at her door.

"Yeah, Magic, come in," she told her sister. Magic came in Sydni's room, closing the door behind her. She sat on the side of the bed, her eyes stopping on the program with Aaron's picture on the front, lying on Sydni's pillow. Sydni looked at her sister's fatigued face and quickly grabbed her T-shirt and pulled it over her head. She sat next to Magic and rubbed her back.

"It's a lot of people downstairs asking about you. You coming back down?" Magic asked.

"Yeah, I just wanted to get outta these clothes. I'll be down in a minute. Where's Mama?"

"She's still down there. Mister Joe is clinging to her arm like it's gonna fall off if he let go. You know he's just trying to put on a good show," Magic informed her. They both disliked their mother's boyfriend of the past year. He was controlling and opinionated, and Sydni didn't like the way he looked at her, especially when she was at work. He was her boss at the dry cleaning shop where she was the cashier/bookkeeper. That was actually how he and her mother had met. She'd come in to see Sydni one day and he invited her to lunch. They had been dating ever since. The only reason Sydni stayed at the cleaners was that he grossly overpaid her and he was only there on Wednesdays and Fridays to pick up the deposit for the bank.

"I'll bet. How you holding up, Magic?" Sydni looked at her sister. She hadn't really said anything. She'd hardly cried during the funeral and Sydni was worried. Magic was usually the most emotional person in the family. While Sydni kept all of her emotions in, Magic had always been the ultimate drama queen, always overly dramatic about any issue, happy or sad.

"I still can't believe he's dead, Syd. I'm waiting for him to come home and cuss me out about my grades or some guy Mama told him about me seeing. I'm waiting for things to go back to normal."

"I know, Magic. It's gonna take some time." Sydni didn't know what else to say. She was still in shock in some ways herself.

"Now, what are you gonna do? I know Aaron was getting the money for you to go back home."

"I don't know, Magic. I don't know."

Another knock at the door caused both sisters to jump.

"Who is it?" Sydni called out.

"It's me, Sydni. Byron," the baritone voice answered.

"It's your *boyfriend,*" Magic whispered teasingly. Sydni was used to the teasing about Byron. It had been going on for years. It was no secret that he had been infatuated with her since high school. He was sweet and smart; what Nana Brown would call well bred, from a good family. He was easy to talk to and Sydni could appreciate his intelligence. Byron was attractive as hell, too. He stood five feet eleven, one hundred eighty-five pounds and he had the most perfect teeth Sydni had ever seen in her life. There was only one problem: Byron was white, very white, and Sydni had never, would never, could never roll like that. No, sir. She made certain that he always knew that, and he respected it. He seemed content to be a part of Sydni's life in whatever capacity she would have him.

"Come in, Byron," Sydni said, giving Magic a look of warning as the door eased open.

"I just wanted to make sure you guys were okay." He had a concerned look on his face. Magic stood up and gave him a hug. She liked Byron. He was really cool, and although she knew that Sydni wasn't feeling him because of the obvious, she thought he was at least do-able. He smelled so good and his arms felt strong; like a man. She closed her eyes and enjoyed the moment. When she re-opened them, Sydni was looking at her funny.

"Thanks, Byron. We're okay. I just wanted to change into something a little more comfortable," Sydni told him as he released Magic and reached for her hand. She knew he was genuinely concerned but she also knew that Magic was hot in the tail. Her promiscuity was one problem she *and* Aaron had with Magic. Aaron had had to beat down more than one guy who she had lured into the wrong place at the wrong time: in other words, their Mama's house when she thought no one was home. Sydni hoped that it was just a passing phase, but it had been years and Magic was still wide open.

"Did you eat anything?" he asked, looking at her sad eyes.

"Not yet." Sydni sighed. "It's too many people down there right now. I'll eat something. I promise."

"You need to eat, Syd. Come on. I'll fix you a plate. I'll even protect you from the masses if you need me to." He pulled her toward the door, smiling. She glanced over at Magic, who watched.

"I'll be down, Byron. Just give me a few more moments," she told him.

"If you're not, I'm coming back up here and carrying you down myself," he warned. He opened the door and stepped into the hallway, bumping into someone unexpectedly. "Oh, sorry."

"Yeah, it's okay," Darrius murmured. He briefly glanced at Byron as he made his way past him. The door to Sydni's room was slightly open and he slowly eased it open. He waited for a signal or sign of some sort from Sydni to let him know that it was okay for him to come in. When there wasn't, he cleared his throat.

"Hey, D, You can come in." Magic motioned for him. He slowly walked into the neat bedroom, trying not to be obvious as he looked around. There were various pictures on the wall, mostly of Sydni and Magic, some including Aaron and their mother, all of them smiling. His heart began to feel heavy as he saw a few that even included him. They had become his second family and he loved them, including Sydni.

"Your moms told me you all came upstairs. I just wanted to—"

"Just wanted to what? Let me guess, see if we were okay? Well, Darrius, we're fine. We would probably be doing better if we hadn't had to bury our brother, but he decided to hang with you last weekend and wound up dead, remember?"

"Sydni, that's not fair!" Magic hissed. "It wasn't his fault!"

"Don't you think I feel just as bad, Sydni? I mean, I lost my best friend," Darrius retorted. He looked at her. He was used to the look of disgust when she looked at him, but the look of hatred she held deepened his pain.

"If he was your best friend you wouldn't have had him with you when you made your so-called run to the strip club," Sydni spat at him. He knew she was hurting. Aaron was her heart and soul and they were closer than any brother and sister he had ever seen. Aaron would do anything for his sister. When he came home last week for Spring Break, all he could talk about was getting dough for Sydni to go back to Atlanta. It was one of the reasons he wanted to take that ride to the club with D that night. He wanted to talk to Dax about flipping some money.

But D kept that bit of information to himself and just let Sydni vent. If he told her Aaron's real reason for going with him that night, she might feel guilty, and he didn't want that. He knew the weight of that guilt and wouldn't want to wish it on anyone. He looked at Magic, who put her arm around his shoulder. The two sisters were so opposite. Sydni with her long, silky hair, oval face, eyes the color of jade and skin the color of wheat. She was a dead ringer for that singer Mya, just a little thicker. He remembered the first time he saw her and mistook her for a Puerto Rican chick. He had never had a female so mad at him. He almost cussed her ass out until Aaron stepped in that day, too.

Ever since then, he and Syd had never clicked. Whenever he stayed at the house, she made it known that she didn't like him and he made it known that the feeling was mutual. She was so fucking stuck up and he hated that. She always referred to him as a thug or a bum and that shit got old. Granted, school was not one of his top priorities once he blew his knee out his junior year and hopes of a basketball scholarship diminished, but he did graduate and had a job on top of that. Shit, he had dreams just like she did and she wasn't the only one hurting because of Aaron's death. But Sydni was Sydni whether Aaron was dead or alive.

Magic was his homegirl. It took both him and Aaron to watch out for her hot ass. The girl seemed to have men on the brain. Every time he looked, there was a different one in her face. In some ways, he couldn't blame them. Magic was a beautiful, darker version of her sister and was by far sexier. Both girls had shapes any nigga would want, but Magic had sexy in her walk, in her talk, in her laugh, and in her hazel eyes. They both shared the same thick lips, but Magic knew how to lick hers just right, and he constantly had to remind himself that not only was she a young girl, she was his best friend's sister. That fact alone kept his libido in check when it came to Magic.

"We're okay, D. We'll be back down in a few," Magic told him. He looked like she felt: lost. She was used to seeing him in jeans and Timbs. Today he wore a gray, four-button suit. It was the first time she had seen him really dressed up. He looked good.

"Cool, I'll check you when you come down," he told her. He turned to leave, pausing as he passed Sydni. He opened his mouth and murmured something.

"What? What did you say?" she asked defensively.

"I said you ain't the only one that loved him. I did too."

# 3

"Sydni, have you seen your sister?" Sydni's mother asked loudly through the phone. It was Friday evening and Sydni was more than ready to go home. She had taken her last final this morning and was glad that the semester was finally over. She didn't know how she had made it these last two months with her brother being gone, but she had. Sydni had to admit that she'd thought about quitting school on more than one occasion after Aaron died, but she had to get her degree. She owed that much to his memory. He had promised her that if she made it through Brooklyn Community College he would make sure she would be able to finish her studies at Spelman. Now, he was gone and she wasn't even excited about her upcoming graduation on Sunday.

Then there was Magic. Her sister seemed to have lost her mind these days. She had begun staying out late at night, barely making it in before the sun came up. At first, no one seemed to notice because they were all mourning in their own way. But it was now apparent that Magic was taking it to a whole new level. Granted, she was eighteen now, but their mother still demanded respect in her household, and that meant coming in a whole lot earlier than Magic had been.

"No, Mama. Did you try her cell phone?" Sydni asked, not wanting her mother to worry.

"Her voicemail keeps coming up." She could hear the annoyance in her mother's voice.

"Her battery is probably dead, Ma. That's all."

"It always seems to be dead when I call it. I don't even know if she came home last night, do you? I swear, I just don't know what I'm gonna do with her. They called and said she ain't show up for work again. She don't wanna go to school. She won't keep a job. If your brother was here—"

"I'll talk to her, Ma. I promise," Sydni said. The bell rang, alerting her that someone had entered the dry cleaning shop. She turned to see Mr. Davis, the owner, walking in and several customers at the counter. "Ma, I gotta go."

"Is Joe there? Tell him to call me when he gets a chance."

"I will, Ma. See you when I get home." Sydni quickly hung the phone back on the wall. She could feel Mr. Joe's eyes taking in every move she made and avoided facing him.

"Evenin', Sydni." His raspy voice greeted her.

"Hi, Mister Joe," she said. She took her time helping the customers so she wouldn't have to be alone with him.

"Was that your mother you were speaking with?"

"Yes," she answered without looking up. "She wants you to call her when you get a chance."

"I sure will. I'm taking her out to Dempsey's tonight for dinner," he said.

"Really? That's nice. She needs to get out." Sydni finished with her last customer and took a seat on the stool she kept behind the register.

"I know. I made reservations for eight o'clock. You have the deposit ready for me?" She could feel him as he walked up behind her, and she tensed up. This was one of the reasons she disliked him. He was always up on her.

"The bank bag is in the safe already. The deposit slip is already made out," she replied. He was so close that she could smell the scent of his cologne. She could not believe his ass still wore Grey Flannel.

"Let me get some bills out of here." He reached across her, opening the register. She quickly jumped off the stool to get out of his way, nearly falling down in the process. Mr. Joe smiled as he reached to catch her by the arm, his hand brushing against her breast in the process.

"Be careful, Sydni," he said cynically. The look he gave let her know that the feel had not been an accident on his part, and she shivered at the thought. She looked at his fat face, with his salt-and-pepper beard and moustache and his bushy eyebrows. She could not see what her mother saw in him.

The bell rang again and Sydni was damn near overjoyed to see Byron walking through the door.

"Quitting time, guys." He smiled. Sydni looked at the clock and saw that it was indeed six o'clock.

"Hey, Byron. I'm ready right now." She smiled and scurried past Mr. Joe.

"How are you, Mister Joe?" Byron asked in his usual friendly manner.

"Fine, Byron. Sydni, I need to see you in the back for a moment." Mr. Joe motioned toward the back of the store. Sydni looked at Byron.

"Go ahead, Sydni. I can wait right here." He grinned. *Wrong answer, jerk,* was all she thought of as she walked past the racks of neatly pressed items to Mr. Joe's office. The smell of starch and plastic filled her nose as she tried to figure out what the hell he wanted to see her about. She entered his small office behind him, making sure the door stayed open. He reached into the briefcase that was on top of the cluttered desk and handed her an envelope.

"I was going to give this to you on Sunday, but I decided to go ahead and let you have it now."

"Thanks," she said, confused by the gesture.

"It's your graduation gift. You are graduating, aren't you?" He licked his lips as he asked her. She took a step back.

"Yeah, I am."

"Open it." He smiled. She carefully opened the yellow envelope and read the card congratulating her. As she opened it, she could see several bills peeking from the inside. She glanced up and saw him taking a step toward her.

"I, uh . . ."

Sydni didn't know whether to continue opening the card or get the hell out.

"Go on, read it."

She opened the card and her mouth fell open as she realized that each of the bills had the face of Benjamin Franklin and there were a lot of them. She was speechless. So much so that she hadn't realized how close he was until he spoke.

"Did you read the signature?"

She shifted the money so she could read what it said.

"Love, your future stepfather?" Sydni read aloud. She could hear her heart beating in her head and tried to clear her thoughts.

"Yes, Sydni. Your mother has been through so much these past couple of months and I have realized how important she and you girls are to me. I want to be there for you all always. I want us to be close. I want us to be one big, happy family." He put his arms around her and pulled her to him. She could feel his face in her hair as he rubbed her back. She tensed her body and then she felt it. It was subtle, but she knew what it was, that small pressure against her thigh, poking her through his pants. *This perverted bastard has a hard-on!* She pushed away from him and nearly bum-rushed Byron as she ran out the store. *I gotta get the hell away from this city,* was all she could think about.

"Where the hell have you been?" Sydni demanded when she got home. Magic was sitting on the edge of her bed, painting her toenails like nothing was wrong.

"What the fuck is your problem?"

"My problem is you! Why didn't you carry your

ass to work today, Miriam? They calling the house, getting Ma all upset. Did your ass even come home last night?"

"Why is she upset? That job was whack as hell anyway. It wasn't like I was making any real money." Magic gently blew her feet.

"That's not the goddamn point. It was a fucking job. And answer the other questions. Where the hell were you and why didn't you come home last night?" Sydni began pacing the floor, still fuming from her perverted encounter with Mr. Joe.

"I was out! Damn, can't a sistah go out and chill? Just cuz you ain't got a nigga and you ain't getting none don't mean that everybody ain't." Magic looked at Sydni, wishing someone would hurry up and give her some dick so she would loosen up. If it wasn't a shame, she would even advise Byron to screw Sydni. Dick was dick, no matter what color it was. Long as you know how to throw it.

"Shut the hell up, Magic. And I mean that shit. I ain't in the mood."

"What has you so pissed? And don't say it's me, either."

"Did you know Mister Joe is gonna propose to Ma?"

"For real? That's nice." Magic reached on her dresser and grabbed the polish remover along with some cotton balls then began on her fingers. Sydni snatched the cotton from her sister and looked her in the face.

"What the hell do you mean, nice? Have you noticed the way he looks at you?"

"He looks the way any other man looks at me. I'm fine as hell, so I'm used to it." She reached for another cotton ball and continued to take off her polish.

"Bullshit. That man is nasty and trifling and I am not gonna let him marry my mother," Sydni said matter-of-factly.

"I hate to be the one to tell you this, but that's not your decision to make. Mama loves him. With everything that has been going on around here, he's been right there for her."

"Then, to top it off, the motherfucker tried to bribe me. Gave me a graduation card with a grand cash and signed it *your future stepfather*. Like I was supposed to be impressed." Sydni finally sat down next to her sister. She brushed her long hair out of her face and sighed.

"Shit! *I'm* impressed. I can't stand his overstuffed ass, but a grand?" When she heard this bit of news, Magic put down the cotton balls and remover and perked up. "Damn, maybe I *should* go to school."

"Please, your ass barely graduated high school," Sydni teased. The phone rang but Magic grabbed it before Sydni could.

"Hello. Hey. Yeah, everything's cool. Yeah, at two o'clock on Sunday. I wasn't out there with them. Who told you that, D?" Magic giggled in the phone.

Sydni frowned and rolled her eyes at Magic when she heard D's name. She could not believe Magic was telling him about the graduation like that nigga cared.

She turned and left Magic's bedroom without saying another word. She went into the kitchen, roaming for something to eat, even though she wasn't really hungry. After Byron picked her up from work, they'd stopped by one of their favorite pizza spots and gotten a slice. She'd vented about her mother and Mr. Joe without mentioning his apparent arousing moment or lecherous looks.

"If he makes your mother happy, you shouldn't worry about it, Sydni," he said, taking a bite of pizza.

"He doesn't make her happy. No man can make a woman happy. That's just a myth. People are responsible for their own happiness," she responded.

"You know what I mean. If he adds to her happiness, then. Is that a better way to put it?" He smiled at her. She didn't return the smile. She just shook her head. "If you would let me, I would do the same for you. I just want to see you happy."

"That won't be happening here. There's nothing in this godforsaken city that can make me happy. The only reason I stayed after high school graduation was because Aaron asked me to stay with Ma and go to BK Community and then he would help pay my tuition to Spelman. Now, he's gone and I'm stuck." She sat back in the booth, looking down at her slice.

"You're not stuck, Sydni. What about financial aid? Or a loan?" he asked. She knew he was trying to be helpful, but his naïve suggestions were beginning to irritate her. He had no idea what it was like to be broke. His parents were well off which meant that he was well off.

His family lived in the prestigious Jewish section of Crown Heights and both of his parents were attorneys. Where he lived, the name Byron Steinhill, II, meant a lot, to say the least. The only reason that his parents accepted Sydni and Byron's friendship was because Sydni had gained their respect with her intelligence. They could not deny that she was the smartest female their only son had ever brought home and by far the most beautiful, despite the fact that she was black.

"Financial aid doesn't cover everything. I would still need some loot to get straight once I get there."

"Well, about how much money would you need, Sydni?"

Sydni looked in his eyes and laughed. He seemed so concerned. "How much? Ten grand would do me right. I could go to school full time and not really have to work. I could maybe get me a little car and still have money to get me some gear if I wanted to."

"Ten grand isn't a whole lot of money." He shrugged.

"For you it's not. For me it's damn near impossible. But let's go. I'm done and tired. I just wanna go home." She stood and grabbed her purse.

She couldn't help notice the ugly looks she got from a group of hootchie bitches who were wearing names they probably couldn't pronounce. Sydni had learned to expect the stares. Byron acted like he didn't see them.

Little did people realize that she and Byron were just friends. They'd shared a lot of the same classes in high school and held many of the same interests, so they gradually became close in spite of their cultural differences. Sydni loved talking to Byron. He could hold her interest, which was more than she could say about any of the other male counterparts who tried to holla at her for a moment.

"Sellout!" Sydni heard one girl comment. It took all she had not to turn around and pull out every track the trick had in her head. She tossed her hair over her shoulder as she walked by their table.

"Jealous," she replied and kept walking. When she got to the door that Byron had opened for her, she made sure they were watching as she put her arms around his waist and kissed him. "Thanks, baby."

"You are so fake." He laughed as the door closed behind them.

"But you enjoyed every minute of it."

"Indeed, I did."

"Why do you do that, Sydni?" Magic asked, walking into the kitchen after she got off the phone with D.

"Do what?"

"Hate on D. You been doing this shit for years and it's getting real old."

"I don't like him; never have, never will. I can't believe he's still calling this house after everything he caused. And then you got the nerve to talk to him like everything is all good." Sydni glared at her.

"What are you talking about, Sydni?"

"Hello, our brother is . . . if he wouldn't have been with him . . . Aaron . . ." Sydni was too frustrated to explain her thoughts about Darrius. "I just want him to stay away from me. That's another reason I wanna get the fuck away from here."

"The problem with you and Darrius is that you two are in love with each other." Magic opened the refrigerator and grabbed a bottle of water.

"You have lost your mind. In love with him?" Sydni was appalled at what her younger sister was saying. She watched as she opened the bottle, being careful not to mess up her nails. After taking a long swallow, Magic put it on the table.

"Ah, that is good. Yes, in love with him. Don't be mad. He's in love with you too. I've been telling him that for years. There's so much sexual tension between you two that it's ridiculous. I think that's the real reason you can't get with Byron."

"You're crazy."

"No, I'm not. His being white ain't got nothin' to do with it. Hell, you're damn near white yourself. Shit, Sydni, Darrius is the reason you can't get with nobody. Have you noticed that you don't go out, date, have fun? You have all these pent up emotions for that brother and it takes all of your energy to suppress them, which is why you are so mean and hateful toward him and all other men. Can't say I blame you, though. That brother is fine as hell."

"What? I can't believe you're saying all of this bullshit."

"It's true. I saw it on Doctor Phil."

"That's why your ass needs to get a job." Sydni pushed past her sister and opened the freezer. The cool air felt good on her face. The sight of a container of Ben and Jerry's Chunky Monkey brought back memories of late night snacks with Aaron. They would sneak down the steps and have ice cream and talk without Mama and Magic ever knowing they were up.

She missed him terribly. They made lists of their goals for life and vowed that they would accomplish everything on them. Her list included graduating from BCC, Spelman and grad school, becoming a marketing executive for a Fortune 500 company, buying a house and a Benz. His list included graduating from college, owning his own business, getting married and being a better father to his kids than their father had been to them. He often teased her for not adding wife and mother to her list. Her face became clouded with sadness as she thought of the things on his list that he never got to complete.

"What's wrong, Sydni, the truth hurt?"

They heard the front door opening and soon their mother was calling out to them. "Sydni, Miriam."

"In here, Mama." They quickly went into the living room. Sydni hesitated in the doorway when she saw Mr. Joe sitting on the couch beside her mother. His arms were around her and she smiled as Magic kissed her on the cheek.

"Hi, Ma, did you have a good time?"

"Yes, baby, I sure did. I'm so full that I could bust. The food was so good." Her mother squeezed Magic's hand. Sydni could see that all thoughts of Magic's disappearing act were gone, and she wasn't surprised. That was why Magic was so spoiled; her mother never stayed mad long enough to say anything. "Hi, Mister Joe," Magic politely greeted him. Sydni watched as his eyes traveled up and down her sister's body as she walked across the room and sat on the arm of the recliner. She could not believe that her mother didn't see it.

"Come in here, Sydni. I need to talk to you all for a minute," her mother called to her. Sydni obliged and sat in the chair next to Magic. She was hoping that the inevitable hadn't happened, but she knew it had. "You wanna tell them, Joe?"

"No, sweetheart. You do the honors." He looked at her mother like she was a priceless gem to be admired. Her mother seemed to bask in his gaze. Sydni tried not to become sick to her stomach, but it was hard. She kept her eyes on her mother as she began to speak.

"Tonight, Joe asked me to be his wife." She paused as she took his hand in hers. "And I said yes."

"Really? Oh Mama, that's great." Magic laughed. She jumped up and hugged her mother and Joe. His eyes never left Magic's bouncing breasts. "Congratulations, Mister Joe."

"Thank you. After all the sadness we've had these past few months, I felt we needed a happy occasion. Right, Sydni?" Joe turned and asked Sydni, who remained quiet. Magic looked at her sister, afraid of what she might say to spoil this moment.

"Well, we have a lot to celebrate this weekend—a graduation and an engagement. We should have a party!" Magic began dancing around like she was on *Soul Train*. Sydni stood up and hugged her mother before she left the living room.

"Congratulations, Mama, Mister Joe," she said quietly.

"What's wrong, Sydni? Joe told me about your gift. I figured you'd be on cloud nine tonight," her mother commented.

"I am, Mama. I'm just tired. You know I took my last final this morning and I been working all day, unlike some people." She gestured toward Magic, who was still dancing in the middle of the floor.

"Whew, anyone taste any haterade up in here, up in here?" Magic stuck her tongue out at Sydni. The ringing of the cell phone on her hip caused her to stop her performance and excuse herself. Sydni took this as her cue to leave her mother and Mr. Joe too. She could hear Magic laughing and making plans for the night all the way down the hall.

In a way, she wished she would have opened up to other females and gained a group of friends like Magic had, but she knew better. She had been burnt more than one time by females who were supposedly her friends, and it wasn't even worth the grief of trying to make any more. Her best friends still lived in Georgia and she talked to them on a regular basis. They did enough bonding on the phone to keep her happy, and she couldn't see herself bonding with a female in New York anyway. She would party and hang out enough when she got back down south, if she ever did.

# 4

"Oh, Sydni, I am so proud of you," her mother cried when Sydni made her way across the auditorium after the commencement. Her mother had already used one roll of film snapping pictures of Sydni in her cap and gown before they left the house. Now, she was still snapping, nearly blinding Sydni with the flash.

"Me too, Syd. You go, girl!" Magic hugged her and thrust a bunch of balloons in her hand.

"Thanks, Mag. You know you're next."

"Ha, I don't think so. Walking across that stage once was hard enough." Magic laughed.

Sydni was grateful that this day had finally come. All her hard work had paid off. Her mother, Magic, Mr. Joe and Byron had applauded loudly as she proudly received her Associate Degree in Business. There was only one person missing as she looked at them sitting in the audience: Aaron.

"How does it feel to be a graduate?" Byron asked as she hugged him.

"It feels good. I accomplished another goal on my list," Sydni answered as she closed her eyes and tried not to think about her brother. She thought she was seeing things when she opened them and saw the tall figure carrying a bouquet of roses toward her.

"What are you doing here?" she asked.

"I came to watch you march." Darrius shrugged and handed her the flowers. She reluctantly took them from him and mumbled a thank you.

"Darrius, thank you for coming." Her mother hugged him for a long time. "You don't know how much this means."

"I wouldn't have missed it for the world," he said, avoiding Sydni's eyes. Magic nudged Sydni and winked at her as she took Darrius' arm in hers.

"Are you coming back to the house with us, D? Mama hooked up a spread for Sydni and she even made your favorite: peach cobbler."

Sydni squinted her eyes in anger, but Magic ignored her. She looked at Darrius and tried not to notice how good he looked in the cream linen pants and ivory shirt he wore. She reminded herself that if it weren't for him, her brother would be standing there with them right now.

"I don't know. I mean, I'm sure that's gonna be a private family dinner. I don't want to intrude on Sydni's celebration." He looked at Sydni for some sign that he was invited, but she looked away from him.

"What are you talking about, boy? You are family," her mother interjected.

"Besides, it's also gonna be an engagement dinner," Mr. Joe added as he stepped beside her mother.

"What? Who's engaged? I know Magic ain't suckered nobody into marrying her yet."

"No, silly. Joe and I are engaged." She held out her hand so he could see the two-carat solitaire she had been wearing since Friday night. Darrius checked out the ring and whistled. He looked over at Sydni, who still had the look of disdain on her face, and he knew that she must not be happy about the situation.

"Wow, congratulations. I think I'm gonna have to pass," he told them, not wanting to add fuel to Sydni's already burning fire. He really didn't want to be around her and her white boy anyway. The only reason he came to the ceremony and brought the flowers was because he knew it was something that Aaron would have wanted him to do for her. That trick didn't even care. She barely said thank you. He congratulated Sydni once again and quickly said goodbye to everyone, promising to see them all soon.

"That was nice of him," Mr. Joe commented.

"It was," Byron added.

"Darrius has always been a thoughtful young man. I always liked him. He was like the brother Aaron always wanted. He would have been so proud of you, Sydni," she said with tears in her eyes.

"I know, Ma." Sydni hugged her again. Magic could feel the emotions building up in her chest as she watched her mother and sister. She quickly diffused the situation.

"Yo, let's go. We got folks waiting at the house, ready to eat."

"She's right. We'd better be going," Mr. Joe reminded them. "Honey, take a picture of Sydni and me before we leave."

"Okay. Go ahead, Sydni," her mother said cheerfully. Sydni eased next to his chunky frame and tried not to cringe as he put his arm around her.

"Say cheese," Byron said. Sydni looked over at Magic, who was distracted by a group of guys standing near them. Sydni managed a weak smile as her mother aimed the camera.

"Cheese." Mr. Joe grinned. Sydni's eyes got big when she felt his hand palm her ass as the camera flashed. She swiftly stepped away from him, totally surprised at his boldness.

"Now that's gonna be a good one, Joe," her mother said.

"Yes, it is," he said, looking at Sydni, licking his lips. "I'll bet it is."

# 5

Sydni thought she was dreaming as the sound of moaning drifted into her room. She sat up in bed when she realized the sound was coming from the room next to hers. She looked at the clock on her nightstand and the numbers read nine twenty-two. She had overslept. She was supposed to have been at work forty-five minutes ago. She jumped up and opened her door, easing toward the noise. She stood outside Magic's room, appalled. She could hear the bed creaking and her sister crying out in ecstasy and a male voice groaning. Sydni stood, listening, growing aroused as she heard them cry out in unison. She felt her heart beating and her breath becoming faster. She turned when she heard footsteps approaching the door and went back into her room.

"I'm takin' a shower. You wanna join me?" Magic

said. Sydni could tell she was right in front of her door.

"Hell, yeah. I'm all about savin' water, boo!" The male voiced boomed out.

"What the hell are you doing?" Sydni scared the hell out of her sister as she opened the door. Magic had stepped naked into the hallway and almost fell the hell out from surprise.

"Wh-what are you doing home, Sydni? Why aren't you at work?" Magic asked, backing toward her room. Her male companion stuck his head out of the room to see what was going on.

"Oh shit," he said and quickly disappeared into the room.

"Who the fuck is that?" Sydni walked toward her sister who began to back up.

"He . . . I . . . Uh."

"Shut up! I don't even wanna know who he is. I want you dressed and him the fuck up outta here, now!" Sydni yelled and stormed back into her room. She could not believe Magic. Her sister ran, naked, back into her bedroom, slamming the door behind her. Sydni could hear the murmuring of their voices. She was so mad that she didn't know what to do. She looked at the clock again and then picked up the phone and called the cleaners, hoping that Miss Donna, the other woman who worked in the cleaners as a presser and steamer, would pick up the phone. She would often work for Sydni when she couldn't make it.

"Good Morning, Davis Cleaners," Miss Donna answered cheerfully. Sydni loved her Jamaican accent.

"Hi, Miss Donna. It's Sydni."

"Sydni, chile, you all right?" the woman asked.

Sydni could hear the closing of the cash register in the background. She knew it was usually slow on Mondays, but sometimes you never could tell.

"Yes, Ma'am. I am so sorry. I overslept this morning."

"Dat's okay. It been really slow dis mornin'. Only 'bout two or three people been in here. Your friend came to bring you your coffee, though. I tink he was kinda disappointed dat it was me in 'ere and not you." She laughed heartily into the phone. Sydni could feel pounding in her head and tension in her neck. She knew that she was not going to make it to work. She still had to deal with Magic and her visitor and she knew that meant spending most of the morning arguing with her sister.

"I'm not gonna make it, Miss Donna. I don't feel well," Sydni told her.

"Dat's okay, chile. I can stay all day. You get some rest. I'll let Joe know for ya."

"Thanks, Miss Donna. I will," Sydni said and hung up the phone. She walked back out into the hallway, listening to see if Magic's company had heeded her words and gotten the hell out. There were no sounds coming from Magic's room as she knocked on the door. She turned the knob and peeked in; the room was empty. The bed was rumpled, but there were no signs of Magic or anyone else. *Where the hell did she go?* Sydni wondered. She searched the rest of the house, but Magic was nowhere to be found. Sydni quickly got dressed and headed out of the house in search of her sister. *She couldn't have gone far.*

Sydni walked up and down her block for about fifteen minutes, and then returned home. She was surprised that her mother was home when she got there. She entered her mother's bedroom without knocking.

"Lord, Sydni, you scared me, girl. What are you doing home?" she asked. Sydni watched as her mother took things out of her dresser drawers and rearranged them.

"I had a headache so I didn't go to work," Sydni answered. "What are you doing?"

"Making room for Joe's things," her mother answered like it was no big deal. Sydni felt the pounding in her head get louder.

"What?" she said without thinking.

"Well, it makes no sense for him to renew his lease on his place another year since we're getting ready to be married anyway. He's just gonna move in here." She continued to shift underwear and socks.

"When did all this happen and why didn't you discuss it with me and Magic first?"

"I didn't know I had to discuss it with you and your sister. Last time I checked it was my name on the mortgage. Is there a problem?" She turned and frowned at her daughter. She loved Sydni, although she was rather overprotective of her family at times, but now she was going too far.

"I'm just saying, Ma. Isn't this kind of fast? I guess I figured that you all were gonna have a long engagement, that's all." Sydni sighed and left her mother before she could say another word. It seemed as if her life could not get any worse than it already was. She walked back outside and sat on the steps. She looked down the busy street filled with people with so much to do and no time for her and her problems. She became lost in her own thoughts. Soon, a car pulled in front of her.

"Sydni, what's wrong? I went to the store and you weren't there. Then I called you and got no answer." Byron jumped out of his silver Audi and ran beside her.

"Nothing, Byron. I just didn't feel like going in, that's all."

"Come on, Sydni. I know you better than that. What's wrong? Tell me, sweetie." He sat next to her and put his arm around her shoulder. She could not stop the tears from falling. She told him about Magic and the guy, then went on to tell him about Mr. Joe moving in.

"I can't take this anymore. I just want to get the hell away from here. God, is that so much to ask?" She cried.

Byron watched as she poured out her heart. He was in love with this beautiful girl who seemed to carry the weight of the world on her shoulders, but she didn't take him or his feelings seriously. Since he had known her all she talked about was leaving New York and going back down south. As much as he didn't want that to happen, he wanted her to be happy. His eyes stared into her soft face, frowning with hurt and anger, and traveled down her seductive body. Her full breasts went up and down as she breathed in anger. He would do anything to touch them, to feel her body against his. She was his angel.

"Sydni, come on. You need to take a ride," he told her, pulling her up.

"I don't want to take a ride. There's nowhere for me to go," she told him.

"Come on. Just get in the car," he pleaded. She looked at him and decided the hell with it. Anywhere was better than sitting there. She got into his car and they drove down the street. Byron put on Maxwell and she sat back and relaxed.

They drove down to the Village and walked around, not really talking, just making comments every now and then. He knew she didn't have a lot to say and respected that. She was glad he did. They paused in front of a building that used to hold one of Sydni's favorite stores. It was now gone, replaced by scaffolds and work trucks, clearly being renovated for something else. The sounds of drilling and hammering echoed as she peered inside the empty building.

"I wonder what they're putting here?" she said out loud.

"Yo D, can you come here and help me install this sprinkler when you finish that one?" A gruff voice called from inside the building.

"Sure thing. Let me grab my other bag out of the truck."

Sydni searched for the source of the sound coming closer and closer to her from the doorway. Darrius was looking down, focusing on some mechanical gadget in his hand; He didn't even see her standing there. He was dressed in some grungy jeans and a ripped T-shirt, his thick arms covered in dust. She looked at his strong face as he concentrated on what he was doing. She could not help but stare at him. Before she knew it, he had passed her, just like that. In the five years she had known him, he had never just walked by her without acknowledging her presence. She stood, watching him reach into the white work van and pull out a tool bag, continuing to work.

As she watched Darrius, Byron watched her. He noticed the look of desire in her eyes as she stared at the man she had always claimed to despise. He had never wondered about their relationship until now. He didn't like what he was seeing. It made him uncomfortable.

"Sydni, come on!" He called out to her.

Darrius looked up at the sound of Sydni's name and saw her standing in front of the work site. He hadn't even noticed she was there, but damn, he saw her now. She was looking as fine as ever in her jean shorts and tank top. As usual, she was with the white boy. He smirked as he glanced over at the punk who followed her around like a puppy. *That's just the kind of man she needs, because I know she can't handle a real man like me.*

"What's up, Sydni?" he spoke.

"Hi, Darrius," was her only response. As she stared at him, she forgot that she hated him and it actually came out sounding like a sincere hello.

"I didn't even see you out here. My bad," he continued.

"I know. You were too busy working, I see."

"Yeah, we're trying to be finished by the end of the week and we 'bout two guys short." He took a few steps closer so he could see her pretty eyes.

"Oh," she said, not looking up at him. She was too afraid he might see the heat she held for him. *Oh, God. There's no way Magic was right.*

"Hey, Darrius." Byron stepped up and interrupted their conversation. He wanted to stop this before it got any further.

"Hey there, Byron. You guys just hanging out?"

"Yeah, just hanging out. You ready, Syd?" He reached and took Sydni's hand in his. She didn't resist; she was too confused by what was going on in her head.

"Huh? Oh, yeah. I'm ready." She nodded. Her eyes never left Darrius' hands.

"Yo, D? Where you at, man?" The gruff voice called from inside once again.

"Here I come, man!" he yelled back. "Well, I gotta go. Yo, tell your moms and Magic I said what's up."

He closed the van door and walked past them and back into the building. Sydni slowly looked up and took a deep breath. Byron knew something was on her mind and it had something to do with Darrius. He decided to remind her of why she didn't like him.

"Have the authorities said anything else about Aaron's killer?"

The sound of Aaron's name caused a shadow to come across her face and she quickly remembered her disfavor for her brother's friend. She looked back into the doorway of the building, her heart heavy once again.

"No, they still haven't said. They're still investigating. Come on, I need to get back home and talk to my sister," she said.

Magic finally returned home after midnight. Usually, Sydni would be knocked out in her room, but not tonight. As Magic crept into her bedroom and flicked on the light, Sydni was sitting in the middle of her bed, eyes wide open. Magic screamed.

"Shut up before Ma wakes up!" Sydni hushed her.

"What the hell are you doing in my room?"

"Waiting to cuss your ass out. What, you thought I was gonna just let that shit go? Think again."

"Look, Syd. I am so sorry about that. I thought you and Mama were gone. Usually no one is home that time of day."

"I don't care what time of day it is. You don't have no business fucking in this house, period," Sydni hissed.

"Oh please, Sydni. In case you didn't notice, I am grown. I don't know why you're on this holier than thou tip, but you'd better get off it and make it quick. No business fucking in this house? Girl, please. Do you know how much pussy Aaron got in his room? And that nigga was in high school. You're crazy." Magic shook her head at Sydni and her self-appointed authority. "At least I respected this house enough to do it when no one was here. The only reason you found out was because you happened to stay home from work. Now, can you get out so I can go to bed?"

"No. You tell me who that was. Who was that guy?"

"A friend, Sydni. Just a friend."

"So you screwing 'just friends' now?"

"Get out, Sydni. I keep telling you, I'm grown."

Sydni looked at her sister and knew that she wasn't going to get anywhere with her. Aaron had always been the only one who could talk sense into her. She reluctantly slid off the bed and walked out of the room. Climbing into bed, she cried herself to sleep. It had been a habit she had become accustomed to over the past few months.

A week later, Mr. Joe moved in. Sydni made it her business to stay away from him at home and at work. She made up excuses for not wanting to spend time with him and her mother. Magic was no help. When she was home, which was rarely, she would have dinner with them, sit around and watch movies, and laugh and talk like they were all one big, happy family. Sydni was not amused. She knew that Mr. Joe was giving both her and Magic inappropriate looks.

But she didn't say anything. As long as he kept his hands off her, she left the issue alone. And it seemed as if her mother was happier than she had been in years. Sydni spent more and more time with Byron to get out of the house. He was her refuge when she needed to escape and her ears when she needed to vent.

"I have something for you," he told her one evening as they sat in Central Park.

"What is it?" she asked him, curious.

He reached into his back pocket and pulled out an envelope. She paused before reaching for it.

"What is it?"

"Open it and see." He laughed.

Sydni took the envelope from his hand and slowly slid her finger under the flap to open it. She pulled out the long slip of paper and read it. She blinked her eyes to make sure she was seeing what she was seeing.

"I love you, Sydni. I want you to be happy. And if

this is what it will take to do that for you, then it's yours." His fingers rubbed the back of her neck as she sat, too shocked to move.

"Byron."

"I mean it, Sydni. There is nothing in this world that I wouldn't do for you. You know how I feel about you. I have always told you how much I love you," he continued. "So now I'm going to show you how much I love you."

"Byron, this is a cashier's check for ten thousand dollars. I can't take this." She finally found her voice.

"Why not? This is for you, Sydni."

"Where . . . how . . ."

"From my trust fund. I convinced my father that I was making a wise investment and he let me take it." Byron smiled.

"You know I can't take this, Byron."

"Yes, you can. Take it and get the hell away from here. That's all you've wanted to do since you got here. But there is one thing I want you to think about as you are leaving." His face got really serious and he sat up in front of Sydni. This time he reached into his shirt pocket. He felt around until he found what he was looking for. He took Sydni's hand and placed the large ring on her finger.

"Byron!"

"I want you to think about being my wife. I have no problem moving to Atlanta. I would follow you to the end of the earth if you want me to. I love you, Sydni."

Sydni could not respond. In one hand she held a check for ten grand and on the other was a ring worth about four. She knew that any other female would die for an opportunity like the one he was bestowing upon her.

"I'm not saying you have to say yes today, this week, this month, hell, not even this year. I will wait forever for you if that's how long it will take."

"Byron." Sydni thought about what she should say. She had always told him that they would only be friends and she thought he understood that. She loved Byron, but she knew she would never be in love with him. She just didn't feel for him like that. She searched her heart for the right words to say. "You don't know what this means to me. No one, and I mean no one, has ever done anything like this for me before. Thank you, but I can't accept either one of these gifts."

"Yes, you can. You don't have to answer me right now, Sydni. But you have to take the check and the ring because they're yours. I want you to have them. If you give them back, I will burn the check and toss the ring into the river, and I mean that!" He was adamant, and she knew he was serious. She thought about the check going up in smoke and the ring being lost forever. She was no fool.

"I will accept the gifts on two conditions. One, this check is considered a loan that I will repay, with interest." She made sure he understood clearly what she was saying before she gave the second condition.

"Okay, and the second?" He smiled at her. He had a look of excitement in his eye and it bothered her.

"I will hold the ring for you. I won't wear it. I can't. This ring isn't for me, Byron. This ring is for the love of your life. I will keep it until you meet her and fall in love and you realize that what you feel for me is nothing compared to how you feel about her."

"I hear what you're saying, Syd. But you are the love of my life. You just don't realize how you feel about me yet because you're so focused on leaving. So, now go. You got the money and you can leave. But I know without a doubt that no matter where you go, you will never find a better friend or a man who will love and care for you half as much as I do. You know the old saying, if you love someone, set them free? Well, the door is open and the world is yours. I love you," he told her with tears in his eyes. Sydni could not stop hers from falling either. He was such a good person and she had always cared for him, but she knew that she didn't want to marry him. She hugged him and they stayed in each other's arms a long time, neither one saying anything.

# 6

Sydni stood in the shower letting the hot water run down her body. Her mind was cluttered with thoughts. She still could not believe that she had the money and she had yet to tell anyone she was leaving. Everyone seemed to be in their own little world. Her mother was always with Mr. Joe and Sydni wanted to tell her in private. Magic was just gone all the time. Sydni had no idea where, but she knew it had to do with a man. She could hear him in the background every time she called Magic's cell phone. And for someone who didn't have a job, Magic was always bringing in something new: new shoes, new purse, new clothes. Sydni knew she had to have a long talk with her sister.

Sydni poured some of the almond scented bath lotion onto her washcloth and began to bathe herself. She inhaled the scent and enjoyed the feel of her hands along her skin. As she ran the cloth across her breasts, she felt her nipples harden under her touch and the heat began to rise between her legs. Her thoughts turned to Darrius and how he looked the day she saw him in front of the building. She imagined his strong hands, wishing they could touch her. She wanted to feel his succulent lips on her neck, his tongue licking her chest. She could feel his arms caressing her back as his mouth went further and further down her body, her hands rubbing his head, guiding him. Her fingers became his hungry mouth and he tickled her clit until she shuddered under the water, moaning as she climaxed.

Her eyes flew open as she realized what she had just done and who she was dreaming about. She turned off the water and reached for the towel that she had laid on the toilet before she got in the shower. It was no longer there. She pulled the shower curtain open and looked. There was no towel. Frustrated, she climbed out and checked to see if it had fallen on the other side of the commode. It hadn't and she was pissed. Water was dripping off her body and she was getting cold. Before she knew it, the door eased open and she squealed.

"Oh, I'm sorry. I didn't know anyone was in here," Mr. Joe said, smiling and looking her naked body up and down. "Is this your towel? It was outside the bathroom door and I was about to bring it back in here."

Sydni quickly jumped back into the tub and pulled the curtain in front of her. Her heart was pounding. No one was home when she'd gotten into the shower and she had absent-mindedly forgotten to lock the door behind her. She knew he had to have come into the bathroom while she was in the shower and taken the towel. She wondered if he had heard her moaning.

"Can you get out please, Mister Joe?" she asked, her face red with embarrassment.

"Sure thing, darling. Here's your towel." He remained in the doorway, holding the towel out to her.

"Just lay it right there, Mister Joe. I'll get it."

"Okay. Sorry about that, Sydni." Mr. Joe raised his eyebrows at her and slowly backed out of the bathroom. His eyes never left her. Sydni closed the curtain and waited until she heard the bathroom door close. A minute later she heard the front door shut. She grabbed the towel and wrapped it around her, making sure she locked the door. She didn't know what to do. She wanted to rush into her mother's bedroom and cry into her arms, but what could she say? That Mr. Joe walked into the bathroom with her towel that he had taken out while she was in the shower? What kind of sense would that make? She peeked into the hallway, making sure it was empty, and practically ran back into her room, again double-checking the lock.

After getting dressed for bed, Sydni reached into the nightstand and removed the envelope that held her check. She knew she could not stay in this house much longer. She needed to talk to her sister. She picked up the phone and called Magic's cell. Magic finally answered after the fourth ring.

"Hello."

"Magic, where are you?" Sydni could hear a lot of music in the background.

"Why? What's wrong, Sydni?"

"I need to talk to you. It's important."

"Sydni, can't it wait until tomorrow? I'm kind of in the middle of something." She giggled. She knew all Sydni wanted to do was lecture her and complain about not going to Atlanta and she was not in the mood.

"No, Magic, it can't. What time are you coming home?"

"Hell, Sydni. I don't know. I don't have a curfew. What the hell is wrong?" Sydni could hear the voices in the background becoming fainter so she knew Magic had left the room.

"When . . . Mister Joe . . . He . . ." Sydni tried to explain what had happened. She was finally able to tell Magic the entire incident.

"It's okay, Syd. So he walked in on you in the bathroom. You know to keep the door locked from now on," Magic told her.

"Yo, Magic, let's roll!" Someone called out in the background. Sydni heard the music and the voices become louder and she tried to make out what they were saying.

"Sydni, I'll be home later, okay? I'll call when I'm on my way so you can be up."

"Okay, Magic. Be careful." Sydni sighed into the phone. She hung it up and then went into the den to curl up and watch television. Her mother called to tell her that she and Mr. Joe would be home after three and not to worry. Sydni shuddered at the mention of his name. She had just curled on the sofa when she heard someone at the door.

"Who is it?"

"It's Darrius."

Sydni's eyes got wide with surprise and she slowly

opened the door. He was standing outside dressed in a SeanJohn T-shirt and denim shorts and a fresh pair of Air Force Ones. She could see the diamond stud he wore in his left ear, gleaming. She could smell his Escape cologne as he walked past her.

"Were you asleep?" he asked, pointing at the blanket lying on the sofa.

"Uh, no. I was just watching some television. Magic's not here," she told him.

"I know," he answered. She looked so pretty, even in her rumpled nightshirt and boxer shorts. Her thick, curly hair was pulled to the top of her head. She smelled sweet and he liked that.

"Well, Mama's not here either," she began as she went back and climbed on the sofa. She didn't want him to look into her face, thinking he would be able to read her mind and see the fantasy she'd had about him earlier.

"I came here to see you," he told her.

"Me? For what?" Sydni became defensive. What the hell did he want with her? There was nothing she could do for him and furthermore, she really didn't have too much to say to him.

"I need to talk to you. It's about Magic."

Sydni sat up on the edge of the sofa, wondering what the hell he was talking about. "What about her?"

Darrius looked around the familiar room, which held so many memories of his best friend. They would hang out here and talk about any and everything, joking and talking until the sun came up at times. He knew that since Aaron was gone, his friend would expect him to look out for his sisters, which was why he was here now.

"You know who Magic been hanging out wit' lately, Sydni?"

"Some guy. I really don't know who he is. Do you know who he is?"

"Yeah, his name's Malik. Malik Fitzgerald."

"I guess I've seen him around. What about him?"

"Malik got a lot of beef wit' Dax. Something to do with that nigga Frido and a deal gone bad. He lost a lot of money. So much money that he was ready to kill Dax," Darrius told her. He took a few moments so she could digest everything he was saying. "One night, somebody told Malik about a meeting Dax was having outside the strip club and he decided to roll up on Dax."

"What are you saying, D?" Sydni knew it couldn't be true. There was no way. Darrius didn't know what the fuck he was talking about.

"That same night, me, Aaron and Dax were leaving the club because they had taken care of some business." He looked down at the floor as he continued. "We were walking to the car, laughing and tripping about the girls in the club."

"No." Sydni knew what he was about to say and she didn't want to hear anymore. "You don't know what you're talking about. I want you to get out."

Darrius ignored Sydni and kept talking, tears filling his eyes as he remembered the details of that night. "Dax had been drinking all night and was too fucked up to drive. I told him I wasn't his damn chauffeur and we laughed. Dax tossed Aaron the keys. He walked to the driver's side of the truck and was opening the door when the car rolled up on him."

"Shut up, shut up." Sydni began breathing harder

and harder. She shook her head from side to side, but Darrius just walked closer to her as he talked.

"The shots came from out of nowhere. We all ducked and hit the ground. The car sped off and that's when we realized he wasn't moving." Darrius was right in front of Sydni, crying as he confessed what he had been holding in for months. He kneeled in front of her, placing his arms on her knees. "I am sorry, Syd. I swear to God I wish I had just shut the fuck up and drove the fucking truck."

Sydni couldn't breathe. She was gasping, trying to understand what he had just told her. She looked at his crumpled body, bending in front of her, and realized he was just as broken as she was. She put her hand under his chin and looked into his face, knowing that he still had more to tell her. "Magic?"

"She's fucking the nigga that shot your brother." He nodded. Sydni began to sob out loud. He slowly stood and walked out of the den. He climbed the steps and continued down the hallway, stopping in front of the closed room that he had not entered in months. He slowly turned the knob and walked in. Turning on the light, he saw that nothing had been touched. The walls still held plaques, trophies and certificates bearing Aaron's name. There were still cutouts of newspaper articles that his mother had framed, highlighting Aaron's basketball career. The room held so many memories for him. Darrius sat in the big beanbag chair that he had always claimed for himself. He leaned back and closed his eyes.

# 7

"What kind of business did Aaron have wit' Dax?" Sydni asked him.

Darrius nearly fell out of the chair. He didn't hear her come in the room. It had taken a lot for her to come in there. She hadn't been in her brother's room since he died.

"Wha-what?" he said, catching himself on Aaron's desk.

"You said Aaron had to meet Dax and take care of some business. What business?" Sydni looked him in the eye and waited for him to answer her.

"He . . . Dax . . . look, it's not important," he told her. Darrius knew she wanted the truth, but he didn't want to tell her the full details.

"Tell me, dammit! What business?" Sydni demanded. She knew that Aaron didn't hang out with Dax that often. He was on a whole other level and Aaron didn't really associate with him outside of general conversation when they ran into each other. She could not figure out why the hell he had even gone to a fucking strip club. Sydni had always believed it had something to do with Darrius.

"He had gotten his refund check from school and he had a little money that he had saved," Darrius told her. He fought the urge to lie and decided that Sydni needed to know the truth. He had told her this much and there was no sense in stopping now.

"And? What did that have to do with Dax? Was Aaron trying to buy some drugs or something? I know that's a lie, because my brother never put a drop of liquor in his body, let alone anything else. Don't even try to feed me some bullshit story like that. Are you sure it wasn't you that had the business with Dax?"

This was the Sydni that Darrius was used to, the bitch with attitude who knew everything. His eyes matched her stare and he made sure they were face to face.

"No, it was Aaron's business," he said slowly.

"What was it?"

"He wanted Dax to flip the money so he could give it to you."

"That's a lie!" Sydni shook her head. She knew Darrius was making it up. There was no way Aaron was killed because of her.

"He wanted to get the money so you could go back home," Darrius responded. Sydni felt as if someone was sitting on her chest and she fell onto Aaron's bed. He was dead because of her. All because she wanted to get the fuck away from New York.

Darrius got up and walked over to the bed. He reached for Sydni and pulled her into his arms. She tried to pull away from him but he refused to let her go. As she buried herself into his chest, he clicked the remote on the stereo, knowing what disc was already inside. The sound of Destiny's Child filled the room as Beyonce crooned out "Dangerously in Love."

Sydni heard the song and could not help smiling. It was Aaron's favorite. He often joked that Beyonce was his future wife and she was going to serenade him with this song at their wedding. Darrius looked down and saw the faint grin on her face. He gently wiped the tears from her cheeks and kissed her forehead. He closed his eyes and inhaled her sweetness. He couldn't resist; he cupped her face in his hands and continued kissing her. He covered her face with small kisses; her eyes, her cheeks, her nose, until he found the lips he had been yearning to taste from the first day he saw her. Sydni was hesitant at first, surprised at his actions, but she slowly opened her mouth, inviting his tongue and savoring his flavor. They explored each other, each one curious, both afraid to stop because this was a moment they'd both anticipated.

Darrius' fingers trailed along Sydni's neck and she tilted her head, inviting his mouth where his fingers had been. He licked along her collar, nibbling and savoring. His hands reached under her shirt and cupped her breasts, his thumbs rubbing across her nipples. He could feel her pressing against his hands, wanting more. He was rock hard now and knew that if they went further, there would be no turning back. He leaned her back on the bed, removing his shirt, enjoying the look of desire on her face. Her heart was racing as he eased her boxers down and she undid his jeans. Her hands found his penis, rigid as she wrapped her fingers around it. They were both naked now, taking each other in with their eyes, both pleased by what they saw. Darrius kissed her again; this time there was no resistance. He wasted no time easing down her body.

Her skin was so soft. He gently took each nipple into his mouth as she moaned. He continued down her stomach, kissing her thighs as he eased them open. His fingers found her wetness and she gasped as he played with her canal, making sure she was ready. Sydni felt his tongue licking where she had once imagined it. She closed her eyes as she arched her back, riding waves of ecstasy. She called out his name, begging him to stop because she couldn't take it anymore, but he took her higher and higher until she felt she was going to erupt. Once she had, he smiled at her, biting his bottom lip. She pulled him to her and it was she that kissed him this time. As she felt the heat begin to rise in her again, she guided him between her legs. He paused, calling her name.

"Are you sure you want to do this?" he asked her, rubbing her neck. Sydni didn't answer him. She reached for the remote and clicked repeat, letting Beyonce answer the question for her. Darrius laughed and stood up completely. Sydni, confused by his actions, sat up to see what was wrong.

"Relax." He smiled and reached into the nightstand, taking out a condom. Aaron had always kept his stash there. He shook his head and said aloud, "Always prepared."

Sydni lay back on the bed, watching him unwrap it, still nervous about what was about to take place. He put the rubber in her hand and she rolled it onto him. She closed her eyes and prepared for the inevitable. She flinched as she felt his hardness enter her. This totally took Darrius by surprise when he saw the look of pain on her face. He tried to stop but she pulled at him, telling him to keep going. Slowly, he entered again and began a steady rhythm. Her tightness aroused him and he could barely control himself.

He made love to Sydni like no woman he'd ever had. She clawed along his back and gripped his ass, wanting him to go deeper, faster and faster, until he couldn't take anymore and she was crying out his name. He could feel her contracting as she told him she was coming. He exploded inside her, satisfied to no end. They held each other, both holding back tears.

"You okay?" he asked her after a few moments.

"Yeah," she replied. He didn't know if her silence was of regret. He looked up at the ceiling and chuckled to himself.

"You wanna hear somethin' funny?"

"What?"

"This is the room I lost my virginity in."

"Me too," she said quietly, turning to face him. He realized what she was saying and his eyes got wide with surprise.

"Why didn't you say something? I mean, damn, Syd. Shit." He lay on his back, shaking his head.

"What? Would it have made a difference?"

"Yeah."

"Why? Would you not have slept with me? Would

you have done something different to me? What, D?"

"I still can't believe this shit. I know Aaron is pissed as hell. He's probably looking down right now saying, 'That mothafucka. I told him to look out for Syd, not fuck her!' " He moaned.

Sydni laughed at her newfound lover. "In a way, you're probably right. But he's not saying that. He's saying, 'Them nasty ass hoes. They got the nerve to be fuckin' in my bed! Sydni got her own damn room!' "

It felt good to laugh about Aaron. They lay for a few minutes then Darrius went to the bathroom. When he returned, Sydni slipped her T-shirt back on and got up to go. As she was coming out of Aaron's room, she ran into Magic.

"Hey, I called you but you ain't answer the phone. What are you doing in Aaron's room?" she asked, surprised.

"I . . . Uh . . ." Sydni couldn't think of anything to say. Magic could hear the music coming from the room and pushed open the door.

"Oh, shit! D! I know y'all didn't!" Magic yelled. Darrius quickly tried to cover himself with the comforter, but he knew Magic had seen enough.

"Magic! We were . . ." Sydni began.

Magic walked in and stood in the middle of her brother's room, tears streaming down her face, which she covered with her hands. She bent over as she convulsed. Darrius sat up, still covered by the blanket.

"Magic, I am so sorry," he said. "I swear we didn't plan for this to happen. We just . . ."

"Magic, please listen to me." Sydni reached for

her sister and turned her so she could look in her face. Magic gasped as Sydni pulled at her hands and she yelled at her sister.

"I knew you were in love wit' each other. I told both of you. I just can't believe y'all screwed in Aaron's bed! I know he is having a fit right about now!" She laughed. This was the funniest thing she had seen in her life. She laughed and laughed.

"This trick is laughing! I don't believe this." Sydni threw her hands up as she left the room. She sat on the toilet thinking about what she had done. There was no doubt in her mind that she loved Darrius. But there was no point in getting caught up now that she was about to be out. She decided to ride it out until she left, having a little fun before she left NY for good.

"I told you, Dr. Phil ain't no joke. You need to pay attention to what he has to say. I know I do!" Magic yelled. She flopped into the bean bag chair and begged Darrius to tell her the details. He refused and told her to get out. There was a click as the disc changer switched and R. Kelly began to sing.

"That's okay. I'll get them later from Syd. Wait a minute. When I came in, Destiny's Child was on. Y'all did it in Aaron's room, in his bed, listening to his favorite CD? Now that is funny."

"Get out, Magic," Darrius told her again.

"Oh, I will. I can't believe this." She continued to laugh as she went into her own room.

"She finally left?" Sydni asked when she returned.

"Yeah."

"I know she wanted a full report."

"She said she'd get one from you later." He pulled her to him, kissing her neck. She laughed and her mouth found his.

"I think we'd better get out of here and go to my room," she said when she finally pulled away from him.

"We need to talk to Magic anyway," he whispered. She couldn't help admiring his sexiness as he stood and pulled on his pants. She stood in front of him and grasped at his crotch.

"Come on, let's go to my room. We can talk to her in the morning. There's no point in disturbing her tonight. I have somethin' else we can do instead."

"Are you sure you were a virgin? You seem kind of freaky." He raised his eyebrows at her as she pulled at him.

"I guess you bring out that side of me, huh?" She led him into her room. They made love and fell asleep in each other's arms.

# 8

The next morning, Sydni went into her sister's room and found that she was not there. She dialed Magic's phone but got the voice mail. She went back into her room and told Darrius that Magic was gone.

"Where did she go? Damn, it's only seven in the morning."

"I don't know. I don't even know what time she left," Sydni told him. She looked at the clock. "What time do you have to be at work?"

"Eight-thirty. Where is Moms?"

"She's still sleep. She got in late and she doesn't have to be at work until eleven this morning."

"What time you gotta go?"

"Eight," she told him as she began rummaging through her closet for something to wear.

"You want me to drop you off?"

"You got time?" she turned to ask him.

"I'll make time for you. I'll be back in thirty minutes." She walked him to the front of the building and kissed him goodbye.

"Thirty minutes. Be ready."

"Ready for what?" She licked her lips seductively.

"I still don't believe you were a virgin." He kissed her again and told her he'd be back after he changed for work.

As she was getting dressed, her phone rang.

"Hello."

"Good morning, Syd. You ready?"

"Uh, hey, Byron. I don't need a ride this morning." Sydni had forgotten that he told her he'd take her to work that morning.

"Really? You're not going in? You're not sick, are you?"

"No, Byron. I'm not sick." She laughed. "I'm just gonna walk. I need to think about some stuff, that's all."

"About my proposal, I hope." He laughed.

"No pressure, Byron. Remember the two conditions," Sydni told him. She didn't dare tell him about Darrius and their newfound friendship. She knew he would want the check back. *Darrius and I aren't serious, anyway. No sense in opening a can of worms.*

"I know, I know. Hey, I'll still bring you your coffee later. How about that?"

"That would be great. I'll see you then," she said cheerfully as she hung up the phone.

The phone rang again and Sydni snatched it up, thinking it was Byron calling her back.

"Yeah."

"Syd."

"Magic, where are you? Why did you leave? D and I told you we needed to talk to you."

"I know, Syd. But I had to get out of that house. I had to."

"Why, Magic? What happened?"

"I have to tell you later. Are you going to work?"

"Yeah. Darrius is coming to get me." There was a lot of hustle and bustle in the background.

"Where are you, Magic? I really need to talk to you."

"I know, Syd, and I gotta talk to you, too. But not at the house. I'll call you later. I love you, Syd. Be careful."

"Be careful of what?" Sydni asked, but Magic had already hung up. She could hear Darrius blowing his horn. She grabbed her purse and ran out. As they pulled off, they never saw the eyes that had been watching them since she'd kissed him outside earlier, nor did they see the car that trailed them.

"Hey, there. Hot coffee, cream and sugar. Just the way you like it." Byron greeted her as he carried the steaming cup.

"Oooh. Thanks. I need it this morning," she told him.

"Wow, you look like you had a rough night. What did you do? You got bags under your eyes," he said with a worried look on his face.

"Dat chile come in 'ere glowin' dis mornin' Whateva happen to her put a smile on her face, I tell you dat much, Mistah Byron," Miss Donna said knowingly. "And what I tell you 'bout comin' in 'ere wit' one cup o' coffee every day?"

Sydni was glad Miss Donna turned the conversation to coffee so she wouldn't have to explain what Miss Donna was talking about.

"I'm sorry, Miss Donna. I totally forgot. I'll bring you a cup tomorrow, I promise." He smiled at her.

"You betta, I tell you dat much. Or don't bring one at all." She waved her scissors at him threateningly and smiled back.

"Well, Sydni, what time do you want me to pick you up this afternoon?" he asked her.

"Well, you really don't have to. I have to meet Magic and we're gonna go get something to eat."

"Okay, where? I can meet you guys there."

"Not this time, Byron. I have to talk to her about some *things* and I want to do it alone," Sydni told him. In all actuality, Darrius was picking her up and they had made plans for that evening.

"Oh, I know. You haven't told her yet." He winked at Sydni. She just nodded like he was right.

"Alright, then. I'll give you a call later."

"Okay, Byron. Talk to you then." She walked from behind the counter and hugged him. She felt guilty about lying and didn't know why she felt that she had to. It wasn't like he or Darrius was her boyfriend.

"Dat boy got a itch for you dat he shouldn't have," Miss Donna said after he had gone.

"What do you mean?" Sydni asked. "He's just my friend."

"Da way he look at you. Like a man wit' a bleedin' heart and only you can save him. Dangerous look. You be careful wit' dat one."

"Careful of who? Byron? He's harmless." Sydni laughed as she stirred her coffee.

# 9

Sydni's mind was filled with images of her and Darrius the night before. She caught herself smiling throughout the day every time she thought about him. She was extremely nice to her customers and Miss Donna teased her about her apparent change in attitude.

Sydni tried to reach Magic on her cell, but got no answer. She left several messages and told Magic to reach her on Darrius' cell phone.

"Why is D hanging outside?" Mr. Joe asked as he came in the door. It was almost six and he had finally come out of his office. He had been holed up in there all afternoon.

"He's picking me up," Sydni answered.

"*He's* picking *you* up? When did you all become friends?"

"I tink dey're more den friends da way she been smilin' round 'ere t'day, Joe." Miss Donna laughed.

Sydni's mouth opened in shock at what Miss Donna had said. She quickly grabbed her purse and wasted no time leaving before Mr. Joe could say anything else. Joe raised his eyebrow as he watched Darrius embrace her and help her into the car.

Darrius took Sydni to Maroon's for dinner. They feasted on jerk chicken, cabbage, and peas and rice, reminiscing about the past.

"This place is my favorite," she told him as they ate.

"I know."

"What? How do you know?" she questioned.

"I know you love this place. I know your favorite color is yellow. Your favorite TV shows are *Boomtown* and *Law and Order.* I know you want to graduate with a degree in criminal justice and then go on to the FBI Academy. I know you hate bananas, which is why you didn't want any plantains, and I know you love R. Kelly as much as Aaron did Beyonce." Darrius studied her face as he told her this. Never in a million years would he have thought that he would be sitting here at her favorite restaurant telling her this.

Sydni sat back in her chair, totally stunned by what he had just told her. All these years she had held on to this hatred for him, not caring if he lived or died, and he knew everything there was to know about her. She was embarrassed that she knew nothing about him and her eyes dropped to her plate, not knowing what to say. He continued talking, not waiting for her to respond.

"Aaron used to joke with me when I would comment about how much of a bitch you were and how I hated you. He would tell me that I was in love with you. I denied it for years, but it was true. He was right, but you know I would never have told him that. I would just tell him he was crazy."

"Magic would tell me the same thing." Sydni smiled. "They were probably in cahoots with each other."

"Probably." He smiled back. They finished their meal and then stood to leave. Sydni excused herself and headed toward the restroom. A familiar face caught her attention and anger engulfed her. She stormed over to the table where a group of four men were sitting.

"Where's my sister, you asshole?" she hissed.

"What?" The man looked at her like she was crazy. His boys looked at him in amusement.

"Where is Magic?"

"Yo, don't be coming to me like that. What the fuck is wrong wit' you?"

"You are what's wrong with me! Where is my sister, you murdering mothafucka?" Sydni's blood was about to boil. She stood facing her brother's murderer, fear nowhere in her body.

"Yo, Malik! Who the fuck is she, man? What is she talking about?" his boys wanted to know.

"It's Magic's sister, the bitch! Look yo, your sister is at my crib. Her ass don't wanna come home and I don't blame her. You need to take that shit up wit' her. Now get the fuck outta my face before—"

"Before what? You gon' shoot me like you did my brother? Is that what you gon' do, Malik?" Heads turned in the restaurant. Sydni was yelling to the top of her lungs, not caring who heard.

"What the fuck are you talking about? I don't know shit about your brother!" He stood up and yelled back at her. Darrius came running to Sydni's side, pulling her back, but she snatched away and swung at Malik, hitting him right in the mouth. Blood appeared from his lip as he touched it. He wasted no time charging at Sydni, but Darrius' six-foot-two, two hundred forty-five pound frame stopped any chance of him touching her.

"Do it," Darrius told him, "and they'll be carrying your ass outta here in a body bag!"

"Man, I don't know what her beef is wit' me. I told her where Magic is. And I don't know who the fuck her brother is!" He stepped back from Darrius, knowing Darrius could easily whip his ass.

"Her brother was my best friend. The nigga you shot when you took an aim at Dax," he told him.

"Oh, shit." Malik frowned at Sydni, remembering that night vividly. Not wanting to incriminate himself, he quickly recovered, adding, "I don't know what you're talking about."

"Whatever, nigga! You know you did it. And I'ma figure out a way to prove it!" Sydni yelled. The manager announced that he had called the authorities and they were on their way.

"Let's go, Syd," Darrius told her, grabbing her and leading her out the door.

"You'll pay for what you did!" She continued to scream at him.

"Check your girl! You'd better watch your back!" Malik yelled back at her.

Sydni was silent during the entire ride home. As they pulled in front of her house, Darrius asked her if she was okay. She nodded. He got out and walked around to her side of the car, opening the door for her. He walked her to the door and put his arms around her, pulling her close. He kissed her gently. She was amazed at his tenderness and the way it made her feel. He put his chin on her forehead and held her for a while.

"Are you gonna invite me in?" he whispered in her ear seductively.

"I don't think I'd be very good company tonight," she answered.

"That's okay. I know you got a lot on your mind. Can I call you later?" He pulled back to look at her beautiful face again.

"Yeah, do that," she told him. He kissed her again and hugged her close.

"I love you, Sydni," he said. Sydni's heart began to beat so fast and hard that she thought he could hear it. She looked at him, knowing that she felt the same way, but the words wouldn't come to her mouth. Darrius turned and walked away. His car had just pulled off when Byron walked up, startling Sydni.

"Hey, there. What's going on?" he asked. Sydni nearly jumped out of her skin. It was as if he had appeared out of nowhere.

"Geez, Byron. You scared the hell out of me!" She sighed when she was able to catch her breath.

"Oh, I'm sorry. Where's Magic? Didn't you guys go to dinner?" He walked up and gave her a kiss on the cheek. She subtly pulled away, not wanting to be bothered.

"Oh, uh, we met at the restaurant. She went to hang out, as usual. She'll probably be home later."

"Did you tell her you were leaving?"

"Huh, wha?" She was still distracted by everything that had gone on earlier and what Darrius had said before he left.

"Did you tell her you were moving back to Atlanta and going to school in a few weeks?"

"Oh, no, I didn't." With everything that had happened over the past two days, Sydni hadn't given moving a second thought. She knew Byron would want to know why, so she added, "I'm gonna tell my mother and her together."

"I understand." He nodded. "So, when did you and Darrius become so friendly?"

"Uh, what do you mean?" She frowned, hoping he didn't catch her blushing. She began fumbling in her purse until she found her keys.

"He was leaving when I walked up, was he not?" Byron tilted his head and watched her reaction.

"He was here when I got here. He came by to see my mother." Sydni shrugged at him. "I told him she doesn't get off until later."

Sydni heard the phone ringing from inside the house. She unlocked the door and rushed inside to answer it, Byron right on her heels.

"Hello," she said.

"What the hell is the matter with you?" Magic screamed through the receiver.

"What?"

"What the hell is your problem going off on my nigga in public like you ain't got no sense? Malik told me you slapped him in Maroon's. Is this true?"

Sydni could not believe that Magic was carrying on like this. She threw her keys and purse down and tried to explain to her the situation that she was caught up in.

"Magic, did Malik tell you why I went off on him?"

"No, he just said you started tripping like you always do and when he tried to check you, you went the fuck off."

"And you believed that shit, Magic? Come on, now. Listen, I need to talk to you about Malik. Come home now."

"You don't need to tell me shit about my man. And I ain't coming home. Whatever you gotta say, you say it now!"

Sydni looked over at Byron, who had taken a seat on the sofa and didn't look like he was going anywhere. She wanted to talk to Magic in private. She took the phone upstairs into her bedroom.

"Look, Magic. I don't know how to tell you this, but you gotta get the hell away from Malik." She told her everything that Darrius had told her about Dax and that night outside the club.

"You really have lost your damn mind, Sydni. First, it was all D's fault that Aaron was killed. Now that you're fucking him, you need someone else to blame. If this is true, then why haven't the police picked Malik up?"

"Because Mag, there is no concrete evidence. No weapon, no motive—just D's word against Malik's. How can it be proven?"

"Exactly, Sydni. How can you prove it to me that Malik shot Aaron? You can't," Magic told her.

"You know what, Magic? It's sad. If anyone would have told me the nigga I was wit' even lived next door to the person they thought had anything to do wit' my brother's murder, I would leave him alone. That's how deep my love for Aaron is. But for you, I guess money and dick are the priorities in your life," Sydni said before she hung up the phone. She was so disappointed in her sister that she could hardly think straight. She lay across her bed and closed her eyes. She heard her bedroom door creak and sat up.

"Everything okay?" Byron asked.

"Yeah, it's cool. Just some family drama going on right now, I guess."

"Don't worry, sweetheart. You'll be outta here soon enough." He smiled at her smugly. The phone rang again and it was Darrius.

"Hey, D, hold on a minute. Byron, look, I really need to chill by myself tonight and think."

"Okay. You want me to pick you up in the morning?" He looked at her strangely, surprised that she was asking him to leave.

"No. I'll call you from work," she said.

"Okay. Are you sure you're gonna be alright?"

"Yeah. Thanks."

"I'll see myself out then." He hugged her and closed her bedroom door behind him as he left.

"Hey, baby," he heard her say as he stood outside her room. He felt his heart slowly begin to break.

# 10

The next day seemed to creep by while Sydni was at work. She was so worried about her sister that she barely said two words to Byron when he brought her and Miss Donna their coffee, and Miss Donna kept having to repeat herself all day. The phone was ringing, but Sydni was so deep in thought that she didn't hear it.

"Git de phone, chile. It's bin ringin' for de past five minutes," she called from the back of the store.

"Oh, I thought Mister Joe was here." She walked over to the wall and picked it up. "Davis Cleaners."

"Sydni, it's me."

"Magic, I'm glad you called." Sydni sighed. She hated arguing with her sister.

"Before you start, Syd, there's something I gotta tell you. I wanted to tell you face to face, but I might as well just come out and say it."

"What is it, Magic?" Sydni tried to prepare herself, afraid of what her sister had to tell her. *Is she pregnant? I hope it's not by Malik. That's all we'd need right about now.*

"I . . . I'm moving out. Today. I'm getting my stuff in a little while."

"What? Why? What the hell is going on?"

"I just can't stay there anymore."

"I know you're not living with that mothafucka Malik." Sydni looked around to make sure there were no customers and Miss Donna wasn't anywhere near her.

"Don't go there, Sydni, okay? I just wanted to let you know. Is that all you care about? Whether or not I'm staying with Malik? You don't even wonder why the hell I'm leaving?"

"Yeah, I'm wondering. That's why I'm asking what the hell is going on. Magic, talk to me."

"I don't know, Sydni." She could hear the distress in her sister's voice. "Look, you know I'm a hard sleeper."

"Hell, yeah. Everyone knows that," Sydni replied.

"Okay. I mean, at first I thought I was dreaming, you know. I could feel someone touching me, feeling on me. Rubbing on my breasts and stuff."

Sydni could feel her heart pounding as her sister kept talking.

"I would just roll over and pull the covers over me. But Syd, the other night, I could really feel the touches. My eyes opened and I swear, Mister Joe was standing next to my bed."

"Oh my God. What did he do, Magic? Did that bastard rape you?"

"No, Syd, he didn't rape me. I looked at him. As a

matter of fact, I was too scared to say anything. He asked me was I alright because he heard me moaning and thought I was having a bad dream. He said that's why he came in my room. I was so spooked that I just dipped. That's why I can't come home, Sydni."

"Why the hell didn't you tell me this before?" Sydni hissed into the phone. She was so angry that she could barely speak.

"Because the way it happened, Syd, I was wondering if I had been dreaming and he just walked in."

"That's the way that sneaky bastard operates. The same way he found my towel outside the bathroom door and walked in on me. I'm telling Mama."

"No! Don't tell her, Sydni. Maybe I was dreaming. It doesn't matter anyway. I'm moving out. Look, I'll call you after I get settled. I love you, Sydni."

"Magic! Magic!" Sydni yelled into the phone but all she heard was the echo of the dial tone in her ear. She grabbed her purse from behind the counter and left without saying a word to anyone.

"Dammit!" Mr. Joe whispered as he hung up the phone on his desk. He had picked it up at the same time that Sydni had answered it, and when he heard the two girls talking, he muted the receiver so they wouldn't know he was listening. He knew that Magic had known what he had done the other night, but when her mother didn't mention anything he thought he was safe. Now he had to come up with a way to stop that bitch ass Sydni from ruining what he had hoped would be a promising future with her mother.

\* \* \*

"Magic! Magic, are you still here?" Sydni yelled as she entered her house. She ran up the stairs and into her sister's room. Her bed was still unmade and there were still a few items on her dresser, so Sydni thought that maybe she had changed her mind. But when she opened Magic's closet and saw the missing clothes and suitcase, she knew her sister was gone. She picked up the phone and dialed Magic's cell phone, but the voice mail picked up.

Sydni was so lost that she didn't know what to do. She tried to reach her mother at work, but she was not there. She paced the floor nervously, trying to figure out what to do next. She called Darrius and left a message for him to come to her house as soon as he could. She ran back down the steps and sat on the sofa. She was deep in thought when the ringing of the telephone caused her to jump.

"Hello."

"Can I speak to Sydni?" an unfamiliar male voice asked. She had no idea who it was.

"Speaking. Who is this?"

"Look, I'm a friend of your sister."

"Where is she?" Sydni demanded.

"She told me to call and tell you to meet her at this address."

"Let me speak to her! Where is she?"

"She ain't here. She just told me to call you. If you don't want the address, then cool."

"Why didn't she call me herself?"

"I don't know. Something about her phone being dead," he told her. "You want the address or what?"

"Yeah. What is it?" Sydni made mental note of the address and realized it wasn't too far. She hung up the phone and was headed out the door when the phone rang again. It was Darrius. She told him about Magic and Mr. Joe and then said she was on her way to meet Magic.

"Wait, Sydni, and let me go with you," he told her.

"It's cool, D. I'll call you as soon as I get back. I'm just gonna go over there and check on her."

"I don't want you to run into that asshole Malik," he replied. "I wish you had a cell phone. At least then you could call me if something did go down."

"I promise you, D, I'll be okay. I gotta go. Bye." She rushed out to find her sister.


Sydni stood outside the building at the address that the guy had given her over the phone. The building looked somewhat empty, but she went inside anyway. She walked down the dimly lit hallway until she came to the right apartment number. She could hear music coming from inside. She knocked on the door, but there was no answer. She knocked again, louder this time.

"Magic, it's me!" she yelled. She turned the knob and the door opened. She hesitated, still calling out as she slowly entered. "Magic?"

The apartment was dark with the exception of a light coming from a room down the hall. Sydni took a few more steps, praying that she wouldn't find her sister's dead body lying somewhere. She thought better of it and decided to leave. As she backed up, she felt someone grab her and put something over her mouth. As she took a breath to scream, the world went black around her.

\* \* \*

"Sydni! Sydni!" Darrius banged on the door. He tried to look through the window, but he knew the house was empty. It was after one and he hadn't heard from her. Darrius was worried. He tried to call Magic's cell, but the only thing he got was the voice mail. He knew he had to find her and see if Sydni was alright. He set off for Malik's house.

"Yo! What the fuck is going on?" Malik said angrily as he opened the door. He was tired as fuck; he had just gotten in the bed when Darrius came banging on the door.

"Where is Magic? I need to talk to her!" Darrius answered. He could tell that Malik recognized him from Maroon's and would understand that Darrius wasn't playing.

"Her ass is 'sleep. You talk to her in the morning." He tried to close the door but Darrius put his arm up and pushed it back open. Malik took a step back and reached for his piece.

"Bitch, please. Don't even think about it!" Darrius grabbed Malik's arm and twisted it, causing him to drop the gun. Malik groaned in pain and he began to sweat as Darrius pinned his arm behind his back.

"What the hell is going on?" Magic said, rubbing her eyes. "D! What are you doing? Let him go!"

"Your bitch-ass boyfriend pulled his gun out on me!" D told her. He released his grip on Malik. Malik fell on the floor in pain.

"What are you doing here, D?" Magic asked him, confused by what was going on.

"I came looking for you. Sydni said she was coming over here to talk to you and I haven't heard from her."

"I haven't seen Sydni. She hasn't been here." Magic began to panic.

"She's not at home. I know something happened to her." Darrius walked over to Malik and kicked him. "Where the fuck is she? I know you did something to her!"

"I don't know what you talkin' about. I haven't seen her, man. I swear!" Malik groaned and grabbed his stomach. He scrambled to reach the gun that was laying across the floor, but Darrius grabbed it and aimed it at him.

"Is this the gun you killed Aaron with, mothafucka? You gon' kill me with the same one?"

"What is he talking about, Malik? Did you really shoot my brother?" Magic stood in disbelief. She had called her sister a liar earlier when Sydni might have been right.

"I didn't know he was your brother. I thought it was that nigga Dax!"

"Where is my sister? What the fuck did you do to her?" Magic began kicking and punching Malik as she screamed.

"I ain't seen your sister, I swear!" he yelled and tried to push her off him.

Darrius pulled Magic off and told her to get dressed and get her stuff. She ran into the bedroom and pulled her clothes on, running back out with her bags. Darrius stuffed Malik's gun into his waistband and then Magic and Darrius didn't waste any time leaving.

"Do you have the number for the detective who's

handling Aaron's case?" he asked as they got into his car.

"Yeah, it's here in my purse somewhere." Magic began digging in her purse, taking stuff out and laying it in her lap. Darrius noticed that her cell phone was off.

"Why the hell is your phone off all the damn time? Sydni may be trying to call you!"

"Because I don't want to waste my minutes, that's why!" she answered, turning the phone on. "And if she couldn't get me then she would try to reach you. Is your damn phone on?"

Darrius looked down at the phone attached to his waist and made sure it was on.

"Here. Here's the number," Magic said, pulling the rumpled business card from her purse. Darrius looked at the card and began dialing the numbers. Magic frowned at him. "It's three o'clock in the morning. You're calling him this late?"

"Hello, this is Darrius Whitman. May I please speak to Detective Schultz? Thank you. Yes, I'll hold." He cut his eyes at Magic, who just shrugged. She listened as Darrius explained the situation that had just occurred with Malik, including the possible murder weapon that he had taken out of Malik's place. Darrius also added that Sydni was missing and that they suspected Malik had something to do with her disappearance. He agreed to meet them at Sydni's mother's house.

# 11

Sydni was scared. She could feel the sweat pouring down her neck as she tried to scream. She was sitting in a chair and her hands and feet were tied behind her back. The rope was cutting into her wrists. She tried to breathe normally, but it was hard with the thick cloth over her mouth. Her eyes were covered, leaving her in total darkness. She heard the door open and then shut. Her heart was racing as the echo of footsteps came closer and closer to her. She began to whine. The gag was slowly loosened, then removed. Her lips began to quiver and she sniffled and cried from the fear.

"Please, please tell me why you're doing this to me," she wailed. There was no answer. A hand slowly tipped her head back and she felt a cup placed on her lips. She shook her head, afraid to drink, thinking it was something to knock her out or even worse, kill her. "No, no!"

"Drink it! It's just water. It won't hurt you," the voice whispered. Sydni tried to figure out who it was, but she couldn't even tell if her captor was male or female. The cup was once again placed to her mouth and she drank. The water felt so cool and good that she began to take it in too fast and almost choked. She could feel a cool towel on her face as someone gently wiped her mouth. The ropes around her ankles were loosened. "Get up!"

Sydni did as she was told and stood. She was led a few feet away and then she was pushed backward. There was no way she could brace herself, but there was no need. Her butt fell onto a thick cushion and she knew it was a bed. Her captor spread her legs apart and tied each one to a post. The same thing was done to her hands. She began to whimper again, pleading to be released. Although she was blindfolded, she squeezed her eyes shut, not knowing what to expect.

"Shhhhh! Be quiet. I'm not gonna hurt you. Go to sleep. I'll be back later." The gag was placed back in her mouth and she could hear the door open and then close. She was once again alone. She began to pray for God to help her, because she knew that He was the only one who could.


Magic tried to think positive, hoping that they would find Sydni asleep in her bed when they arrived at the house. She wasn't; the bed was empty. No one was there; not even her mother and Mr. Joe. As they waited for the detective, she went into Sydni's room to search for any clue as to Sydni's whereabouts.

The detective finally arrived and took a statement from each of them, then said he would have the gun checked out. This could be the lead that they had been waiting for in the case of Aaron's unsolved murder. Unfortunately, he also informed them that they would have to wait until Sydni had been missing for twenty-four hours before he could file a missing person's report. But he promised to keep his eyes and ears open and let them know if he heard anything.

"What time is it?" Magic asked after he finally left.

"Almost seven," Darrius answered, rubbing his eyes.

"Where the hell is she? Why hasn't she called?" Tears began to form in Magic's eyes as she thought out loud. "And where the hell is my mother? She hasn't called or come home either."

"She's probably out with Mister Joe, because he ain't here either," Darrius said sleepily.

"Oh shit! I'll bet that bastard has something to do with this. Sydni probably went to him about what I told her. Oh God, we gotta go find him!"

"What are you talking about? What does Mister Joe have to do with any of this?" Darrius asked in obvious confusion.

Magic grabbed his hand in a panic. "We don't have time for me to tell you right now, D. Just trust me, okay? I'll explain it to you later. Right now we just gotta find my sister."

"Alright, Magic, but even if Mister Joe had something to do with this, we don't know where he is," Darrius told her.

"We can start at the cleaners. He has to go there some time today."

"Let's go." Darrius followed her out of the door and they set off for Davis Cleaners for some answers.


Sydni had no idea what time it was. She didn't even realize that she had finally fallen asleep until she heard the creak of the door and the footsteps echoing once again. She raised her head off the bed, once again trying unsuccessfully to free herself. She felt the hand on her head as the gag was removed, and this time she drank from the offered cup without resistance. Her face was wiped as it had been before. There was something about the tenderness that the person used with her that made her think that this was not a stranger, yet Sydni could not imagine who could be doing such a thing.

To her horror, Sydni could feel her captor unbuttoning her blouse. She could feel the breath of her abductor against her skin and she began to cry as she felt hands running across her breasts, softly at first, then pinching her nipples. She could imagine the eyes on her body as the fingers rubbed along her thigh. She had felt that stare on her body before.

"Mister Joe, please don't do this to me. You need to think about this. Please, stop." The hands were coming closer and closer to her essence and Sydni was nauseated at this point. "Mister Joe, stop!"

The movements suddenly stopped and the only sound was heavy breathing. Sydni tried to raise up again. She could feel him putting her blouse back on hastily. She was confused.

"What did you call me?" the voice asked.

"I . . . I called you by your name," Sydni answered. It was her own breathing that she heard now as she felt the blindfold being removed. She could not believe her eyes when they fell upon the face before her.

"He touched you? Did he?" He didn't wait for Sydni to answer. Her eyes told it all. "I am gonna kill that mothafucka!"

"Noooo!" Sydni yelled as he ran out of the door. She used every ounce of strength she had and managed to free one of her arms. She moved quickly to untie the rest of her body, knowing that she had to prevent a murder from happening.


"Miss Donna, where is Mister Joe?" Magic asked as she burst into the store.

"Good mornin' to you too, chile. Who done gone an' took your manners dis mornin'?" Miss Donna frowned at her and Darrius.

"Sorry, Miss Donna, but we need to see Mister Joe. Where is he?" Darrius asked her.

"He not 'ere. Told me last night that 'e wadn't gon' be 'ere. Was takin' yo Mama to Atlantic City or sumtin'. I had to open de store myself. Where's your sistah dis mornin', anyway? She went flyin' outta 'ere last night witout even sayin' goodbye."

"We don't know where she is, Miss Donna. That's why we need to see Mister Joe. We think he may have something to do with her being gone." Magic began to cry. She told Miss Donna everything that had happened between her and Mr. Joe.

"Dat lowlife scumbag! When I see 'im I gon' ta

whip his ass me self. But chile, I don' tink he got nuttin to do with Sydni not bein' 'ere. I know he and yo Ma gone to Jersey. They called me dis mornin'."

"Then where the hell is Sydni?" Magic sniffled.

"Dere's sumtin else wrong too. It's after eight an dat dere boy ain't 'ere wit no coffee fer her!"

"Who? Byron? Byron would never do anything to hurt Sydni. He loves her," Magic replied. As if on cue, the doors to the store burst open and Byron ran in.

"Where is he? Where is he?"

"Where is who?" Magic asked. She was immediately frightened. Byron was beet red and his hair was wild all over his head. His clothes were rumpled, like he had been in a fight, and he was acting like a madman.

"Joe. Where is that bastard? I need to see his ass right now! Now!" He ran past the counter into the back of the store, searching for Joe, but he was nowhere in sight.

"Byron. Calm down, man. What's this about?" Darrius walked over and tried to touch Byron, but he jumped away. "Byron, do you know where Sydni is?"

Images of Darrius and Sydni kissing and holding hands filled his mind. He saw them walking into Maroon's and then could hear Darrius telling Sydni he loved her. Byron reached into his pants and pulled out the gun, pointing it at Darrius.

"Byron, what are you doing?" Magic yelled. Everyone remained frozen as Miss Donna began praying out loud.

"Shut up!" he yelled at the mumbling woman.

The sound of the door opening caused all heads to turn.

"Sydni!" Miss Donna said.

"Byron, don't do this. Please give me the gun." She walked toward him. He shook his head, eyes still on Darrius.

"Sydni, what are you doing?" Magic cried out. "He's crazy."

"He's not crazy. Come on, Byron, give me the gun," Sydni continued.

"All I wanted to do was make you happy. That's all. I did everything, *everything,* to prove that to you. But it wasn't good enough, huh? I just wanted you to love me, that's all. But instead, you chose to love him. He doesn't love you, Sydni. I do." Byron continued to shake his head. "Don't you know I would do anything for you? Do you know that?"

"I know that, Byron. And you're right. Just give me the gun," Sydni pleaded.

"You said you wanted to move back to Georgia. I didn't have a problem with that. I gave you everything I had to prove my love for you, Sydni." The tears flowed down Byron's flushed cheeks as he talked.

"I know, Byron. And we can go back to Georgia together. Just you and me." Sydni was crying just as hard as he was. He looked at her to make sure she was telling the truth.

"Together?" he asked.

"As man and wife, Byron. I love you," she whispered as she stepped within his reach. "But you've got to give me the gun."

Byron turned to place the gun in Sydni's hand. He had finally heard the words he had waited an eternity to hear. Sydni was gonna marry him. The door opened again and a man and a woman walked in. Byron frowned at the gentleman's face.

"What the hell is going on up in here?" the man growled. Byron's actions were smooth and swift as he lifted the gun and pulled the trigger. Screams filled the air as the bullet went into motion and people ducked for cover. When it made impact into the chest of its target, life as they all knew it stopped instantaneously, once again.

"You ready to go, sweetheart?" Byron asked Sydni as she quivered on the floor. He placed the gun to her head and grabbed her arm to help her get up. "He won't be touching you or hurting you like that ever again. I promised you, remember? Now let's go get some of that southern comfort in Georgia that you always brag about."

Sydni tried not to freak the hell out. She smiled weakly at Byron and took his hand. She looked over at the blood spilling out of Mr. Joe's body as she stood up. No one else moved.

"Come on, sweetie." Byron smiled. She could see the craziness in his eyes.

"Sydni, no!" Magic screamed.

"Shut up!" Byron took the gun from Sydni's temple and aimed it at Magic. With swiftness, Darrius was up and grabbing Byron from behind. Sydni moved away from Byron and reached for the gun that was aimed at her sister. She struggled with Byron with all the strength she had, determined to keep him from hurting anyone else. The sound of the gun firing again resounded and she looked into Darrius' eyes.

"Sydni!" She heard the words coming from his mouth. Sydni frowned as the pain gripped her side.

"You mothafucka!" She could hear Magic screaming as her eyes began to close.

"Oh my God, Sydni. Sydni!" She could feel Byron's arms around her as she fell.

"You killed her! You killed her!" Magic yelled.

Sydni could hear a lot of commotion in the distance, but her eyes remained closed.

"I . . . Uh . . . Oh, God, please. No." She heard Byron crying, but she knew not to open her eyes. She was in his lap and he was rocking back and forth. "Baby, I'm so sorry. Please don't leave me. I love you. Please don't leave me."

"Don't do this, Byron. Give me the gun," Magic pleaded.

"I loved her. Oh, God, what have I done? What have I done?" Byron whispered. He leaned over her and kissed her on the cheek. "I am so sorry, baby. I love you."

"Give me the mothafuckin' gun! Do not do this!" Darrius yelled. For the third time, a shot rang out and Sydni felt the wetness splatter on her face. She still didn't open her eyes, too afraid of what she would see. Magic and her mother cried out in horror and Darrius quickly picked up Sydni's body. Miss Donna was in shock and could not move.

"Sydni, Sydni." She heard the pain in Darrius' voice and her eyes fluttered open.

She looked into his tear-streaked face and whispered, "I just wanna go home."

That was the last thing she said to him as her world went black.

# Epilogue

There's no place like home. I know exactly how Dorothy felt when she said that in the *Wizard of Oz*. Since I've been back, my life has taken a three hundred and sixty-degree turn. And today, for the third time in my life, I am graduating. All my friends and family will be watching as I receive my degree from Spelman College.

I think the move back home has done wonders for everyone, including Magic. Believe it or not, she is back in school, majoring in Massage Therapy. I'm quite sure she has ulterior motives, but school is school, I guess. Mama is glad to be back here too. She missed her family and they missed us. Come to find out, Mr. Joe had everything put into her name, including his life insurance and the dry cleaning business. So after giving him a cheap burial, she cashed it all in and sold the cleaning business to

Miss Donna for two dollars. She is still running it, but now it's Donna's Cleaners.

Malik Fitzpatrick is serving a life sentence for murder. It turned out that not only was the gun that Darrius had confiscated the one that was used to murder Aaron, but it was connected with two other shootings. He will never be free again.

I have been accepted into the FBI Academy in Charlotte, Virginia. All of my hard work and studies have paid off. I only wish my brother were here to see me check off my list. I miss him dearly. But at least I have his best friend, my lover, my hero, and soon to be my husband, Darrius. We are getting married in three weeks. Everyone thinks that I am shelling out too much money for this event but hey, I had ten grand saved that no one ever knew about. And wait until they see the ring that I got for D, which was bought from the proceeds from the sale of the one they never knew I had.

New York may be the city of dreams for some folk, but as for me, all I need is some southern comfort.

# Played

## by Dwayne S. Joseph

# 1

Ray was about to die. That's the first thought that came to my mind as I watched in shock as Frido pointed his .45 down at Ray. Jesus Christ. This was all my fault. Just a few weeks ago, I was a happy-go-lucky fly girl on the block, running things. My shit was tight and on point. I was the shit and I controlled my own destiny.

Then I met Frido. Fucking Frido.

Frido is the reason I was paralyzed and shaking with fear. I'd always been in control of things until he stepped into my world. It was a Friday night when we met and I started to lose my mind. I was out clubbing with my boys, Raymond and Stevie, and my only real girl friend, Shanice. We were out getting fucked up, dancing our asses off and scheming. This is what we did every Friday, Saturday, Sunday, Monday, Tuesday, Wednesday, and Thursday.

We were always getting into some crazy shit, and that night was no different.

We were at the Latin Quarter getting our salsa on. Salsa is my shit. Tito Nieves, Johnny Rivera, India, Grupo Niche, and of course Marc Anthony. These are just a few of my favorites. Put me on the dance floor and I just start twirling, shaking, gyrating, causing guys' necks to break and their eyes to pop out of their heads. Like I said, I'm the shit. I've always known it. And I love that fact. There's no better feeling for me than to make a male or female sweat the hell out of me while I'm doing my thing. That's the very essence of control. When I'm working it, I know that I can get what I want, when I want it, in the way that I want it, from whoever I want. That's me. Angel. A devil in disguise. I like to tease and have a good time. Occasionally my teasing causes some drama. But for those times, my boys Raymond and Stevie are always around to pull me out of the fires I create. That's why I hang with them.

Raymond is 5'5", about two hundred pounds with a face full of zits. He's a Trini-Rican. His mother is from Trinidad, his father obviously from Puerto Rico. Raymond is not the prettiest brother on the block. Shit, if you want the truth, he's a few clicks away from Craig Mack. He even has the same medium-sized Afro. But what Ray lacks in looks he makes up for in personality. He's one of the realest, sweetest guys I know. He's twenty-nine, has his own legitimate business, and has taught me more about guys than anyone. He's taught me how to tell the difference between a player and a playa. He's showed me how to see past the bullshit that men spit and read between the lines to get the true meaning behind their words. Ray keeps it real and he's a true friend. He's only ever tried to press up on me once, but once I let him know what was what, we developed a fast, devoted friendship. When it comes to someone knowing about all of my dirt, Ray's the one and only one. He's always talking shit about writing a book about me. Shit, maybe someday I'll let him do it.

Stevie is Ray's boy from high school. He's Ray's opposite. He's tall, about 6'3", with rugged, pretty features. Stevie is Nuyorican to the core. He's your full-blooded, Bronx born and raised Puerto Rican guy who thinks he's God's gift to women. Unlike Ray, Stevie's always trying to spit mad game at me, trying to get in my panties. It doesn't matter how many times I shut him down. He still tries. I ain't gonna lie, though. Stevie is fine as hell. But you know how Ray makes up for his looks with his personality? Well, Stevie doesn't do that. He's so full of himself that there's no room for any kind of personality. Not only that, but it's all tits and ass with him. That's all he sees and that's all he wants. That's why I'll never give him a taste of my candy.

Although he's got a big ass head and gets on my nerves sometimes, Stevie is cool. The best thing about him is that he's a loyal motherfucker. He'd put his life on the line for any of his friends, no questions asked. How could you not have love for a guy like that?

Shanice is the final piece of the puzzle that I call my extended family. She's black, with dark, smooth, chocolate skin, a shapely figure with a big ass and small titties, and she sports a Halle Berry hairstyle.

Brothers are always sweating her. Shit, I would too if I was a dude. Like me, she's got it going on. Shanice is the only female that I completely trust, next to my mother and abuelita, of course. I've known her since we were in the seventh grade. She's had my back since the first day we met. A couple of girls wanted to beat me up because their boyfriends were sweating me. Shanice, who'd just moved to Brooklyn from Queens, didn't know shit about me, but she jumped right in and helped me kick those bitches' asses. We've been tight since then. I normally don't hang with too many females because they get on my fucking nerves with their petty-ass attitudes; Shanice is the only one I can really stand to be around. She's a lot like me. Shanice is my girl. Mi hermana. The only difference between us is that I like my dick primarily Black, while Shanice loves her dick thick, long and Latin. Other than that, we're like twins.

We were on the floor shaking our asses while Stevie and Ray made their rounds around the LQ, scoping females. That's how it always worked. Me and Shanice went our way while the fellas went another. We were there to back each other if need be, but for the most part we all had our own agendas and we all knew not to cramp each other's flow. "Shanice, I am fucked up," I said, dirty dancing with a guy to the salsa jam "La Agarro Bajando" by the group Puerto Rican Power. I really was, too. I'd lost track of the number of cosmopolitans I'd had. Dudes just kept buying me drinks, trying to get some. Of course I wasn't giving them shit, but I wasn't about to turn down free drinks. Shanice was next to me, getting her own groove on with a guy. If you didn't know that she was Black, you would swear she was a Latina just by the way she moves.

"So am I," she said, spinning around and looking at me. "I'm horny too. I think I'm fucking him tonight."

I looked at her dance partner, a tall guy. He seemed all right: nice build, nice eyes. Looked like he could handle himself in the bed. "Make him scream your name," I said.

Shanice high-fived me. "You know this."

We laughed and then turned back to our partners, who had no idea what had been said. Shanice grabbed her man by the hand and disappeared with him deeper onto the dance floor. I knew that I wouldn't see her until the club closed—if at all.

I looked at my guy. Like Shanice, I was feeling horny as hell. Alcohol always did that to me. My guy was cute. A little on the skinny side, but fuckable. Shit, another couple of drinks and it was gonna be his lucky night. I gave him a look and a smile with purpose, letting him know that sex was on my mind.

Then I saw Frido.

He was standing at the side of the dance floor, by the bar, with two sexy-ass females attached to each arm. I'd seen him around in other clubs before, checking me out, but I never really gave him a second thought, because I knew from word of mouth that he was a major player in the drug game. As crazy as I can be sometimes, the one thing I don't do is fuck with dudes like that. Usually, he'd check me out for a couple of minutes and then roll, but that night he was staring the hell out of me.

Dressed in some black leather pants and a sleeveless black top, he looked like the Puerto Rican version of P-Diddy, only with long hair, slicked back into a ponytail. My feet and hips kept moving, but for some reason my eyes were frozen on Frido. He always had a presence about him, but that night his aura was demanding attention and I couldn't look away.

Pissed off that Frido was getting my full attention, the guy I was dancing with decided to walk off to save face rather than look like he'd been dissed. I didn't give a shit. He wasn't the greatest dancer and if it weren't for the alcohol, he had no chance of getting my pussy. I was horny, yeah, but I was never pressed. Besides, I could find another guy to satisfy my urge. And from the way we were staring at each other, even though it went against my better judgment, I had a feeling that guy could be Frido.

I didn't care that I was out there alone. I was dressed in a hot pink halter top, skin-tight black leather pants and my ankle-high, black leather boots. I'd come to dance, guy or no guy. Besides, I had an audience; Frido wasn't the only one watching me.

I shook my ass with venom to the Sean Paul jam "Get Busy" that the DJ was now playing. I shook, I bounced, I gyrated; I dropped it like it was hot. I was in my element, feeling myself and the heat that I was emitting. I looked to see if Frido and his girls were still watching me. Frido's girls were, but he was nowhere to be seen. I continued to show my ass, getting hornier by the second, feeding off of the testosterone around me, feeding off of the females' attention. I worked it like the girls in Sean Paul's video did, rocking my hips, making my ass bounce, teasing, twirling, sexing the hot air around me. Yeah, there were other females in the club getting their shit off too, but you couldn't tell me I wasn't the shit.

Suddenly, someone stepped behind me, merged his body with mine and began to move to the music with me. Normally I don't let strangers press up on me without an invitation, but I was drunk, the music was tight, and whoever it was behind me knew how to move. So I just said fuck it and kept on moving. We danced, his crotch to my ass, in sensual syncopation.

"You got nice moves, Angel," my dance partner said. I didn't recognize the voice. I turned to see who my partner was. Staring at me with a set of sinfully sexy eyes was Frido. I backed away a step.

"How you know my name?"

Frido smirked. "I know everybody's name," he said easily.

"Is that right? And does everybody know your name? Because if they do, I'm not one of them."

Frido smiled just as smoothly and easily as he spoke and then he put his hand out. "I'm Frido." I shook his hand. "And now everybody knows my name." Without warning, he spun me around as the DJ played Sean Paul's other jam, "Glue", and began to grind into my ass again. I had to admit he was smooth. We danced in silence, sweating up a frenzy. Every now and then Frido's hands would roam along my torso, his fingers softly grazing me at the side of my breasts. His teasing touch was a definite turn on. So was the hardening of his dick. I reached my hand up and placed it behind his neck. Frido lowered his head and brought his lips down on the back of my neck. "You smell good, Angel," he said, pecking me and licking me at the same time.

"Thank you," I said, nibbling on my bottom lip. The alcohol, his light kiss, and the cologne that he was wearing were all making my body heat rise even more. I closed my eyes as the kissing and licking went from my neck to the back of my ear, while the exploration of his fingertips became bolder. When I opened them, the two females who'd been attached to his arm were watching me. One was a Latina like me with long, straight black hair, and flawless, bronze-colored skin. Her body was lethally curved. The other was a white female with blue eyes, brown hair, and large, C-cup sized breasts. I'm not into women, but I can't front, they were both off the hook. Especially the Latina, who was looking at me with slit eyes. "I don't think your friends are happy that you're over here giving me your time," I said. "Especially the Latina. She looks a little pissed off."

Frido kissed my neck again. "Don't worry about them."

"I don't want no drama," I said, enjoying the kiss. "I came to party. Not kick a bitch's ass."

"I told you not to worry about them." He kissed me again and I followed his instructions and ignored the females' staring. We danced for a few more songs and then Frido whispered in my ear. "What are you drinking?"

"Cosmopolitan," I said.

"I'll be back," he said, stepping away from me.

"Hurry," I said. "Another dude might try to take your place."

Frido smiled slyly. "I'll be back."

I stood out on the floor, a little unsteady but still moving, smelling Frido's cologne on my neck. If there was any one guy who could get some, it would be him. He was a pretty, bad boy with a mysterious nature to him that was more intoxicating than the drink he went to get me. He was good, but I planned to take things up a notch when he came back. After fifteen minutes, though, I had a feeling I'd been played. I looked around the club, but didn't see Frido or his girls anywhere. "His loss," I said, feeling like it was mine. I was about to step off to go and get my own damn drink when I felt a hand touch my ass. I smiled and then turned, expecting to see Frido. But it wasn't him at all.

It was the Latina who'd been staring me down. I knew she was attractive, but I was seeing her from a distance. Now that she was up close, I could really see how much she had it going on. She was holding a drink in her hand. "What's up with you touching me like that?" I asked.

She cut her eyes at me, pursed her lips and then lifted the glass to me. "Here's your drink."

"Where's Frido?"

"Frido had business to take care of," she said.

"What kind of business?"

"Important business. You want your drink or not?"

I stared at her hard for a second and then took the glass. "So where's your friend?" I asked, taking a sip of the strong drink.

The Latina started to move seductively to the music in front of me. "She's around," she said, moving closer to me. I backed up and took another sip. "What's wrong?" she asked. "You don't dance?"

"Yeah, I do. But I'm strictly dickly."

The Latina smiled and swayed closer to me. I took another step back, took a sip of the cosmo that was starting to taste better and better. "Yo, chill with that," I said. "I told you I don't get down like that." The Latina smiled again and continued to move. I swallowed the rest of my drink and then stared at her as she moved her waistline to the old school reggae jam "Flex" by Mad Cobra. I was suddenly beginning to feel hot again, just like I had with Frido. Then I felt another pair of hands on my ass. I turned around again, expecting to see Frido, and again I was disappointed. It was the other female. She smiled and then started to move her own hips to the music.

It was obvious that they were challenging me. Seeing what I was made of. The way I saw it, I had one of two options. I could either bounce and leave them to do their two-girl tango out on the floor, or I could join them and show them what it was to really move. Obviously, I wasn't about to let them get the best of me. I nodded and then began to move in step with them. I don't know if it was just the alcohol or if something had been placed in my drink— Ecstasy, maybe—but with every pulsating beat, with every one of their motions, I found myself becoming more and more turned on. There was something about the way the Latina's ass was against me and the way my ass was pressing against the white female that had me grinding and swaying in a way I never had before. I'd never fucked with chicks before, but that night, right there on the dance floor, I did.

The DJ must have been watching us out on the

floor because it seemed like he turned up the music to match our antics. The Latina turned around and faced me, never missing a beat, and put her hand on my breasts while the white female palmed my ass. She took my hand and guided it to her crotch. She was wearing a mini-version of a miniskirt, so it was nothing at all for me to slide my hand underneath and toy with her clit. I wanted to stop myself, but I just couldn't. My fingers went exploring and discovered that she was wearing no panties.

*Flex, time to have sex.*

The song's melody played while we played. I was burning from the sensuality of what was going down. My panties were soaked from it all. I would have never pictured myself doing what I was doing, but there I was unable to stop, oblivious to anyone around me, tonguing the Latina, fondling the white female's pussy while she sucked on my neck.

*Flex, time to have sex.*

"We're leaving," the Latina whispered, nibbling on my bottom lip. "You coming?" She kissed me again as the white female orgasmed from my touch, then she stepped around me and grabbed the white girl by the hand. They stood watching me, waiting for my answer. I felt like I was a top spinning around and around. Nothing seemed to make sense, yet did at the same time. While the intensity of the lights seemed to grow brighter, the music rose in volume, I got hornier and my panties got wetter.

"What about Frido?" I asked.

"What about Frido?" the Latina said, eyebrows raised.

I turned toward the bar, looking to see if I'd spot Frido anywhere.

"Coming?" the Latina asked again.

I turned back to them and stared at them through my blurred vision.

*Flex, time to have sex.*

I stumbled forward a step. "Let's go."

We hopped in a cab and fondled each other the whole time it took to get to wherever it was we were going, not giving a shit about the Indian cab driver who I'm sure was having a hard time concentrating on the road. For brief moments here and there I tried to stop what I was doing. I knew that I was about to do some lesbian shit, but I just couldn't stop. I was gone.

We didn't waste any time once we reached our destination. We started in the living room, fondling, kissing, grabbing, poking, while we made our way steadily to the bedroom. I don't remember every little detail about my surroundings, but I do remember the mirror above the bed. I remember that because I was lying on the bed facing up, watching our reflection as the Latina spread my legs and began to lick at the walls of my pussy while the white female ate her out. The Latina sucked and nibbled on me until I erupted and when she was finished drinking, she looked up at me in the mirror. "Your turn," she said. "But lick her first."

I didn't say anything as the white female lay on her back and spread her legs while the Latina caressed her own breasts. I just got on my knees and began to do to her what had been done to me. Up until that point, I would have sworn the white female was a mute, because she hadn't uttered a single word. But as I stuck my tongue deep inside of her, she moaned and begged me in a Catherine

Zeta Jones type voice to bite it. I did, soft at first, until she demanded that I do it harder. I did as she asked and bit down on her flesh, making her squirm and yell out in pleasure.

"My turn," the Latina said. Once again positions were switched and pussy was eaten. I don't know how many times I came that night, but I had a feeling I came more than I ever had before. Whatever else happened after that I don't remember. I just remember waking up in the bed in between the two females with a splitting headache, a dry-ass mouth, and in shock and disbelief. I'd just had sex with two females. And from the way my pussy felt, it must have been good. Shit.

I got out of the bed as slowly and gently as I could. I didn't want to wake them. This shit was awkward. *I'm not a fucking dike,* I thought. Shit. Where the hell were my friends? I know I was drunk, but I'd had more to drink before and I'd never done some shit like this. I was almost positive I'd been drugged.

I found my clothes and dressed as quickly as I could and then left, not even bothering to close the door. *I'm not a fucking dike,* I thought again. Shit. I looked at my watch. It was fucking twelve o'clock in the afternoon! This was one of those times when I wished I had a cell phone. My mom was always strict about me not having one. She said a cell would corrupt me. Imagine that shit.

I found the nearest pay phone, threw thirty-five cents into the slot and called Shanice. I hung up before the first ring. There was no way I could explain this shit to her. I gathered my change, threw it down the slot again and then dialed Ray's number. When he answered on the third ring, I said, "Ray, I need you to come and pick me up."

"Angel? Yoooo! Where the fuck have you been, dog? We been tryin' to reach your ass all morning. Shit, your moms called me at like six in the morning looking for you."

"I'll explain later," I said, shaking my head. "Just come and pick me up."

"You a'ight?"

I sighed. "I don't know," I said, thinking about waking up in that bed. "Just come and get me."

"A'ight. Where you at?"

I gave him my location and told him to hurry.

"A'ight. I'll be there."

"Thanks. Oh, and Ray," I said before he could hang up. "Don't tell anyone that you talked to me."

"But Angel, peoples is looking for you."

"I don't give a fuck, Ray. Don't say shit to nobody. Not Shanice, not Stevie, and definitely not my mom. Just come and get me and then take me to the hospital."

"The hospital? What's goin' on, dog?"

"I told you I'll tell you later. Now hurry and come get me. I'm scared."

"A'ight, a'ight. I'll be there. Just sit tight."

"Don't say shit, Ray," I warned again.

"Yeah, yeah. I got you. I'm a fucking mute."

I hung up the phone and covered my face with my hands then quickly pulled them away. I didn't like the stench coming from them.

# 2

I didn't say anything to Ray right away. I just got in his jet black Escalade, reclined in the seat and closed my eyes. I was still tripping off of what I'd done. *I'm not a fucking dike.* I kept thinking that over and over. Shit. I felt dirty. As soon as I was through at the hospital I was gonna head straight the hell home and scrub myself down under some hot water. Of course that wasn't gonna happen until after I dealt with my mom. I know she was probably having a fit and going crazy with worry.

"So what's up, dog?" Ray said after a couple of music-only minutes. "Why we rolling to the hospital?"

I pressed my lips together, frowned and sighed. I didn't even know how to begin. I sighed again and turned my head to the window. I didn't want to look at him. "I got into some crazy shit last night," I said somberly.

"Yeah, no shit. I figured that out when you asked me to take your ass to the hospital. So what's up?"

"I think I was drugged last night."

"Drugged? What do you mean you were drugged?"

"You gotta keep what I say between you and me," I said, raising up in the seat and looking at him.

"A'ight."

"No, don't give me no fuckin' a'ight, Ray. I mean you can't say shit to nobody. This shit goes with you to your grave."

"I said a'ight, Angel. Damn. What you want, my blood?"

"I'm just sayin', Ray, this is some serious and embarrassing shit."

Slowing the car down as the light changed to red, Ray said, "Just tell me what you did."

I shook my head. I couldn't believe I was about to say what I was about to say. "I had sex with two females last night."

It's a good thing Ray had already come to a complete stop, because he turned his head so fast toward me that if the car had still been moving, no doubt we would have crashed into something. "What did you just say?" he asked.

I exhaled. "I had sex with two females," I said again.

Ray nodded. "That's what I thought you said."

*Honk!*

"Shit!" Ray got off the brake, hit the gas, pulled over to the side and double-parked the car. As he shut off the engine, he said, "Yooo! I didn't know you were a dike. Not that there's anything wrong with it. You're still my girl, but damn!"

I shook my head. "I'm not a fucking dike!" I yelled.

"You're not?"

"Fuck, no! I like dick."

"Then what was last night all about?"

"Like I told you, I think I was drugged."

"Drugged into sleeping with two chicks?"

"Yes. I think some Ecstasy shit was put in my drink."

"Ecstasy? By who?"

"I think by this guy named Frido."

"Frido? Who the fuck is that?"

I sighed. Fucking Frido. For a second my mind went back to the night before, out on the dance floor with him. I could still smell his cologne, still see his dark eyes and his sexy smile. He'd sent the Latina and the white female to me. Why? "He's some guy I met last night."

"And you think he slipped the E in your drink?"

"Yeah."

I could tell that Ray was skeptical about my story.

"And instead of fucking him, you did some porn star shit with two females?"

I nodded slowly. "That about sums it up."

"So how do you know you were given E?"

I cut my eyes at him. "I slept with two women last night."

"So? Maybe you just had too much to drink."

I shook my head. "No way. I've had more to drink before and I've never been as gone as I was last night."

"And you think you got E?"

"How many times you gonna keep asking me that shit, Ray?" He was annoying the hell out of me.

"Chill, Angel. I'm just asking questions."

"Well, stop asking fucking questions. I told you I got E last night. Shit, if it wasn't E, I'm positive it was something, because when shit was going down, I wanted to stop but I couldn't. My mind was gone, and I was so freaking horny. I never lose control of myself like that. Even when I'm drunk."

"Damn, Angel," Ray said.

"Yeah, I know. That's why I wanna go to the hospital. I want to get myself checked out."

"Damn."

"You said that already."

"You slept with two females."

"Yeah, yeah. No need to remind me. Just make sure you keep that shit under lock and key."

"Yeah, a'ight." We were silent for a couple of seconds and then Ray said, "Yo, I gotta ask. How was it?"

I looked at him. "How was what?" He better not have been asking me what I knew he was asking me.

"Come on, Angel. You know what I'm talking about. The sex. How was the sex?"

I punched him hard in his arm. "How the fuck are you gonna ask me that?"

Rubbing his arm and laughing, he said, "What? You just banged two chicks. Do you have any idea what kinda pictures that puts in a ma'fucka's head? So come on, fill me in. How was it? What kind of shit did y'all do?"

"Ray, shut the fuck up and start the fucking car and take me to the hospital."

"So you not gonna tell me?" he asked, turning the key in the ignition.

"Hell, no, I'm not telling you. Just drive and let's

drop this subject. Damn. And get rid of whatever pictures you got in your fucking mind."

Ray laughed again. "A'ight, a'ight."

I punched him in his arm again. "You're fucking stupid," I said.

Ray laughed out loud. "I got some crazy pictures, ma."

"Whatever."

"So anyway, what's up with this Frido cat?"

I shrugged my shoulders. "I don't know. One minute me and him were on the floor getting our groove on, the next minute he was leaving to go get me another drink. Next thing I know the two females he rolled in the club with were bringing me my drink. You know the rest from there."

"Yeah, you got your freaky freak on."

I shook my head as Ray chuckled. I thought about Frido and his fine self. I couldn't believe I'd let myself get played like that. For real, I thought I was gonna be fucking him that night. The Latina said he was handling some business. No doubt it was some illegal shit. I didn't know what kind of game he was playing with me, but he'd better hope I didn't see him again, because if I did, I was gonna make sure he knew I wasn't the bitch to fuck with.

Ray and I drove in silence for a little while. Every now and then he'd chuckle and I'd groan. I can't lie; even though what happened wasn't funny, it was so crazy and unreal that I wanted to laugh sometimes too. Idiot. Asking me if it was good.

When we got to Beth Israel Hospital I jumped out of the car and went straight to the emergency room. I was glad I had insurance because I knew this shit would be expensive if I didn't. I could have gone to the free clinic around my way, but I didn't want to wait. I also didn't want to take the chance that I'd see someone I knew. "I need to see a doctor," I said to the receptionist behind the counter.

"What's the problem?" the receptionist, a heavy-set black woman, asked.

"I think I was drugged."

She looked at me. "Drugged? What kind of drugs?"

"I think I was given Ecstasy."

The receptionist nodded and then handed me some forms. "Fill these out and we'll call you."

I wrote down all of the information I needed to and then went to sit in the waiting area. Ray was chilling in his car, which was cool with me, because I wanted to be alone for a little while. I didn't know how long I was sitting there waiting, but when my name was finally called, I'd been asleep. I got up and followed a nurse to a curtained station where she checked my blood pressure and asked me a bunch of questions about my health and sex history. I always hated answering questions about my sex life. With all the shit I'd done, I always ending up feeling guilty for having fun.

After the nurse was done with the preliminary work, she left me alone for another long-ass time until the doctor, a fine-ass black man wearing a pair of Malcolm X-type glasses came in. "Hello," he said in a deep, baritone voice. "I'm Doctor Jeffries."

"I'm Angel," I said, checking out his long, lean frame.

He picked up my chart of information the nurse had left behind and flipped through it. He closed it after a few minutes. "So you think you were given Ecstasy?"

"Yeah," I said, snapping out of infatuation mode and coming back to reality. "I think somebody slipped it into my drink last night."

"Mm-hmm. Aren't you too young to be drinking?" He gave me a fatherly stare. I didn't say anything. "Alright, well let's do a urine sample and see if we can find anything."

"Can we do some other tests, too?" I asked.

The doctor looked at me. "Other tests?"

I nodded. "Some other stuff happened last night."

Giving me another paternal gaze, Doctor Jeffries asked, "Like what?"

I hated to talk about what I'd gotten into, but I told him all about what I did with the females. When I was finished the doctor said, "Okay, we'll have some blood work done, but it'll be a little while before the results are ready."

"No problem," I said. Shit, I didn't care how long it was going to take. Thankfully, after having my blood drawn, I only ended up having to wait for forty-five minutes before Dr. Jeffries came back and told me that all of my blood work had come back negative, which was a big relief. He also told me that they hadn't found any trace of drugs in my system. That shit fucked me up. I guess I was more drunk than I thought. I thanked the doctor and then went back to Ray's car, where he was sleeping. I knocked on the glass, waking him. He unlocked the door.

"You a'ight?" he asked as I got in.

"Yeah, I'm cool."

"And what about the E?"

I sighed. "They didn't find shit."

"Damn," Ray dragged out. He was about to say something else when I cut him off.

"I ain't no fucking dike," I said. "I was just more fucked up than I thought."

"A'ight," Ray said. I could hear the skepticism in his voice.

"Yeah, a'ight. I was fucked up and that's all there is to it. Now get me home, please. I got to deal with my mom."

Ray looked at me for a sec and then shrugged his shoulders and started the car. When I got home, my mom ripped into me, yelling about where the hell had I been and why couldn't I call. Then she went on to tell me how irresponsible I was and how my priorities were all screwed up. I let her rant and rave without saying too much and then after apologizing, I went to my room and laid out on my bed and fell asleep. I didn't wake up until my mom came into my room to give me the phone. It was Shanice, asking me about where I'd been. I told her that I'd hooked up with the guy she saw me dancing with and left it at that. She told me about hooking up with her dance partner. We talked for an hour or so, and before we hung up the phone, plans were made to hook up with Ray and Stevie later that night and go clubbing again.

# 3

I managed to put the craziness from Friday night behind me and partied hard on Saturday and Sunday. By the time Monday rolled around, I was exhausted. The last thing I felt like doing was sitting behind the front desk at the law firm where I worked, greeting potential clients and answering phones. But I had bills to pay and partying to do, so that's what I did. I was so used to partying that even though I was tired as hell, I busted my ass. When lunchtime rolled around I was more than ready for a break. I was also starving because I had woken up late that morning and since I couldn't afford to miss my train, I had to skip breakfast.

I signed out for lunch, grabbed my purse and then stepped outside. I was in the mood for some pepperoni pizza and a Jamaican beef patty, so as I always did, I headed to my usual lunch spot—the pizzeria around the corner. The owner, a short,

Italian guy with jet-black hair and a crooked smile, liked me and was always hooking me up with free food. He'd asked me out a couple of times, but I always turned him down. First of all, I'm not into dating white guys. But the main reason I wouldn't go out with him was because he's just too damn old. Shit, he has a daughter who's older than me. I've met her. She's cool—just a little stuck up. Thinks she's fly but she ain't. Not like me, anyway.

"'Sup, Angel?"

I stopped dead in my tracks. Double-parked and leaning against an all-white Benz with his arms folded across his chest was Frido. He was wearing a gray Sean John tank top and some Sean John calf-length shorts. His long hair was out and lying on his shoulders. A pair of stylish black shades concealed his eyes. I hadn't noticed before, but his arms were well defined, and covering the side of his right arm was a tattoo of a snarling black panther. On his left arm he had a tattoo of the Puerto Rican flag with the words *Boricua born and bred* etched underneath. I can't front; he was looking hella fine. But I hadn't forgotten about Friday night.

"What the fuck are you doing here? How you know where I work?"

"I came to talk to you," he said smoothly.

"You ain't got shit to talk to me about, maricon."

"What's up with the attitude?"

I slit my eyes. I know I was outside of my job and should have kept my cool, but I didn't give a fuck. "What the fuck do you mean what's up with my attitude? What, you think I forgot about that shit you pulled Friday night? Pulling a disappearing act and then sending your bitches over to me with a fucking spiked drink? What, you think I don't know you put some shit in it? I know your hoes told you all about what went down that night. You're lucky I didn't catch shit from them. I swear, y'all better not be putting my fucking business out in the fucking streets. I ain't the one to fuck with, maricon. And don't be fucking trying to talk to me no more." I flipped him both my right and left middle fingers and then stepped. He was lucky I wasn't a little bit more hardcore or else I would have tried to beat his ass down. Stupid, pretty motherfucker. Trying to come at me like Friday never happened. Shit.

I walked, pissed, and with my appetite gone. I was so mad I didn't know where I was going. Right foot. Left foot. Blood boiling as I thought back to when I woke up in the bed with the Latina and the white female beside me. Right foot. Left foot.

And then Frido grabbed my hand. I hadn't even heard him run up to me.

"Angel, hold up," he said.

I pulled my hand away quickly and turned around. "What the fuck is your problem?" I snapped. "Don't put your fucking hands on me." I may not have been as hardcore as some bitches I knew, but if he touched me again I was gonna throw down.

Frido must have sensed that and threw up his hands in surrender. "Alright, ma, chill. I ain't gonna touch you. Just hear me out for a sec."

I tightened my lips. It was obvious from the look on his face that he wasn't gonna let me go until I let him talk. "What do you want?"

Frido flashed a panty-dropping smile at me and lowered his hands. "I want to take you out tonight."

I looked at him like he was crazy, which he must

have been. "Were you not listening to a fucking word I said? You really expect me to go out with your ass after the shit you pulled? You're lucky I didn't see you out the next night. I would have had my boys beat on your ass."

"Who, your friends Ray and Stevie?"

"Yes." How did he know about them?

Frido laughed and shook his head slightly. "That wouldn't have been a good idea, ma."

"Why, because you're a fucking drug dealer? I ain't stupid, maricon. I know your game. I got news for your ass—I ain't impressed. I don't give a shit about your clothes, your jewelry or your car. I ain't a stupid bitch that you turn out like your two friends from the club. Now leave me the fuck alone with your wannabe Puerto Rican P-Diddy ass." I rolled my eyes and turned around.

As I walked away, Frido said, "I'll pick you up at five o'clock, ma."

"Be here if you want," I said, walking away. And I meant it. He could be there all he wanted. The last thing I was gonna do was go out on a date with his ass.

**4**

I walked around the city for a while, trying to calm down after my confrontation with Frido. I couldn't believe he had the balls to ask me out. And then he took his arrogance a step further and said he'd be there when I got off even after I basically told him to go to hell. Arrogant ass. His attitude pissed me off. What's worse was that cocky-ass attitude only added to his sexiness.

Damn.

After not eating lunch, I went back to work and called Ray when I got a free moment. "He came to my job," I said as he answered his cell.

"What's up, dog? Who came to your job?"

"Frido."

"You mean the cat from the LQ?"

"Yeah."

"You told him where you work?"

"Hell, no, I didn't tell him. I hardly even spoke to him."

"So how'd he know where your job was?"

I sucked my teeth. "According to him, he knows everything and everyone."

"Oh, yeah? What does he do?"

"He's never told me, but I'm sure he's a dealer."

"Why you think that?"

"Because he drives a Benz, dresses in nothing but expensive clothes and got two bitches to step to me."

"Shit, he sounds like a pimp if you ask me."

"Nah, he's too slick to be a pimp," I said.

"So what'd he come by your job for? He trying to get in on the action now?"

"Get this. He came to ask me out tonight."

"What?"

"Yeah, I know. That's some bugged out shit. He asked me out after I went off on his ass. And to make things even worse, after I turned him down he actually said he'd be here by five."

"Word?"

"Yeah."

"So what are you gonna do? You going out with him or what?"

"Hell, no, I ain't going out with him! I made it perfectly clear to his ass that despite what happened with those females, I am not some bitch that he can turn out."

"I don't know, Angel. He kinda turned you out that night," Ray said, laughing.

I didn't find anything funny. "You know what, Ray? I'm done talking to your stupid, Trini-Rican ass."

I hung up the phone without saying anything else. For the rest of the afternoon I worked and tried my hardest not to look at the clock. Five o'clock. That's when he said he'd be there. He had said he'd be right back after he left to get the drink, too. I *hmph'd* as the phone rang. I didn't care how sexy or how smooth he was. I wasn't going anywhere with him.

"You ready to go?"

It was quarter after five and I'd just stepped outside. I sucked my teeth and curled my lips. "You're hard of hearing, aren't you? I told you earlier that I wasn't going nowhere with you."

"Yeah, you did," Frido said, pushing himself off of his Benz. He was wearing an all-black suit with a light blue shirt underneath. His hair was once again slicked back into a tight ponytail. I couldn't help but wonder if he ever looked bad. He walked to the passenger door and opened it. When he did, sounds of salsa escaped from the inside. Frido stepped to the side with his arm draped on the opened car door. "You ready, ma?"

"I told you I'm not going nowhere with you." I sucked my teeth and started down the block. If he thought I was some easy trick he had another thing coming.

"Yo, ma, hold up," Frido said, jogging beside me. "Why you being like that? I feel bad that I had to disappear the way I did. I just wanna make it up to you."

I stopped walking and turned to him. "You feel bad, huh?"

"Yeah."

"Why, because you missed out on all the action after the club?"

"Nah, ma, it's not like that."

"Yeah, right."

"For real, ma. Believe me, when action goes down between you and me, nobody else is gonna be around to enjoy it." Frido licked his lips and stroked his goatee. As much as I didn't want it to, my willpower was weakening.

"When? What do you mean, when?"

Frido smiled. "You coming, ma?"

I stood still and stared at him as he stood waiting for me while the music played from his car, which he'd left open a few feet away. Damn it, he was smooth. I know I told him that I wasn't impressed by the shit that he had, but it was hard not to be just a little impressed. Shit, his clothes were on point, his ride—at least what I saw from the outside—was bad as hell, and he was iced out with a couple of simple but dazzling and expensive pieces of jewelry. He had it going on. That was obvious. Shit, after what happened Friday, I should let him take me out, wine me and dine me and make up for it. Besides, I was already dressed to impress in my black skirt and red silk blouse, with no place to go but home. I sucked my teeth again. "You better get me home by twelve."

"It's all good, ma. I'll have you home by eleven. I got things to do at twelve."

I swear I could have fallen right to sleep after I got in Frido's Benz. That's how comfortable his leather seats were. "You like the ride?" he asked, getting in.

I put on this indifferent face. "It's alright. I've been in better, though."

"Is that right?" Frido said, pulling off and laughing.

"What's so funny?"

"You, ma."

"Me? Why you say that?"

"Because you're sitting there fronting."

"Fronting?"

"Yeah, fronting. Acting like my ride ain't shit."

"So it is, huh?"

Turning up the music, Frido said, "You know the answer to that, ma."

I sucked my teeth and rolled my eyes, but I didn't say anything else because he'd been right. I was fronting big time. Never in my life had I been in a car as bad as Frido's. The pillowy leather seats were just a small part of the off the hook interior. His steering wheel and dash were made of the same leather as the seats. He had a navigation system that talked; a CD changer that was hidden in the dash; the shit was bad as hell. The drug trade was obviously treating him right. "So, where you taking me?"

"You hungry?"

"Yeah."

"We're going out to eat."

"Where?"

"You'll see."

"How you know I'll like where you take me?"

"Because I know," he said, full of confidence.

"I forgot—you know everything."

"Remember that, ma."

Frido took me into Greenwich Village to a hidden Italian restaurant that I'd never seen before. It was small, private, and romantic. We were seated at a private table in the corner that had a RESERVED sign on it. To my surprise, there were also a dozen red roses in a crystal vase with a card attached to it, sitting in the middle. I looked at the card and saw my name stenciled on it.

"You like roses, right?" Frido asked.

I smiled. "Yeah, I like roses." I had to fight my smile from getting any bigger as Frido nodded knowingly. I'd never been out with a guy as smooth or as confident as Frido. I mean, shit, he had a dozen roses waiting for me. Guys had given me roses before but never like that. He definitely scored some points with that.

The waiter came to take our order and before I could say anything, Frido went ahead and ordered both his and my meal, along with a bottle of white wine. When the waiter walked off I said, "So how you know I want whatever it was you ordered?"

Frido smiled. "Relax and let a man treat you, ma.

"So you're a man, huh?"

"As real as they come."

"So what was that shit about at the club last Friday?"

Frido smiled his sexy smile again. "I had business to take care of."

I straightened my lips. "Business, huh?"

"Business."

"So you sent your hoes to make sure I wasn't lonely?"

Again he smiled. "No. I sent them to give you the drink I'd promised you. I had nothing to do with whatever went down after that."

I slit my eyes at him. "You really expect me to believe that bullshit?"

"Like I said, Angel, I was handling some business."

"Right, right, business." We sat silent for a few minutes while soft Italian music played from speakers above us. "So what's up with those two bitches anyway?" I said after a while.

"Reina and Simone. That's their names. And nothing's up with them. They just handle some business for me from time to time."

*Again with the business,* I thought. "So I was business, then?" Frido didn't answer me and stared at me intensely. I was about to say something else when the waiter came with our food. I didn't know what it was that he ordered, but it smelled damn good. Before walking off the waiter poured two glasses of wine and handed one to me and one to Frido. When he left, Frido lifted his glass.

"A toast," he said.

"A toast to what?"

"To pleasure."

"I thought business always came before pleasure."

Frido touched his glass to mine. "That all depends on how you handle your business." He sipped his wine while keeping his eyes locked on me. We ate after that, not really talking much. Normally silence on a date is a bad sign, but for some reason, the lack of conversation never bothered me. It was eight o'clock by the time we were done eating. I was full from the delicious food and a little buzzed from the four glasses of wine I'd had.

"So where are we going now?" I asked, my nature higher than it had been before the wine.

"Home," Frido answered.

I liked the sound of that. "How far do you live from here?"

"I live in Jersey."

"Where at in Jersey? I have to be home by twelve." I'd had enough grief from my mom this past weekend, so I'd decided to be good for the week.

"I never said I was taking you to my place, ma."

I looked at him suspiciously. "I thought you said we were going home."

Frido stood up. "We are."

"So what home you talking about?"

"Your home."

"My home?"

"Yeah."

"So what happened to having me home by eleven? It's only a little after eight."

"I got some things to do."

"I thought you said that was at twelve."

"Business is unpredictable and always changing, Angel. You'll see."

"Oh, will I?"

Frido smiled and held out his hand for me to take.

"Aren't you gonna pay for dinner?" I asked, taking his soft hand and standing.

"It's already paid for."

We walked out of the air-conditioned comfort of the restaurant into the humid but bearable night air. I was feeling nice. Shit, I'm not gonna lie, I was feeling so nice and Frido was looking so good that if he were to say he was taking me to his place, I would have been down for the ride. I could handle my mom. But instead of suggesting the trip, Frido got on his cell, made a call and said something to somebody about hooking up in forty-five minutes.

After the parking attendant brought the Benz, we got in and rode in jazz-only silence until we got to my house on Jamaica Avenue in Brooklyn. Frido never asked me for a single direction.

"You have a good time?" Frido asked, pulling to a stop in front of my house.

I smiled. "Yeah. It was nice."

Frido nodded and then said, "I'm gonna be there at five again tomorrow."

I looked at him. "Oh, really? And how do you know I don't already have plans?"

Frido leaned over and gave me a slow, sensual kiss on the base of my neck, sending chills up my spine. "You do now, ma," he said, backing away.

I looked at him again but didn't say anything. I didn't know what to say after a move like that. That was an ultimate playa move that had my panties wet with desire. I got out of the car horny as hell and walked to my door.

Unlike most guys I'd dealt with, Frido didn't pull off until I stepped inside. I went to bed and took care of myself that night, imagining my fingers as Frido's tongue and my dildo as his dick.

# 5

It was hard for me to stay focused the next day at work. I kept thinking about the date I'd had with Frido and the kiss he'd given me. I'd been with a number of guys—some younger than me, but most of them older, and none of them had done to me what Frido had done. Shit, his tongue on my neck alone got me moist. I could only imagine what he could do to me in bed. And that's what I did all day long. In between the phone calls and while staring in the faces of clients, all I could do was imagine and fantasize.

When five o'clock finally came, although it was unusual for me, I practically ran outside. Frido said five and I expected him to be there on time waiting like yesterday. But when I got outside, his Benz was nowhere in sight. I looked up and down the long Manhattan block, but saw nothing. I went back inside, sat down in the AC for a few minutes and then stepped back out into the heat. Still no sign of Frido. Damn. I looked at my watch. It was five-fifteen. I'm not one to be sweating dudes, but I decided to wait until five-thirty. If Frido didn't show up then he was done. He'd get no more chances to play me. When five-thirty came and went and Frido was still missing in action, I shrugged my shoulders. "Fuck it. It's his loss." I headed to the subway. I still had time to catch the J train.

"So were you looking for me?"

I was waiting for the light to change to continue on to the subway when Frido pulled up in front of me and lowered his tinted windows. Drivers blew their horns at him angrily but he obviously didn't give a fuck. He got out of the car and walked around it and stepped to me.

I rolled my eyes. "I wasn't looking for you," I lied.

"You weren't?"

"No."

"Don't you usually catch the J train earlier?"

I sucked my teeth. "I worked late."

*Honk!*

"Get in, ma," Frido said, ignoring the car horns.

I stood still and pouted my lips. Frido was wearing a white linen button-down shirt and a pair of khaki linen pants. He had brown sandals on his feet and shades covering his eyes. His hair was loose on his shoulders again. "Why were you so late?"

"Business, ma."

"Right, right."

*Honk!*

"Get in, Angel," he said again.

"Where we going?"

"For a walk."

"A walk?"

"Get in."

I thought about walking off and leaving him there for a second but then my mind flashed back to the restaurant, the roses and the kiss. "I have to be home by twelve."

Frido nodded. "I got you."

We went to the Bay Ridge area of Brooklyn, parked by the Verrazano Bridge, and walked while the Hudson River crashed against the rocks near the railing. Being there wasn't exactly my idea of a good time. He was lucky there was a steady breeze blowing in from the river to keep the heat at bay, or else I would have told him to take me home.

"So what are you thinking about?" he asked. This was after a few minutes of silence passed.

"Honestly?"

"Yeah."

"I'm wondering why you brought me out here. This isn't what I imagined when you said you were gonna take me out."

"Is that right? So what'd you imagine?"

"I expected something like yesterday. A *date* date."

"So walking and talking isn't a date?"

I shrugged my shoulders. "I guess it is if you want it to be."

Frido nodded and walked to the railing, leaned on it and looked out at the river. I didn't know what to make of his silence. After yesterday and the kiss, walking and talking was the last thing I thought we'd be doing. *Whatever,* I thought to myself, staring at Frido's back. If he didn't like my answer he could take me the hell home. I could find other things to do. I was just about to tell him that when he called out to me. "Yo, Angel."

"What?" I said with a lot of attitude.

"Come here."

I reluctantly walked over to him. "What?"

"Look out there and tell me what you see."

I didn't even bother to look. "I see water."

Frido shook his head. "That's not what I see."

"Oh really? So what do you see?"

He looked back to the water. "My thoughts," he said.

I looked at him curiously. "Your thoughts?"

"Yeah."

"Okay?" I said, starting to wonder if for all of his looks and style, perhaps he wasn't as together upstairs as I thought he was.

"See, I come here all the time to think about shit. I'll just lean here like I'm doing now, look out at the water and let the waves take my thoughts, questions and dilemmas away in the current. This is how I meditate. You meditate?"

"No."

"You should try it, ma."

I sucked my teeth. "That's not my thing."

"Try it some time."

"Maybe."

Frido turned away from me and looked back to the river. I exhaled loudly, not caring that he could tell I was frustrated. Shit, he had me in my bed playing with myself after yesterday, and then he brings me out here to talk some guru meditation bullshit. Damn, I was irked.

"You ready to go?" Frido asked, stepping away from the rail.

I didn't hesitate. "Yes. Where we going now?" I hoped it was somewhere better than this.

"Home."

"Home?" I looked at my watch. "It's only seven."

"I got some things to do."

"So wait a minute," I said, putting up my hand. "You pick me up late because you had business. You bring me *here* for a date. And now you're taking me home all early and shit? Damn. This was a fucking waste of my time. Bringing me to stare at the fucking Hudson River, talking meditation bullshit. I should have taken the damn train and left your ass." I was pissed the hell off. First he was late and now this. "Take me the fuck home then!" I stormed off to his car. I couldn't see his face, but I think I heard Frido snickering behind me.

I didn't say shit to him when he took me home. I just sat in his comfortable-ass leather seats with my arms folded tightly across my chest. I hoped he didn't think he was gonna kiss me after this. When we got to my house I was all ready to storm out of the car, but before I got a chance, Frido wrapped his fingers around my wrist. "Angel, hold up for a sec."

I tried to pull my arm away but his grip was too tight. "Let go of my hand!" I demanded.

"I got a question to ask you."

"I don't have any answers. Now let me go."

"Not until I ask my question."

I tried to pull my arm free again, and when I couldn't, and because I knew I couldn't kick his ass, I sighed and said, "What's your fucking question?"

Frido's grip remained firm as he asked, "Why you mad at me?"

I turned my head and looked at him. Was he for real? "What do you mean, why am I mad at you?"

"I mean why does it bother you that I wanted to adore your beauty underneath the glow of the sunlight out by the water?"

Frido paused and waited for me to say something, but his question had caught me completely off guard. I'd heard I was fly, fine, phat to death, the shit, sexy as hell, off the hook, banging, kapow, heaven sent, chula, and a bunch of other over-used, played out compliments before, but that was by far the smoothest, most romantic, and most original thing anyone, guy or girl, has ever said to me. Damn. In a matter of seconds he'd done it to me again: he made me melt. Caressing my arm he said, "I'm gonna be there at five tomorrow. And I won't be late. Wear a dress."

"A dress?" I asked as his fingers snaked up my arm to my shoulder, and then to my cheek.

"And don't do the ponytail tomorrow."

Breathing short breaths as his fingers moved down to my neck, I said, "Okay."

Frido leaned toward me. I held my breath in anticipation of another sensual kiss. He cupped the back of my neck and pulled me toward him slowly. Goddamn, his lips hadn't even touched me yet and he already had a pool forming in between my legs. He pulled me closer to him and stared at me. I held his fiery gaze for a second and then closed my eyes and readied my lips for his. "I'll see you tomorrow, ma," he said. Then he kissed me slowly and softly—on my cheek. When he was done, he sat back up. I didn't move for a hot second. Was he for real? I opened my eyes and looked at him to see if he was.

I couldn't believe it when I saw him pulling out his cell phone and making a call. I shook my head and opened the door. He barely said goodbye as I stepped out. This time he didn't wait. He pulled off before my foot hit the curb.


"Yo, dog, where the hell you been? I thought you were supposed to call me yesterday."

I lay back on my bed and looked up at the ceiling. I called Ray a few minutes after I'd gotten inside. "I've been busy," I said.

"Yeah, yeah, whatever. So what's up, mami? You never called to tell me what happened after you got off yesterday. Did your boy show up or what?"

I smiled as an image of Frido appeared in my mind. "Yeah, he showed up."

"And?"

"And what?"

"What do you mean, and what? Why you holding out on a brotha? What ha . . . Wait a minute. You went out with him, didn't you?"

I thought about the restaurant and the roses. "Yeah," I said after a few seconds.

Ray exploded with laughter. "What the hell happened to 'hell, no, I ain't going out with his ass'?" he asked, doing a terrible job of imitating me. "I see that was just all talk."

"Shut up, Ray."

"What you mean shut up? You was all mouth yesterday. What happened?"

"Nothing happened."

"Don't even try it, ma. Something happened. You went out with the ma'fucka."

I sucked my teeth. "Will you stop riding my clit? It was only a couple of dates." *Shit. I didn't mean to say that.*

"A couple of dates?" Ray boomed out. "I thought you only went out with him yesterday."

Me and my big mouth. "I went out with him after work today, too."

"Damn! The nigga got you open like that?"

"Shut up, Ray. He don't got me open like nothing." I couldn't hold back my laughter.

"Yeah, whatever," Ray said, laughing heartily. "Talking big shit and now look. Your shit's open like a can of sardines."

"You're an idiot!"

Ray laughed. "Yeah I am, but the nigga still got you open. So when's the next date?"

"What next date?"

"What next date?" he mocked. "I know your ass is going out with him again, so stop fronting."

"Whatever."

"Yeah, whatever. So when is it?"

I shook my head and covered my face with my hand. "Tomorrow," I admitted.

"Tomorrow? Are you for real?"

"Yeah."

"Damn. The nigga really got to you."

"He didn't get shit," I said, putting on a terrible front.

Ray laughed again and I joined him. After a few seconds Ray said, "Yo, I gotta be serious for a sec. You sure you wanna fuck around and get all caught up with a drug dealer?"

I didn't answer his question right away. Messing

with bad boys was never a big deal for me. Shit, I preferred their excitement to boring ass guys who never crossed the line. But fucking with a guy who was involved in the drug game, no matter how big or small, was something I never thought I'd ever do. I'd seen too many chicks get so caught up with the money, the glamour, and the status of a dealer that they allowed themselves to be disrespected. But I knew one thing: I wasn't like any of those chicks. Drug dealer or not, Frido wasn't getting me like that. "It's all good," I said. "I'm just having some harmless fun."

"Yeah, it's harmless for now."

Having lost his brother to the drug game, I knew Ray wasn't really feeling my decision to mess with Frido. But the one thing about Ray that I always liked was that whether he liked it or not, he never got in my business.

"It's straight," I said.

"A'ight. I trust you. But you know, there's only one major problem."

"What's that?"

"Stevie's gonna be jealous. Especially if you give up the ass to Frido."

I rolled my eyes and sucked my teeth. "First of all, I ain't giving up no ass. Second of all, fuck Stevie!"

Ray laughed out loud. "Yo, he may never 'fess up to it, but the nigga is sprung on your ass. He's been feeling you for the longest time. For real, ma, I think the nigga's in love with you."

"Whatever," I said. "The only thing Stevie has love for is tits and ass. And I got plenty of both. That's why he's always trying to get with me. And you know I'm telling the truth. Shit, both of you are the same. Y'all both hoes. The only difference between you and Stevie is that you don't be trying to get in my pants."

"Yeah, you set me straight once and that's all it took."

I laughed as I remembered how I went off on Ray in front of his boys—Stevie included—when he tried to run game on me. "I did let you know what was what, didn't I?"

"Yeah, yeah. Me and everybody else. Stevie must have had earplugs on that day."

"And all of the other days after that," I added. "I just wanna know if he'll ever understand that unlike the tricks he's used to, I don't want his pretty ass."

"You know Stevie, ma. He's a glutton for punishment."

"Yeah well he's gonna be a hurting fool if he keeps trying to run his weak-ass game on me."

Ray chuckled. "Yeah, it is weak. He just pulls mad honeys because he's a pretty ma'fucka. It's all good, though, because once I start going to this dermatologist that my mom's cousin recommended, Stevie'll be eating up my sloppy seconds."

"Ray, you're my boy and I love you, but come on, you know it'll be a couple of years before your shit clears up." I busted out laughing.

"Whatever," Ray said. "I still pull honeys, though."

"Yeah, because they all be drunk in the clubs!"

"Yeah, yeah," Ray said as I laughed until my sides hurt. "Anyway, ma, speaking of pulling honeys, I got a question to ask you."

I wiped tears away from the corners of my eyes. "What?"

"Yo, since you're down with Frido, why don't you hook me up with those two females you were with?"

"What?"

"Come on, Angel, you know it's every man's fantasy to bang two chicks at the same time. Shit, you could join in if you want to."

"Fuck you, Raymond. Not even if yours was the last dick on this earth."

"Come on, ma. Hook me up. I'll give you the cam. That way you can just watch and record me in action."

I shook my head and laughed. "You're stupid, Ray. Loco en la cabeza."

"So you hooking me up or what?"

"Sure, I'll hook you up."

"Word?"

"Yeah. I know how I'll do it, too. You wanna know?"

"Hell yeah, I wanna know."

"Alright, listen to this."

"I'm listening."

*Click.*

I tossed the phone on my pillow and cracked up with laughter. He might have had his own printing business, but he was stupid and immature as hell sometimes. That's why I had mad love for Ray. I stood up as a car banging some loud hip-hop cruised by in the street, and I went to my closet. Frido said to wear a dress. Shit. Most of the dresses I had were too hoochie for work. I looked at my clock. My mom had left a message saying she was working late and would be home around nine-fifteen. I still had twenty minutes and she was the same size as me. I smiled and went to find my outfit.

# 6

Five o'clock couldn't come fast enough the next day. Before stepping outside I went to the bathroom to make sure I looked right. I checked myself in the mirror, checking out my curves in the fitted, calf-length, black spaghetti-strap dress that I'd borrowed from my mother. Hopefully she wouldn't miss it. Frido wanted me to wear a dress, which meant that he wasn't taking me out on some walk bullshit. He was taking me out. To dinner, to a club—wherever. He was taking me out and I made sure I was looking good. Shit, if there's one thing I love about being a Latina, it's the curves. Only sisters can match us in that category, except they tend to have more ass. My idol, J.Lo, doesn't have to worry about that, though.

Satisfied that the dress and I made a lethal combination and that my hair, which was down and curly, was on point, I headed outside. As he said he would be, Frido was waiting. I fought to keep from smiling as I walked over to his car. Unlike the day before, he didn't lower the window. I tried to focus a little harder, trying to see inside, but the tint was too dark and all I saw was my own reflection. I tried the handle but the doors were locked. I knocked on the glass but got no response. "Open the door, Frido," I said, knocking on the glass again.

Nothing happened.

I was starting to sweat from the heat and from the embarrassment I was feeling as people walked by and looked in my direction. "Open the fucking door, Frido," I said again.

Still nothing happened.

I sucked my teeth. I couldn't believe he was doing this shit to me. I knocked and called out his name again, and when I got no answer, I bit down on my lip to keep from really going off, because people were still leaving my job. I wanted to kick his car I was so pissed. "You know what? I don't need this bullshit." I turned to leave. It was eighty-eight degrees outside and I was wearing my black pumps; I couldn't believe I was gonna have to take the train home dressed the way I was.

"Yo, Angel." I was just about to step when Frido called my name. I should have just left. Instead, I turned around. Frido's window was cracked slightly, not enough for me to see inside, though.

"Why you playing games, Frido?"

"I was handling some business, ma."

"You always handling some damn business," I yelled. "It's fucking eighty-something degrees out and I'm here sweating, waiting for your ass to open the damn door."

"You look good, ma," Frido said when I stopped to take a breath.

I straightened my lips and folded my arms across my chest. *Oh, no he didn't*, I thought. *He did not just try to feed me some wack compliment like nothing was wrong. Damn.* He hadn't even bothered to lower the window any farther. I was really about to go off when the window rose and the doors were unlocked. At first I didn't move. I just stood still and asked myself if all of the bullshit he was putting me through was worth it. I'd never taken a guy's bullshit like this before. I didn't know why I was now. Suddenly the window cracked open again. "Come on, beautiful. We got someplace to be."

*Beautiful.* I'd heard that comment before. But why the hell did it have to sound so good coming from Frido? I wiped beads of sweat and opened the car door and got inside. I couldn't believe what I saw when I closed the door.

Frido was wearing a pair of Sacramento Kings shorts, a Sacramento Kings basketball jersey, and a pair of basketball sneakers on his feet. What the—?

"Why you dressed like that?" I asked.

Frido pulled away from the curb into the traffic. "I got a game to play."

"A game?"

"Yeah, down in the Village at the basketball court on West Fourth."

"So you're taking me out after the game, then?"

"Nah. I gotta take you home, ma. I got some things to do."

"Taking me home? So what the fuck am I wearing a dress for?" This was some real bullshit. Playing basketball? Oh, hell no. The games stopped here.

"You know what? Stop the fucking car. I didn't put on a fucking dress so that your ass could play basketball and then take me home. Stop the car and let me the hell out."

"Why are you tripping, ma?" Frido asked, as calm as the humidity was high.

"What do you mean why am I tripping? You told me to wear a damn dress today!"

"Yeah, I know. And you look good, too," he said, smiling.

I cut my eyes at him. I'd had enough of his nonchalant, arrogant attitude. In a voice laced with venom, I said, "Pull the fucking car over, Frido."

"You sure, ma?"

"Do it!" I yelled.

With a shrug of his shoulders, Frido signaled and then made his way over to the side and double-parked the car. I grabbed my purse and put my hand on the handle to open the door, but before I could, just as he did before, Frido grabbed me by my wrist. Oh nooo. I wasn't falling for any more lines.

"Let go, Frido," I demanded.

"Hold up, Angel. I wanna say something."

I shook my head. "Unless it's about you canceling your game and taking me out, I don't give a shit about what you want to say." I looked at him and waited for his response.

"I can't do that, ma. I got money on this game."

"Fine," I said, snatching my hand away. "You can go play your fucking game. But I'll tell you one thing. This is the last fucking time you play games with my ass." I pushed the door open and stuck my foot outside.

"So you're not coming?"

"Hell, no!" I said as I got out.

"That's a shame, ma. I was looking forward to having my girl there to cheer me on."

I was just about to slam the door when he said that. *His girl?* I looked at him. He was watching me with those intense brown eyes of his. "What'd you just say?"

"I said I was looking forward to having my girl cheer me on as I schooled some fools on the court."

His girl. He called me his girl. Damn. Frido was the kind of guy my mother warned me about. They lived on the wrong side of the tracks, she said. They were smooth and sexy. They knew what to say, when to say it and how to say it. Dudes like Frido would only bring drama and trouble into my world. I could hear my mother's voice in the back of my head as Frido watched me. She'd never met him, had no idea he existed, but she was there, warning me, telling me to close the door and leave.

He called me his girl.

"So I'm your girl, huh?"

"My number one, ma."

"Your number one what? Trick?"

"Nah. My number one girl."

I gave him a skeptical look and then said, "So if I'm your girl, why you gotta take me home?"

"It's business before pleasure today, ma."

"So when does the pleasure come in?"

Frido licked his lips like LL Cool J. "Soon, ma."

I looked at him and then let my eyes roam over his lean, cut frame. My mother and my own conscience were telling me to step. I should have listened.

"So, you coming or what?"

"Yeah, I'm coming." I got back in the car and Frido pulled off. I was his girl. I kept thinking that over and over in my head. I was Frido's girl. I liked the sound of that.

Usually when I'm dressed the way I was dressed, I easily become the center of attention. So when we arrived at the courts and I saw that there were no other females around, that's what I expected. I was actually looking forward to flaunting what I had and making the guys break their necks trying to concentrate more on me than the game. But the neck breaking and eye popping that I was accustomed to didn't happen at all. Actually, just the opposite happened. From the moment Frido and I made our entrance, it seemed like every guy there—black, white, and Latino—went out of his way to avoid looking at me. They stared at the ground or each other, they dribbled their balls, dug in their bags; they did anything they could to keep from giving me attention.

Frido acknowledged a couple of guys and then pulled me over to the side. "You're looking damn fine, Angel," he said, looking me up and down. "You're gonna bring me some money today."

I smiled. "You think so?"

He put a finger underneath my chin. "I know so."

"Why?"

"Because you're my girl, ma." Surprising the hell out of me, he leaned forward and planted his lips on mine and grabbed me by my ass. Normally I didn't let guys feel up on me like that in public, but shit, it was hard not to let Frido do what he wanted. His lips were softer than I'd imagined they would be, his tongue thicker. He massaged my ass like he was kneading dough and kissed me aggressively yet gently at the same time. If I hadn't been wearing my thong, I swear I think someone could have seen a drip, drip falling from between my legs.

"Do me a favor, ma," Frido said, stepping away from me.

I took a deep breath and released it slowly. I was wet as hell, and it wasn't from the sweat. "What?"

He reached behind his back and removed a .45 from his waistline. He held it out to me, not caring if anyone saw. "Hold this for me."

I looked at the gun but didn't take it right away. My mother's words popped into my mind immediately. Damn. I knew what he was about before this moment, but seeing the gun somehow made everything real. He was a drug dealer. He'd never admitted it because he never needed to. My mother would kill me if she ever found out. My eyes stayed locked on the .45. I couldn't help but wonder how many times it had been fired, and how many people had been killed by its wrath. I had a nervous but excited feeling bubbling inside of my stomach.

I took the gun. "Where you want me to keep it? I don't have any pockets."

"Keep it tucked under this." Frido removed his shirt, revealing a sculpted torso covered with tattoos. On his midsection was a tattoo of the Virgin Mary praying up to Heaven. On his right and left breast were two names with thorns wrapped around them. One was a woman's name, the other a male. I pointed at them.

"Whose names are they?"

Frido pointed to the name on the right—
Carmen. "This was my mother. She was killed when
I was fourteen."

"How'd she die?"

"My father beat her to death after coming home
drunk one night."

I bit down on my lip. "I'm sorry."

Frido shrugged.

"Who's the other name?"

"That was my father. He died when I was fourteen, too."

"How'd he die?"

"I shot him in the head after my mother died in
my arms. I used his gun to do it."

Frido turned around and walked away toward the
court while I stood stunned. His father killed his
mother and he killed his father; that was a vicious
ass cycle to live through. As he walked off I stared at
a huge tattoo covering his back. It was a picture of
the Grim Reaper standing over a pair of dead bod-
ies, holding a pair of .45's in his hand. Blood was
leaking from the muzzle of the guns. Underneath
the detailed and colorful picture were the words
*Madre de Dios, salvajame.* Mother of God, save me.

I wrapped up Frido's gun in his shirt. I didn't
have to wonder about how many people had been
killed by it anymore. My mother's words and my
conscience spoke to me again. *Leave Frido alone,
Angel. He will bring nothing but trouble into your life.*

I finished wrapping the gun and then leaned
against the fence as the warnings whispered to me
over and over. I watched Frido move fluidly up and

down the court, his chest bouncing, the muscles in his cut arms flexing with each dribble. I smiled. I'd been involved in mad drama and craziness in my life, but nothing had been as exciting as this moment.

Frido was a dealer.

But I was his girl.

To hell with the warnings.

**7**

*To hell with the warnings.*

I thought about that statement while Frido stood over Edwin Torres, holding his .45 inches away from Edwin's forehead. I stared at Edwin as he bled from the mouth and nose. I trembled with fear, with my eyes wide and my mouth open, while I replayed in my mind how everything went down.

I'd been standing, leaning against the fence, watching the sweat glisten on Frido's body as he schooled guys just like he said he would. I was so lost in Frido's raw sexiness that I had no idea Edwin was standing next to me until he grabbed my hand.

"Yo, Angel." I recognized the voice before I even turned around. It was my ex, Edwin. If there was any one guy I could say was my man before Frido, it would be Edwin. I was a freshman in high school when we started dating. He was a senior. We had a love-hate relationship that lasted for three years.

Edwin was my first love and my first mistake. He was one of the main reasons I stayed away from trying to be someone's girl. Edwin is your typical Puerto Rican male: possessive, jealous and insecure as hell. I couldn't do shit or enjoy life when I was with him. If a guy looked at me, he swore it was because I gave him a reason to look. If a guy didn't look at me, he swore the guy was trying to avoid making eye contact with me because I was doing something with him on the down low. He was crazy. He accused me so many times of cheating on his skinny ass that after a while I said fuck it and started doing just that. And those were never the times he accused me. Over the course of our relationship we had so many physical and verbal fights that when we weren't fighting things didn't seem right.

Things weren't always insane. In the beginning, our relationship was everything that a relationship was supposed to be. Edwin was sweet, sincere, and put my happiness above anything else. In return, I was faithful and gave all I could give. That included my virginity.

But then things changed. Actually, I did. I was what you call a late bloomer, and midway through ninth grade I started to bloom. And when that happened, all of the attention that other chicks used to get came to me. Edwin hated that. It irked the hell out of him that my body became off the hook as I filled out. Little by little he began to change, and that's when we butted heads. I'll love a guy and be everything to him, but he's got to respect me and let me breathe. He can't be all up in my space, and he definitely has to respect my womanhood. Those were two things Edwin couldn't do. I couldn't do shit without him interrogating me and I couldn't wear anything without his ass getting on my case about showing too much of this or too much of that. Day after day he became more my father than he was my boyfriend. Eventually I got tired of his insecurity and broke up with him. Told him he had to step.

That's when he went crazy. He'd show up at my house begging me for another chance. When he wasn't at my house, he was calling me all hours of the fucking night, crying over the phone about how much he loved me and how he couldn't live without me. He even threatened to kill himself unless I took his ass back. I did once, but that shit didn't last long. We weren't meant to be. I knew it, accepted it, and was ready to move on. Edwin just lost his mind. After a while I just didn't give a shit about his suicide threats, and when he'd threaten to kill himself I'd tell him to do it and leave me the fuck alone. I don't remember when he finally woke the hell up and realized that I was through with him, but one day he just stopped calling me. I hadn't spoken to him or seen him since then.

"Edwin," I said, snatching my hand away. "What the fuck are you doing here?"

Edwin smiled. As tall as he was pale, he was still scrawny. That was one thing about him that I was never attracted to. "I came to play some ball."

"So you came all the way from Brooklyn to do that?"

"Nah. I don't live in New York anymore. I been living in D.C. for the past two years. I'm just visiting my cousin here in the city. I was walking over to his job when I saw you standing here. You look good as shit, Angel. It's crazy that after all this time we bump into each other like this, right?"

I looked out of the corner of my eye to the court. I could see that the game had halted. Shit. I looked back at Edwin. "Yeah, real crazy," I said. I didn't say another word to him, hoping that he'd get the hint and leave.

Instead of catching my hint, he grabbed my hand again, and again I snatched it away. "'Sup with that? Can't I get a little love? Why you acting like you don't know me?"

I shook my head as I saw Frido approaching us. "No, you can't get a little love, and how about we forget that we know each other?" I said.

"Damn, Angel, it's been a long-ass time. Why you still gotta be a bitch?"

*What? He did not just flip on me like that. Oh, hell no!* I was just about to go off on his ass when Frido stepped into the picture.

"Yo, ma," he said standing beside me but keeping his eyes fixed on Edwin. "Is there a problem?"

I was about to say, "Yeah, there's a fucking problem," but then I thought about Frido's gun that I was still holding. "No, there's no problem," I said. "Edwin's just somebody I used to know, and he's leaving right now. Right, Edwin?"

Edwin looked at me and then Frido. They stood almost eye to eye. Edwin was just a little taller. My muscles got tense; there was a look in Edwin's eyes that I knew all too well. "Who the fuck are you?"

Damn.

"I'm Angel's man," Frido said, his voice calm. I'd never seen Frido be anything but calm, cool and collected, but as I stared at him, I began to understand why none of the guys on the court fucked with me. For all of his good looks, Frido was dangerous.

"Her man?" Edwin asked.

"Why don't you fucking leave, Edwin?" I said, watching Frido's eyes turning black.

"I ain't leaving until we talk, Angel."

"We don't have shit to talk about, Edwin. Leave."

"You can do better than this pretty motherfucker, Angel," Edwin said, looking at me. "For real, if you want the truth, you and me need to be together again."

"Will you fucking leave?" I said as Frido's body language changed.

Edwin looked at Frido. "Yo, man, I know you say she's your girl and shit, but for real, me and her got history. She don't realize it yet, but us being here together is fate. So why don't you bounce so I can talk to my girl?"

*His girl?* I shook my head. He was still fucking insane. "Edwin," I started. And then I was cut off by Frido's laughter. I looked at him. "What's wrong with you?" Frido cracked up and wiped tears from the corner of his eye. I looked around the court at the spectators standing around, watching us. They were all doing the same thing; shaking their heads. "Why you laughing?"

Frido laughed for a few more seconds and then stared at Edwin. "You a funny motherfucker," he said, the tone in his voice becoming lethal.

One characteristic of Edwin's that I always hated was that he never knew when to back down. "Is that right?" he said, taking a stupid, defiant step toward

Frido. In an instant, Frido stopped laughing and an ominous look suddenly crossed his face.

"Do what Angel says, *Edwin*, and step."

"Or what?" Edwin asked.

Frido took a step forward. They were almost nose to nose. "You don't know who you're fucking with, nigga. Trust me. You don't want to find out."

I didn't care if they came to blows. Shit, Frido could kick Edwin's ass all he wanted. But as they stood, squaring each other off, I had a very bad feeling brewing in the pit of my stomach. Especially when Frido's gun seemed to get hot in my hand. "Edwin," I said, pushing him back. "Why don't you stop with the bullshit and just get the fuck out of here? I ain't your girl and we don't have shit to talk about."

"Come on, Angel. I'm a different man now. I got my shit together in D.C. Drop that nigga and let's do this."

"I don't give a shit what you got together or where you live. I broke up with you because you are fucking crazy. I broke up with your insecure ass because I didn't want you then and I damn sure don't want you now. Now, for the last time, before some shit happens that you'll regret, leave!" I pushed him back again as hard as I could for extra emphasis. But he wouldn't give up.

"Don't be like that, Angel," he said, sounding like the pathetic, crazy fool I remembered. He pointed to Frido. "That nigga ain't shit. I love you! I wanna marry you." He looked at Frido. "You hear that, nigga? I love her and she belongs with me!"

*Jesus Christ*, I thought. I couldn't believe this shit

was happening. I knew Edwin was crazy, but we'd been apart for two fucking years! There was no reason for him to still be tripping like this. I exhaled and dragged my hand down my face. His shit had to stop and stop now. I opened my mouth, ready to spit Spanglish fire at him, but never got a chance.

What happened next happened within a matter of seconds, but it seemed like an eternity as it all happened in ultra-slow motion. Before I could speak, Frido grabbed his .45 from my hand, unwrapped it from his shirt and pistol-whipped Edwin in the face with it twice, splitting his lip wide open and breaking his nose. By the time Edwin fell to the ground, Frido was standing over him with his gun pointed directly at Edwin's forehead.

*To hell with warnings.*

The statement went through my mind again. *To hell with warnings. Shit.* "Frido!" I yelled out as Edwin moaned. "What the fuck are you doing? Put the fucking gun down!"

"I told this fool he didn't want to fuck with me. I warned you, didn't I, motherfucker?" Frido kicked Edwin in the ribs viciously. "You should have just left like she told you to, nigga. Now your ass is gonna pay for your stupidity. Talking about how I ain't shit. Bitch, you should've kept your ass in D.C." Frido kicked him again in the mid-section and then cocked his gun. *Shit.*

"Frido, no! Don't shoot him!"

Never turning to look at me, Frido said, "This nigga disrespected me. Nobody fucking disrespects me."

"Frido, please!" Tears were streaming down my face as I shook with fear. Edwin was a pain in the ass and was messed up in the head, but he didn't deserve to die. "He's crazy, Frido. He's a fucking jealous, insecure, insane ass, but he's harmless. He's got issues."

"Damn right the motherfucker's got issues. And his main issue is me."

"Please, Frido. Don't do this. Don't kill him. He's not gonna fuck with you or me anymore. Right, Edwin? You're gonna leave me alone, right?" I looked at Edwin through my tear-filled eyes. Blood was flowing from his mouth and nose like a faucet on strike. His eyes were wide and filled with tears from pain, shock, and I'm sure, fear. This was horrible. The muscles in Frido's arm flexed as he strangled his gun tightly. Unless I found a way to convince him to put the gun down, he was going to shoot Edwin. "Frido, don't do this, please. I'm fucking begging you." Frido pressed the muzzle of his .45 against Edwin's forehead. Edwin moaned. I cried. *Warning, warning.* I should have listened to the voices in my head. "Please," I begged. "Don't kill him."

All was quiet around the court as everyone stood paralyzed. Frido's muscles flexed again. I closed my eyes, not wanting to see anything, and expecting to hear the bang of the gun when it went off. Seconds of silence went by. And then, instead of hearing gunfire, I heard Frido's voice. "The only reason you're not dead, motherfucker, is because my girl begged for your life. This is the only chance you'll get. Make that shit count and don't fuck with her no more. But you got an open invitation to fuck with me." Frido punched Edwin in the face and then moved away from him.

I stood speechless and in shock over what had happened. I looked at Edwin, who lay on the ground curled up like a baby, spitting blood.

*Warning, warning.*

Frido picked up his jersey, slipped it on and tucked his gun back in his waistline. "Let's go, ma," he said, his voice once again calm, as though nothing had happened. I didn't move. I couldn't stop looking down at Edwin. I felt horrible. I never meant for this shit to happen. "Let's go," Frido said again, his voice more forceful. I stared at Edwin for another couple of seconds and then looked at Frido. Blood was sprinkled on his knuckles. If he hadn't listened to me there could have been a lot more. I didn't know why, but Frido's violence shocked me. I know it shouldn't have. I mean shit, he was involved in the drug game, and if you're playing to win then violence is natural. I guess I'd just been so out of my mind and caught up by his suave ways and good looks that I had him on a slight pedestal. He was Frido: expensive ride, stylish clothes, smooth-as-silk personality. He was what every other guy wasn't.

Now I knew better. He was a thug, just like the rest of the other thugs in the game. He just carried himself differently. And the way he handled himself made him a more dangerous thug. Too dangerous for me to be around.

"I ain't going with you," I said.

"What?" Frido grabbed my arm but I pulled it away.

"I said I'm not going with you. I don't need to be around this shit." I walked off and headed out to the street. Frido came up beside me and grabbed hold of my wrist again. This time he wasn't letting go.

"So what, ma? You mad because I put that nigga in his place?"

"Edwin weighs a buck fifty wet, Frido. He's stupid, he's insecure, and yeah, he's a little psycho, but he's fucking harmless. You didn't have to hurt him like that."

"Come on, ma. You know what's up. You know how the game works. The nigga disrespected me. I couldn't let that shit go unpunished."

"Punishing is one thing, but killing is another. If I wouldn't have begged, you would have killed him!"

"The law of the streets is like that, ma."

I shook my head and forced him to let go of me. "You know what, Frido? You can live by those laws all you want. I don't need it." I turned my head and took one last look at Edwin. He was sitting up now, holding his nose. I wanted to help him, but I knew that Frido's reaction to that wouldn't be too cool. I turned back to Frido. "Don't show up at my job tomorrow. And if you do, trust me, I ain't going nowhere with you." I walked away without saying anything else.

I took a cab home because I didn't want to deal with any bullshit from guys on the train. I'd had enough for the day. When I got home I changed right away and put my mom's dress back where she had it, and then I called Ray and told him about what had happened.

"What'd you expect, Angel? He's in the fucking drug game. That's the kind of shit that happens.

Shit, actually it's worse. God was looking out for Edwin's ass today, because that crazy nigga should be dead right now."

I wiped tears away from my eyes. I could still see Edwin on the ground, hurt and bleeding. "I know," I said softly.

"Stop fucking with that nigga, Angel. I kept my mouth shut before, but you know how I feel about ma'fuckas like him. They don't give a shit about nobody and nothing but the almighty dollar."

"I know."

"I lost my brother, Angel. I don't feel like losing you too."

I smiled. It was nice to have a friend as real as Ray. "Don't worry. You won't lose me. I'm not gonna mess with Frido no more. That shit scared the hell out of me."

"Good. I'm glad it did. You needed something like that to wake your pretty ass up. Your brain's been MIA since that nigga came along."

"Yeah, I know. But it's back. It's all good."

"A'ight, cool. So what's popping for tonight? It's hump day and we got some clubbing to catch up on."

I nodded. He was right. My brain had been MIA and there was definitely some partying I needed to do. "I don't know. Let me call Shanice and see what she's doing."

"A'ight. I'll hit Stevie up on his cell. I know that nigga'll be happy to see your ass." Ray laughed out loud.

I sucked my teeth. "Whatever."

"Don't front, Angel. You know you like him."

I sucked my teeth again. "Go call Stevie, dumb-ass."

"A'ight, ma. Hit me up after you talk to Shanice. And don't be taking forever. I know how you females are."

"Yeah, yeah." I hung up the phone and shook my head. Ray was stupid sometimes. I lay back on my bed, looked up at my ceiling and thought about what went down at the courts. When we were dating I'd wished for Edwin's death I don't know how many times. But my wishes were never serious. I was just pissed off over the bullshit he gave me and put me through. Damn. What if Frido hadn't listened to me? What if he had pulled that trigger? I gave a quick thank you to God for sparing Edwin's life and then got on the phone and called Shanice.

# 8

I was back in my element.
Ray, Stevie, Shanice and I all hooked up and went clubbing in the city. The DJ was playing some fierce hip-hop, and when I say I was back in my element, I mean I was back in my fucking element. On the floor—Shanice at my side—shaking, bouncing, gyrating, I was wearing a white tube top and a pair of black leather pants, making dudes pant and sweat. For the first time all week I felt like my old self. In control. I looked over at Shanice. We were both feeling nice from the several drinks we'd had. I smiled at my girl. She was working it too. I put my back to hers and together we created fire as the DJ rocked R. Kelly's new song "Snake." Shanice and I moved like Siamese twins while guys watched us with scheming eyes. I worked my middle and my chocha and made all the guys want to get to know me.

After I had gotten off the phone with Shanice, I went straight to my closet to pick out my outfit for the night. I was intent on having a slamming-ass time and forgetting all about Frido and his good looks and smooth ways. I knew the chances of him showing up at my job were pretty high, but whatever. He could do what he wanted because I was damn serious when I told Ray that I wasn't gonna fuck with him no more. Frido was history as far as I was concerned. So let him show up at work. I was ready. Too bad I didn't prepare myself for running into him at the club. I was dancing, making guys' temperature rise when Frido stepped behind me and slid an arm around my waist.

"You still mad, ma?" he said into my ear.

I turned around immediately. "What are you doing here?" I said, pushing his hand from around me.

"I came to see you."

"Came to see me? How'd you know I was here? What are you, following me?"

"Nah, ma. My peoples called me and told me you were here."

"Your peoples? So what, you're checking up on me?"

"I told you that you're my girl."

I sucked my teeth. "I ain't your girl anymore," I said defiantly. I walked off past people on the dance floor and went over to the bar. I had to get away from him. He was looking too damn fine and smelling too damn good and it was making it hard for me to blow him off.

"So you're still mad, huh?" Frido said, coming up to me.

Damn. I folded my arms. "Look, Frido, why don't you find another female to get with? One who wants to deal with your shit."

"Look, ma," Frido said, grabbing hold of my arm. "Don't be pissed off at me because your boy don't have any sense. He had more than enough time to step before I put him in his place for disrespecting me."

I tried to pull away from Frido but his grip was too tight. "Let go of my fucking arm," I said.

"Let's bounce outta here, ma. I got someplace I want to take you."

"Where? To the fucking courts again? Or are you gonna pick someplace better, like a playground?" I jerked my arm again, trying to get free, but it didn't work. "Let go of my fucking arm! I ain't going nowhere with you."

Frido stared at me but didn't say anything.

"Yo, is there a problem here?"

I looked past Frido. Ray and Stevie were standing behind him, their arms folded across their chests. Frido let go of my arm and turned around. At six feet even, Stevie was just a couple of inches shorter than Frido and was about the same size. Ray, of course, was towered over by both guys. But what he lacked in height he made up for in balls. He stepped forward. "Angel, this dude messing with you?"

"I'm having a talk with my girl," Frido said calmly.

"Yo, it don't look like she's in the mood to talk," Stevie said. He looked at me. "You feel like talking to him?"

I looked from Stevie and Ray, who both had menacing looks on their faces, to Frido, who stood as relaxed as could be. My mind instantly flashed back to Edwin's near fatal beat-down at the court and the gun that I had no doubt Frido had with him. I'd convinced him not to pull the trigger once; I knew I wouldn't be so lucky twice. "It's cool," I said. "We're just talking."

"Come on, Angel," Stevie said. "I saw you trying to get your arm away from the nigga."

"It's cool, Stevie. For real."

"Yo, Angel, you don' have to lie to us," Ray said, looking at me long and hard. I took a quick look over at Frido. He was still calm, but his body language had changed. It reminded me too much of earlier.

"Everything's cool, Ray."

Ray gave me a disappointed look. "Come on, ma. You don't ha—"

"Yo, nigga, didn't you hear her?" Frido cut in. "She said everything was straight. Why don't you and your sidekick do the right thing and step?"

"You gonna make us, ma'fucka?"

Stevie opened his arms wide. "Yeah, nigga, what you wanna do?"

Frido shook his head. "Y'all don't want to fuck with me. Y'all niggas want to live."

"Fuck you, ma'fucka," Ray said. "We can do this right now."

"Let's do this shit," Stevie added.

"This is the last chance I'm giving y'all," Frido said calmly.

*Warning, warning.*

I didn't even hesitate this time.

I jumped in between Frido and Ray and Stevie. "Why don't you guys just chill the fuck out and relax?" I said, looking at my boys. "I told y'all I got everything under control."

"Angel," Ray said, looking at me with concern in his eyes.

"It's cool, Ray," I insisted once again. I just wanted them to back off before something happened.

"Angel," he said again.

"She said it's cool, midget," Frido said.

"Bitch!" Ray yelled. "I got your midget right here."

"You about to catch a beat-down, nigga," Stevie said.

Damn. I pushed against both Ray and Stevie, who looked like they were about to charge forward. He hadn't pulled it out yet, but I could feel that Frido was seconds away from reaching for his .45. "I told you guys to fucking relax." I gave a quick glance at Frido. He was glaring at Ray and Stevie with nothing but malice in his eyes. "Just let me talk to him— alone." I looked at Ray and begged him with my eyes to back down.

Ray looked from me to Frido. I knew he wasn't afraid of anybody and would defend me to his death, but his demeanor surprised me. He knew all about Frido's .45 and his willingness to use it, yet he was still trying to get into it with him. The alcohol had obviously taken away his common sense. He looked back at me. "You sure?"

I nodded. "I'm sure. I got this."

"A'ight," he said after a few seconds. "You go ahead and talk to him. But we'll be close and we'll be watching."

I exhaled a long sigh of relief as he and Stevie

walked over to the end of the bar and stood watching Frido and me intently. I turned back to Frido.

"Your friends don't know who they're fucking with, ma," he said.

I slit my eyes. "What the fuck do you want, Frido?"

"I told you I have someplace I want to take you. I also have something to give you."

"What is it?"

"It's a surprise."

"I don't like surprises."

"You'll like this one."

I stared at Frido. He had a mysterious glint in his eye. "What's the surprise?" I asked again.

"You'll see it when we bounce outta here, ma."

I looked at him and sucked my teeth. I can't lie; as much as I didn't want it to be, he had my curiosity piqued. He said I would like the surprise. Why? What kind of surprise was it? I watched him watching me, waiting for a response. His eyes were intense and inviting. He licked his lips slowly and I swear I could feel his tongue on my pussy. A surprise. One that I'd like.

Frido's eyes.

His lips.

The Ralph Lauren cologne wafting from him.

*Damn. How the hell does he make me want him so bad?*

I looked over to where Ray and Stevie stood. Shanice was with them now. They were all watching me closely. Frido. My friends. A surprise. "You can't tell me what it is?" I asked.

"Nah. You have to see it in person."

"You ain't right, Frido," I said, my spirit breaking.

"I don't like to spoil surprises, ma."

"I came with my friends," I said, trying to find a way to break myself from his air of raw sexiness.

"They can get home without you."

"So you just expect me to leave them like that?"

Frido shrugged his shoulders. "It's up to you, ma."

"Can't you give it to me some other time?"

"Maybe. But I really want to give it to you tonight." Frido touched my cheek lightly with his finger, sending chills up my spine.

"You're not pulling no park or walk bullshit, are you?" I asked as he slid his hand from my cheek to my neck. His touch was all that.

"Nah."

"And I'm gonna like the surprise you give me?"

Frido flashed a devilishly sexy smile. "I guarantee it, ma.

I looked back to Ray, Stevie and Shanice. It was obvious by the looks on their faces that they weren't happy that I was talking to Frido for so long. I locked eyes with Ray as we stared at each other for a few, long seconds. It may not have been the right thing, but I was gonna go with Frido and I knew I owed it to Ray to tell him. "I'll be right back," I said.

"A'ight, ma. But don't take too long."

I walked away and went over to my friends. Shanice looked at me, then at Frido, and then back at me. "Angel, since when you been messing with him? Girl, he is fine as hell."

"Just a little while," I said, looking at Ray, who stared back at me with a disapproving frown.

"You're leaving, aren't you," Ray said more than asked.

"Leaving where?" Stevie asked. "You're not leaving with that nigga, are you?"

My eyes on Ray, I said, "Yeah."

"What!" Stevie yelled. "We was just about to beat that nigga down for you and now you're leaving with him? What's up with that?"

"I thought we talked about this earlier, Angel," Ray said.

"It's cool, Ray."

"It's cool? Did you forget what that nigga almost did today?"

"What'd he do?" Stevie asked. "Ray, you know about that nigga?"

"No, I didn't forget," I said, ignoring Stevie.

"So why you rolling with him?" Ray asked.

"What are y'all talking about?" Stevie asked.

Shanice sided with him. "Yeah, what are y'all talking about? What happened earlier? Angel, you gotta fill me in."

"Ray, you know about him?" Stevie asked again.

"Angel, how come you didn't tell me you were talking to him?" Shanice asked.

"Don't roll with him, Angel," Ray said.

I shook my head and frowned. The music, everyone's rambling, and the questions in my head all blended together to create confusion that was really frustrating the hell out of me. I looked back at Frido; he was still waiting, but I could tell that he wasn't gonna wait too much longer. I turned back to everybody. They were all looking at me, waiting for answers. Answers that I just didn't feel like giving. I exhaled. "Look, I gotta go, y'all."

"Angel, don't roll with that nigga," Ray said.

"I can handle myself, Ray."

"Is that right? You're a big girl, huh?"

"Yeah, I am."

"And what happens when you get in a worse situation than before?"

"I told you I can handle myself, dammit! I'm not a fucking little girl!" I looked at Ray with hard eyes. I know he was only saying what he was saying because he cared, but shit, he was supposed to be my friend, not my fucking father. "I gotta go. Shanice, I'll fill you in later. Stevie, Ray can fill you in if he wants. Ray, I'll talk to you later." I turned to leave.

"Don't come crying to me when you run into some shit, Angel," Ray said as I started to walk away.

I turned around and looked at Ray. "What are you saying, Ray?"

"I'm saying, ma, that if you roll with that nigga, don't come trying to holla at me."

"So it's like that?"

"You're a big girl, ma. You handle your own shit from now on."

I looked at Ray. We'd had disagreements before where we didn't speak to each other for a few days, but there was something in the tone of his voice that bothered me. There was a finality in it that I didn't like. "I'll call you later, Ray," I said.

Ray stared at me and frowned. "You call if you want to, Angel. That don't mean that a nigga's gonna pick up the phone."

His last comment stung. Was our friendship over? I turned without saying anything else and walked over to Frido. He took my hand without a word and led me out of the club.

# 9

"Where are you taking me?" I asked. Frido was driving, and we were headed toward the Holland Tunnel.

"Home."

"Home? I thought you said you had a surprise to give me."

"I do."

"So why the fuck are you taking me home? And why are you driving this way?" I was getting pissed off. I couldn't believe I'd left my friends hanging the way I did so Frido could play me for a fool again.

"The surprise is at home, ma. My home."

"Your home?"

"That's right."

"I can't go to your home."

"Why not?"

"Because I have to work tomorrow."

"So call off sick."

"Sorry, but I don't have it like you. I need the money."

"It's only one day, ma."

"Like I said, I don't have it like you. Besides, I gotta be home or my mother will kill me."

Keeping his eyes on the road, Frido pulled his cell phone out of his pocket and handed it to me. "Here. Call your mom and tell her you're sleeping over at a friend's house."

I shook my head. "My mom won't go for that. I gotta be home."

"Sorry, ma, but as you can see, I'm about to head through the Holland Tunnel. And after that I'm hitting the turnpike. There's no turning around."

"I need to be home, Frido."

"I'll get you home, ma. After your surprise."

I looked at him but didn't say anything. Whether I liked it or not, he obviously had no intention of turning his car around. I sighed. He was taking me to his home. What kind of surprise did he have for me? I sighed again and then sucked my teeth and took the phone from his hand. It was crazy, but I was about to call my mom and tell her that I was gonna spend the night by Shanice's house.

After making the call to my mom and leaving a message on Shanice's voice mail, I looked over at Frido. "This better be a good ass surprise."

"Relax and enjoy the ride," Frido said, touching my cheek softly. I reclined in the seat while he turned up the volume on the radio. Except for the CD's that he had playing, the rest of the ride was a quiet one. Somewhere along the turnpike I fell asleep. I didn't wake up until we got to his place.

After being with him by the basketball court in the Village I knew he was deep in the drug game, but I didn't realize just how deep until we got out of the car and were greeted by three bodyguards carrying semi-automatic weapons. They flanked us as we walked from Frido's car to the elevator and headed upstairs to his condo—a three-bedroom condo decorated stylishly with expensive, modern furniture. That's what greeted me when he opened the front door.

The color scheme was black and silver and was banging. He had a matching black leather sofa and love seat with dark gray pillows. A dark gray rug underneath an onyx coffee table sat in the middle of the living room. His lamps were tall, silver halogen lamps—the kind that bend to wherever you need the light. He had a big screen TV and an onyx entertainment center stacked with stereo components, a DVD player, a VCR, a PlayStation2, and a camcorder, which was pointing directly at the couch. A mini-bar sat by the far wall, and hanging from the walls were framed pictures of Al Pacino as Tony Montana from *Scarface,* and the rappers Big Pun, Notorious B.I.G. and Tupac.

"You like?" he asked, closing the front door.

Trying my best to seem unimpressed, I shrugged my shoulders. "It's alright," I said flatly. "It ain't a mansion."

Frido smiled and nodded his head.

"So where's my surprise?" I asked.

"You'll get it soon," Frido said.

"How soon?"

"Depends on how good you are, ma," he said, stepping to me. Suddenly, before I knew it was happening, he leaned forward, wrapped an arm around me and planted his lips on mine. His kiss was different from the one he gave me at the courts. Where that one was a little aggressive, this kiss was smooth and controlled. His tongue, which I'd only briefly enjoyed before, slid into my mouth and slowly entwined with mine. I breathed out softly as he snaked one hand underneath my halter top and lightly squeezed my nipples while holding onto me securely with the other. It was a damn good thing he was holding me the way he was because the longer the kiss lasted, the more his tongue explored, the more his fingers played with my hardening nipples, the weaker my knees got. I was about to reach for his zipper when he suddenly pulled away from me. I looked up at him. "What's wrong?"

"Nothing, ma."

"So why'd you stop?" Damn, he had me wet and worked up.

Frido smiled slyly. "We got all night, ma. Besides, I thought you wanted your surprise."

"I do," I said.

Frido smiled again and then reached into his pocket and pulled out a slender, black jewelry box. "Here you go, ma," he said, holding it out for me.

I looked at the box and then at him. "What's that?"

"It's your surprise."

"You mean you had that on you the whole time?"

"Yeah."

"So why didn't you give it to me back at the club?"

"Wasn't ready to."

"Yeah, right," I said, sucking my teeth. "I bet you figured you'd get some ass if you gave it to me here. That's some real bullshit. You should've given that to me when I fucking asked you for it. I dissed my friends and lied to my mother all because you're playing fucking games. I should make your ass take me the hell home." I looked at him through slit eyes. Stupid, fucking games. I couldn't believe he played me like that.

"You done?" Frido asked, staring at me.

"What do you mean, am I done? Maricon, you made me come all the way out here when you had that shit on you the whole time."

"I didn't make you do shit, ma," Frido said, his tone darkening. "I didn't make you dis your punk-ass friends back at the club. I didn't make you call your moms and lie to her ass. And I damn sure didn't drag your ass into my car and bring you here. You did all of that shit on your own. So stop fronting and talking shit. Your ass came here for this." He paused and opened the box, revealing a diamond neck-lace with a diamond-studded F hanging from it. "This is what you dissed your friends, lied to your moms, and got in my car and buckled up for."

Frido stopped talking but continued to hold the box open, giving me a full view of the necklace. I could feel my eyes and mouth wanting to widen as I watched the diamonds intensify the halogen bright-ness of Frido's living room. I've had dudes give me jewelry before, but that was always some small shit like a ring, bracelet, or earrings. I'd never gotten a piece of jewelry like what he was holding. "Is that real?" I asked, my eyes staring intensely at it.

"What you mean, is this real?" Frido asked, slamming the box shut. "How are you gonna insult me like that, ma?"

"I . . . I'm just saying," I said, stumbling on my words.

"Yeah, well don't say," Frido said, obviously annoyed. "I'm Frido Rivera, baby. I run shit. And shit don't run without me. Is this real? This shit's as real as it gets. But you know what? Since you don't respect the fact that I didn't do what other niggas would've done, by bringing you here to give you your real gift, I'll do what you suggested and take your ass home. I'll find another female who will appreciate this shit. Shit, I'll find several." He shoved the box back into his pocket and then said, "Let's go, ma." He turned his back to me and walked to his front door and opened it. I hadn't moved. "Let's go, ma," he said again. "I got calls to make."

I looked at him and then at the pocket where he'd put the necklace. Damn. I swear I could see a sparkle. The shit was off the hook. Any doubt I may have had about it before was gone completely now. Like Frido said, it was as real as it gets. And it would look damn good around my neck. "Hold up," I said softly. "Let me see that necklace again?"

"What for, ma? You don't want the shit."

"I never said I didn't want it. Just let me see it."

"Why? Aren't you in a rush to get home and call your bitch-ass boy, Ray, to let him know you a'ight?"

I pursed my lips. "First of all, I don't have to call Ray and tell him shit. He ain't my fucking father. Second of all, I never said I wanted to go home. I just said I should make you take me home."

"You're not making any sense, ma. You either

want to go home or you don't." Frido stared at me with callous eyes. I knew what his game was. He wanted my ass and the necklace was the bait he was using to get it. I wasn't stupid. I looked down at his pocket again. Damn. How many carats did it have? I took a deep breath and let it out slowly. Diamond necklace or not, I was probably gonna give up the pussy to him anyway. He was that fine and I wanted some. So why should I let another bitch get my prize?

"Give me my necklace," I said.

Frido eyed me for a second and then smiled. "Oh, it's your necklace all of a sudden?"

"It's definitely mine," I said, walking up to him.

Frido licked his lips. "You sure you want it, ma?"

I was standing directly in front of him now. "I want it," I whispered.

"I want it too, ma," he said, letting the door close.

"You can have it."

No more words needed. Frido stepped away from the door, grabbed me and lifted me in the air. I wrapped my legs around his waist as we kissed ravenously. We made our way to the couch, where, after setting me down, Frido laid me back and lifted the bottom of my shirt, exposing my belly button. I exhaled as he licked at it as though it were a lollipop. I reached down for his belt buckle but he stopped me. "Lay back and enjoy, ma."

I did as he said and raised my arms above my head. Without missing a beat, Frido moved from my belly button to my breasts and enjoyed the fullness of them with his hands while running his tongue over and around my hard nipples. "Your titties are the shit," he said, sucking on them.

I smiled and gnawed down on my bottom lip. "They're all yours," I said breathlessly.

Frido licked, nibbled, pinched and caressed my breasts so good that if they could have, I know they would have creamed.

Speaking of cream, that's exactly what happened after he removed my leather pants and thong, spread my legs wide and dove into my pool head-first. He licked on the walls of my pussy and nibbled on my clit with so much skill that it was impossible for me to keep from erupting. "You're gonna . . . make me . . . cum!"

"Good," he said, pushing his tongue deeper inside of me.

"Ay, Papi! It's so . . . so good!" I yelled as I came. I crossed my ankles behind his neck and pushed my pussy harder into his face. My pussy was sensitive as shit, but I didn't want him to stop. I'd never been eaten out like that before. The way his tongue probed and licked, I swear it was almost like he'd built my pussy himself. He licked me a few more times and then stood up.

"I want it, ma," he said, unbuckling his belt. I removed my top while he stripped and exposed his muscular frame.

My eyes on his, his eyes on my pussy, I said, "Take it."

Frido nodded, licked his lips and then took it as deep, as hard, as fast, as slow, and as long as he wanted to. His skill with his tongue was unmatched, but the science with which he worked his dick was unexplainable. I'd been with dudes who could fuck. Hell, one or two of them actually made me come back a second time. But no guy, and I mean not a

single motherfucker, had accomplished what Frido
had just accomplished. With his dick, his tongue, and
his Kama Sutra-like movements, he had me completely dick-whipped.

We fucked two more times that night. First on
the couch again, only this time we utilized his camcorder, which was a first for me. The second time
was in his bedroom on top of his black satin sheets,
while our action from the living room played on his
TV screen. For the first time ever, after we were
done the last time, I actually passed out.

Frido was on his cell phone when I woke up an
hour later. I tried not to let him know that I was
awake, though. I just lay still with my eyes opened a
fraction—just enough for me to see him. He was sitting on the edge of the bed with his back to me.

"Yo, that nigga Wise is a stupid motherfucker,
kid. How the fuck can he be so stupid to think that
he can pull shit behind my back without me finding
out? Word? He said that? A'ight, that's cool. The
nigga wanna play games like that, we can play.
Boricua, baby. I don't take shit from no motherfucker. He'll get his. Yo, anyway kid, I'ma be out. I
got company. Yeah, I'll holla at you later. Yeah, Wise
is on my list of priorities now. A'ight. Peace." Frido
ended his call, stretched his neck, and with his back
still facing me, said, "You get all that, ma?"

I opened my eyes wide. "How'd you know I was
awake?"

"Your breathing pattern changed."

I sat up. "What are you, a ninja?"

Frido laughed and turned around and looked at
me. "I gotta be a ninja to protect myself, ma. You
don't survive in this game if you don't."

I nodded. "What time is it?"

"It's four in the morning."

"Damn. What time are you taking me home later?"

"I'm not," Frido answered.

"What do you mean you're not?" I asked, looking at him.

"Change of plans, ma. You're on a mini-vacation now."

"Mini-vacation?"

"Yeah. You're gonna stay here with me until Sunday."

"Until Sunday?" I shook my head. "I can't do that."

"Why not?"

"What do you mean why not? First of all, I have a job. I'm already missing today. I can't be out tomorrow, too. Second of all, are you forgetting that I live at home? My mother's not going for that shit."

"Just tell her that you and Shanice are going away for the weekend. Tell her it was a last minute decision."

"Estas loco? She won't wanna hear that."

"Well, then tell her something she'd wanna hear," Frido said, crawling toward me. "I want my girl here with me for a few days." He flashed a smile and kissed me on the base of my neck and then sucked on my shoulder as if he were going to give me a hickey. I leaned my head back and touched the necklace that was hanging around my neck.

"Frido," I said as he ran his tongue from my neck to my nipples.

" 'Sup, ma?"

"Why'd you pick me to be your girl?"

"What do you mean?" he asked, moving the sheets from around me and guiding his fingers in between my legs.

I moaned as he made me wet all over again. "I mean what was it about me that made you come after me in the first place? What made you give me this necklace? Why'd I get to be your girl over everyone else?"

Frido paused with his finger-action and breast sucking, and looked up at me. "You want the truth, ma?"

"Of course."

"You're the shit, ma. I mean, I know there are fly girls out there, but you are by far the finest female I've ever seen."

I smiled. "Thank you."

"But it's not just your looks that got me, ma. It's the way you handle yourself. You're young, but you don't act like it. For real, you're the type of female that makes a nigga fall in love and want to settle down."

"Really?" I said, blushing.

"Really," Frido answered. "That's why I want you here for the weekend."

I looked at him as he went back to kissing my breasts and fingering my clit. Damn. He said I was making him fall in love. "I don't have any clothes," I said softly.

"We'll buy clothes, ma."

"And shoes?"

"And shoes."

"And things for my hair?"

"I got you, ma."

I nibbled on my bottom lip as his fingers went exploring. *I'm making him fall in love,* I thought again. "My mother's probably gonna kick my ass out after this," I whispered, laying back and pulling him on top of me.

Frido looked at me with those eyes of his. "Don't worry, ma. You got a place right here."

I smiled again and then took a quick breath as he slid inside of me. "Papi," I whispered. He didn't know it, but I'd already fallen for him.

Or did he?

# 10

The rest of the day with Frido was more of the same thing: sex, sex and more sex. Shit, the only time we didn't fuck was when he took me shopping. Other than that, it was on. We didn't even go out Friday night. We just ordered some take out, rented some movies, and then fucked on the couch and on the floor. When it came to sex, I'm not gonna lie, I thought I knew my shit. But Frido put a serious reality check on me. In just twenty-four hours I learned more about sex and fucking than I ever thought possible. Positions, touches, pushes and pulls; Frido was a fucking master, and I was willing to be his student for as long as my pussy could handle it.

So the next night, when he said he wanted to go to a strip club back in Brooklyn, I was too ready. I'd gone to strips clubs with guys before, and if there was one thing I knew it was that the after-strip-club sex was always off the hook. After looking at tits and ass for a few hours, the guy was usually horny as hell and ready to do some undercover work. If Frido had managed to turn me out the way he had performing under normal conditions, I could only imagine what he would do to me when we got back to his place. Wearing some hip-hugging white jeans and another tube top—black this time—I strolled into the smoke-filled and marijuana-laced High Rollers strip club with Frido's arm around my waist, anxious to get back to his place and get the party started.

Party.

That's just what Frido had in mind too. Only it wasn't the kind of party I was expecting. We were sitting in the VIP section of the club, more than halfway drunk, watching the females strip and shake their asses on stage when, out of nowhere, the Latina I'd messed with the week before appeared. "What's going on, Frido?" she asked, standing in front of him but staring straight at me. She was wearing a tight black shirt with the word *sexy* written in silver across her breasts, and a pair of tight blue jeans and black ankle boots.

Frido looked up at her. "What's up, Reina?"

Reina looked at me for another split second and then at Frido and smiled. "Not much," she said, bending over and planting a long kiss on his cheek.

"What are you doing here?" I asked, staring up at her.

"I told her to meet us here," Frido answered.

I turned and stared at him. "Why'd you do that?"

"She's gonna party with us tonight," Frido answered calmly.

"Why? I thought this was supposed to be our weekend."

"It is, ma."

"So what's she doing here?"

"I told you I told her to meet us here. You got a problem with that?" Frido gave me a hard glare, daring me to complain about Reina's presence one more time.

I sucked my teeth. "I just thought it was our weekend," I said again.

"Like I said, ma. It is. Reina's just here for some fun. So relax and enjoy. Reina, ma, sit next to Angel."

Reina looked down at me then smiled and grabbed the vacant chair next to me. I couldn't believe she was there. After what happened, I knew that the chances of running into her and the white girl were high, but I'd still hoped I wouldn't. As much as I didn't want it to, her presence took me right back to that night at her place. Although I couldn't remember everything we did, I still remembered a few things, and that shit made my skin crawl. I'm *not a fucking dike,* I thought to myself. I sat up in my chair and stared blankly at the stage where a female was doing a terrible *Flashdance* impression. I was uncomfortable as hell. I looked over at Frido, who had a subtle smirk on his face. What did he mean Reina was here for some fun? He's lucky I didn't have a car, because if I did, I would have left and taken my ass home right then and there. We all sat quiet for a few minutes until a naked waitress with C-cup sized breasts came over and took our orders for drinks. When the waitress walked off, Frido stood up. "I'll be back."

"Where you going?" I asked, looking at him.

"Gotta make a call, ma." Without saying anything else, he walked off, leaving me alone with Reina, who was sitting entirely too close to me. I didn't even hesitate; I slid my chair away from her a few inches. I didn't want to give her any ideas. Reina looked at me and smiled but didn't say anything.

I sat stone still for the next fifteen minutes, moving only to drink the Hennessy that the waitress had brought for me. Finally, after twenty minutes went by, I sucked my teeth, exhaled and stood up.

Reina looked up at me. "Where are you going?"

"I'm going to find Frido," I said, my tone laced with attitude.

"What for?" Reina asked.

"Because he's been gone for the past twenty minutes." I was worried that he'd pulled the same disappearing trick that he pulled before.

"Sit down and relax," Reina said. "Frido's taking care of business. He'll be back. Besides, he don't like when women come looking for him."

Reina stared at me and downed the Long Island iced tea she was drinking. I looked at her for a few seconds and then looked around the club, trying to see if I could spot Frido anywhere. After a few seconds I gave up. The place was too packed. I sat back down and exhaled. "He better be coming back," I said.

Reina smiled. "Why are you so worried about Frido coming back anyway?" she asked, laying a hand on my thigh. "You don't like my company?"

I shoved her hand off of me. "Look," I said harshly. "Let's get one fucking thing straight. What happened last weekend was a fluke."

"Oh, really?"

I curled my lips. "Yes, really."

"You could have fooled me. You sure knew what you were doing. Made me want to do it again."

I clenched my jaws and shook my head. "Look, bitch, I'm sorry to burst your bubble, but believe me when I say that that shit will never happen again. I ain't no fucking dike. If you want to swing that way, you go right ahead. Call up the white girl and do whatever the fuck you want, but count me the hell out."

The waitress came by as Reina and I stared hard at each other. Reina ordered another Long Island iced tea, and without asking, another Hennessy for me. When the waitress walked away, Reina said, "What makes you think I'm a dike, Angel?"

"What?"

"What, you think I'm a dike because I ate your pussy?"

"Of course."

"And you eating my pussy. What does that make you?"

"I told you that was a fluke. Personally, I think you put some shit in my drink."

"Oh, really? And that's why you got your groove on with two females? That's why you begged me to eat you out more than once? And that's why you forced me to keep my legs open while you tongued and fingered me at the same time? Because I drugged you?"

"Damn right."

"And you being curious had nothing to do with what happened?"

"Hell no, I wasn't curious!" I said, aggravated

over the details she gave me. The waitress came back with our drinks and then walked off. Why did my eyes wander to her ass? I shook my head. *Hell no, I wasn't curious,* I thought. "You put some shit in my drink," I insisted.

Reina nodded her head and looked at me over the rim of her glass as she put it to her lips. "Sorry to burst your bubble, Angel, but I didn't put anything in your drink. And for the record, I'm not a dike either. I like dick. But I wanted you that night." She smiled at me and then swallowed her drink in one gulp.

I didn't say anything. I grabbed my Henny and downed it. I don't know why, but when I put the glass down, my eyes wandered down and lingered on Reina's full breasts. *I'm not a dike,* I thought again. But was I curious?

"You ladies ready to go?"

I turned my head and looked up at Frido through slightly blurred vision. "Where have you been?"

"Business, ma."

"Always business," I said, licking my lips as my eyes went over his lean frame and then stopped at his crotch.

"That's right, ma. Now it's time for pleasure." Frido put out his hand. I took it and stood.

"What about her?" I asked, looking back at Reina.

Frido looked at Reina with an obvious wanting in his eyes. "She's coming with us," he said. Then he looked at me. "You got a problem with that?"

I turned and looked at Reina, who was standing

now. She watched me with intense eyes. I turned back to Frido. "I'm your girl, right?"

Frido leaned forward and drove his tongue into my mouth and slid his hand under my shirt. When he pulled away from me, he smiled that sexy smile. "You know you're my girl." Frido smiled again and then put an arm around my waist. "Take her hand," he said to me. I stared at him for a long second as the smoke-filled air around us became sexually charged. "Take it, ma," he said again. I watched him. He watched me. I turned and looked at Reina. *I'm Frido's girl,* I thought. Then I took her hand, and together we walked out of the club and went back to Frido's.

# 11

I was at home lying in bed, looking up at the ceiling. It was Sunday and I'd been home for the past hour. Luckily my mother wasn't home when Frido dropped me off. Even though she'd bought my lie about going away with Shanice, I wasn't ready to face her. After the wild, uninhibited weekend I'd had, and even though I'd showered, I was a little worried that my mother would have been able to smell how freaky I'd been. Shit, I did things I never thought I'd do, especially after Frido, Reina and I got back to his place. I was still high from all the scandalous shit we did. Food, candle wax, toys, wine; you name it, we probably used it. And we videotaped the whole damn thing and then went at it again while it was playing! Never in a million years did I ever think I'd be involved in a ménage a trois. But there I was.

I stretched out on the bed and looked over at the

clock. It was six o'clock. Normally I'd be on the phone making plans to hang out, but I was exhausted. Besides, I knew that if I called Shanice she'd be asking me a million questions about Frido and what we did. And the last thing I felt like doing was giving her the 411. I thought about calling Ray to let him know that I was back, but I had a feeling that if I did call his cell, he wouldn't answer. That feeling was based not only on the argument we last had at the club before I left with Frido, but primarily on the fact that I didn't have any messages from him waiting for me at home. That was something that never happened. No matter what we disagreed or fought about, Ray always called to check up on me. To know that I was gone for practically four days and he hadn't called really meant that he was pissed and that our friendship was in trouble. Whatever. I know he was trying to be a good friend by trying to convince me not to go with Frido, but he's not my father. Like I told him, I'm a big girl, and I can handle myself. Besides, he didn't know how I felt about Frido, and he didn't know how Frido felt about me. He didn't know that I was Frido's girl and that I was wearing an expensive-ass necklace with the letter F on it. Frido had claimed ownership of me, and I didn't mind one bit. Dealer or not, Frido was my man.

I smiled to myself as my eyes closed. I couldn't wait to see him again. Before he pulled off, he kissed me on my neck and then said he'd see me tomorrow after work. I touched my necklace and then shrugged my shoulders. If Ray wanted to end our friendship because I was involved with Frido then that was his problem. I was happy and that's all that mattered. To hell with what Ray thought. With the crazy weekend on my mind, I fell asleep and didn't wake up until the morning came.

The next day at work was a hard one because I had a lot of catching up to do after being out for two days. But playing catch up was expected, so that was no real big deal. What really made the day hard was that I wanted it to be over so badly that time just seemed to creep by. I tried not to do it, but I must have looked at my watch every five minutes. I couldn't help myself. Frido was coming to get me and I was excited and horny as hell. This was the first time I'd ever tripped over a guy like this. It was just never in my nature to be pressed. But as smooth and as fine as Frido was, and especially after the necklace and the way he worked my body, I couldn't deny it if I wanted to—I was tripping. So when five o'clock finally came, I practically bolted out the door and looked for his car. It was nowhere in sight. I shrugged my shoulders. I should have expected him not to show up on time. I went back inside and decided to do what I should have done; I neatened my desk while I waited for him, thinking that he'd be there in about a half-hour.

When a half-hour passed and Frido still hadn't shown up, I started to get a little upset. Walking back inside of my building, I cursed myself for never getting his number. I usually always got a guy's number. That way if I felt like talking to him, I'd call. It never dawned on me until that moment that I hadn't thought of doing that with Frido. I sat down and flipped through the pages of the *Vibe* magazine that was on my desk. I'd give him another half-hour and that was it. If he didn't show up, then oh well, it would be his loss.

When six o'clock came and went and he still hadn't shown up, I had no choice but to head home. I took slow steps on my way to the subway, hoping that I'd hear him calling out to me, but that never happened. *Maybe he's waiting for me at home,* I thought, trying not to get pissed. When I got home and I didn't see his car anywhere, I shook my head. *Where the fuck is he? I* took one last look up and down the block before I walked through my front door. I was so pissed that he wasn't there; I never even bothered to call Shanice like I had planned on doing. For a split second I thought about calling Ray, but like the day before, there was no message waiting from him, so I didn't even bother to waste my time.

My sleep that night was a restless one filled with questions.

*Why didn't he show up?*

*Why didn't he at least fucking call me, or come by?*

*Why didn't I ever ask for his cell number?*

*Why am I tripping?*

*And again, why didn't he call?*

Over and over the questions came and went. I was so pissed off and disappointed that I didn't get to see him that I was up half the night. I think it was somewhere around two-thirty in the morning when I finally fell asleep. I woke up the next morning, tired but with a new attitude. Maybe he'd gotten involved in some shit that he had to handle. Yeah, I thought, he was handling some business. That's why he couldn't get to me. I went to work with a smile on my face and my spirits high. I was confident that Frido was gonna be waiting for me when I got out of work.

I was feeling so good that I called Shanice and gave her all the details about my weekend with Frido. Of course I didn't mention Reina, but I did talk about the camcorder.

"Girl, you're making me hot. You know that, right?" Shanice said, laughing.

I laughed with her. "Shit, I'm making myself hot just thinking about it again. Frido can fuck, Shanice."

"Mmm. Can I get some?"

"Hell, no!" I said, exploding with laughter. "Frido's dick is all mine."

Shanice chuckled. "You gotta come over and show me that necklace."

I smiled. "I will."

"When? Today?"

"I can't today. Frido's coming to pick me up," I said hoping that he'd be there.

"Going to get your freak on again, huh?"

"You know it."

"Are we going away again?"

I laughed. "No. No trip this time. I can't afford to miss any more days."

"Shit, keep giving Frido some and you'll be able to. He's already given you the necklace."

"Damn right."

Shanice and I laughed and then I looked at the clock. It was a little after three o'clock. "Hey, let me get off this phone before someone says something. I'll call you when I get home."

"Okay. Go on and get yours. Shit, get some for me too."

I laughed and shook my head. "Please, you get enough on your own already."

"You ain't lyin'!"

"Alright, chica, let me get out of here."

"Hey, before you go, have you spoken to Ray?"

"No. Not since I left you guys at the club."

"You mean not since you dissed us?" Shanice said with a laugh.

I sucked my teeth. "Whatever. You know it wasn't like that."

"Yeah, yeah. Shit, if I had a chico as fine as Frido waiting on me, I would have dissed your ass too." Shanice laughed again and I joined her.

"So have you talked to him?" I asked.

"No. He was so pissed after you left with Frido that he went home. I haven't seen him since then."

"Damn. Really?"

"Yeah. He thinks Frido's gonna bring you nothing but trouble."

"Whatever," I said, rolling my eyes.

"You know he's just looking out for you, right?"

"Yeah, I know, but I ain't a little girl. I can take care of myself. Besides, I know what kind of drama I can run into by being with someone like Frido. I'm not stupid."

"He just doesn't want to see you get hurt, that's all."

"Yeah, well I ain't gonna be hurt. That nigga gave me a diamond necklace, Shanice. And he said I was the type of female to make him fall in love."

"How do you know that wasn't just a line?"

"Because I looked at his eyes. He wasn't lying. Frido's all about me, and I know he won't let anything happen to me. If Ray don't like my decision, then fuck him. It's my fucking life."

"So you're willing to give up your friendship with him?"

"I gotta live my life, Shanice. If Ray's part of it, that's cool. If not, oh well. I'll still be getting mine."

"I hear that."

"Alright, girl, I gotta go. My boss is coming."

"Call me later with details," Shanice said.

"I will. Bye."

I hung up the phone and smiled. I missed talking to my girl. Ever since I hooked up with Frido, I really had been unintentionally neglecting her. But that happens when you're in a relationship, and I know she understood that.

Talking to her really made me miss Ray, though. I know I said that I didn't give a damn if he and I stayed friends or not, but the truth was I did. Ray was like the big brother I never had. I could always count on him to be there whenever I needed him. I know he was pissed about me being with Frido, but I never thought he'd stop talking to me over it. I picked up the phone and dialed his cell. Maybe he wasn't as mad as I thought. Maybe he'd been busy. Shit, as unattractive as he was, maybe he found love, too.

"Hello?"

"What's up, Ray?" I said, smiling. It was nice hearing his voice.

" 'Sup," he said with little excitement.

Ignoring his cold tone, I said, "I guess you forgot my number, huh?"

A few seconds of silence took over the conversation and then in a deadpan voice, Ray said, "Why are you calling me, Angel?"

"What do you mean why am I calling? Don't we always call each other?"

"You still seeing that nigga Frido?"

I pursed my lips. "Yeah."

"Then we got nothing to talk about."

*Click.*

I looked at the receiver in my hand. *Did he really just hang up on me?* "Stupid ass," I said, putting the receiver down. *To hell with Ray.* If that's the way he wanted to be then fine. Like I told Shanice, I'd still get mine. Just as soon as Frido showed up. Shit. I hoped he did.

When five o'clock came, like the day before, I went outside hoping to see him double-parked. But once again, I was disappointed; he wasn't there. I waited until six again before going home. I didn't know whether I should have been pissed or worried, so I was a little of both. *What if something happened to him?* I asked myself that question that night as I lay in bed.

The next day when again he didn't show, I took a walk over to the basketball courts on West Fourth Street. Frido wasn't there, so I asked a few of the guys there if they knew where he was, or if something had happened to him. Had the game caught up to him? Nobody knew where he was, but one answer they all had in common was that Frido was alive and still running things.

No longer worried, I was straight pissed.

*Where the fuck is he?* I asked myself that question over and over for the rest of the week and the entire weekend. Shanice didn't realize what I was doing, but as we went out club hopping, without Ray and Stevie, I was on a straight manhunt. Barely dancing, barely drinking, I searched high and low in whatever club we went to, hoping to see Frido. But no matter where we went, Frido was never there. I tried not to stress over his disappearance, but it was hard not to. After all of the shit we did together, this was the last thing I was expecting. As each day passed, I got more and more pissed off. And eventually I started to wonder if he'd been playing me this whole time.

*Was the weekend just part of the game?*

*Did the necklace mean anything?*

Those were the new questions I asked myself as the next week approached. Monday, Tuesday; Wednesday through Friday; there was absolutely no fucking sign or trace of Frido anywhere. If I had known how to get to his place, I would have tried to go there. But I was asleep the whole way to and from his condo, so I had no clue as to where he lived.

Damn.

This shit was really fucking with me. So bad, in fact, that my mood changed and I started to become a real bitch to everyone around me. I couldn't help it, though. I was on a cloud after my weekend with Frido. I felt special. Now I was just feeling used and I was depressed. So depressed that I just stopped going out. Normally, Ray would be there to cheer me up, but since he and I weren't speaking, I leaned on Shanice. She tried her best to lift my spirits, but no matter what she tried, nothing worked. I had it bad, just like Usher said. Every now and then I thought about taking off the necklace, but I never did. A small part of me still held onto the hope that I'd see Frido again, and if that happened, I didn't want to be without it. But after the second week passed, I started to really think there was no point to keeping it on.

And then I saw Frido.

It was during my lunch hour and I was on my way to the pizzeria around the corner to get a slice when I saw him. Windows down, salsa blasting, shades on, he was driving in the opposite direction. My mouth practically dropped as I turned and followed his car. He must not have seen me walking, because he didn't slow down. I watched his car until it disappeared, making a right turn. He was heading in the same direction as the basketball courts. Forgetting all about the pizza, I caught a cab and went to find out where the hell he'd been.

When I got to the courts, I took a deep breath in an effort to calm myself before stepping out of the cab. I didn't know what kind of explanations he was gonna give, but they had better be good. I paid the cab driver, stepped out and walked onto the court. Frido's back was facing me as he talked to a couple of guys. "Frido," I called out as I walked up to him. He didn't answer me, so I called his name again. "Frido."

He turned around. "What's going on, ma?"

I looked at him strangely. "What's going on? Why don't you tell me? Where the fuck have you been for the past two weeks?" My heart started beating heavily. "How come I haven't heard from you?"

"I been busy," Frido said bluntly. I waited for a second to see if he'd have anything else to add. When he didn't say anything, I opened my mouth.

"Yo, is that the mami from the video?" one of the guys behind Frido asked before I could speak.

"Yeah, that's her," another guy, this one black, said with a smile.

The first guy, a tall Puerto Rican, put a closed fist to his mouth. "Yooo! Damn, mami, you got a fat ass!"

*Video? I* looked at the guys, who were both staring at me like I was a plate of rice and beans. "Excuse me?" I said. "What video?"

Both guys chuckled and then the black guy said to Frido, "No wonder you was MIA that weekend. I woulda been smashin' that too." He turned back to me. "Yo, ma, I got a cam too. How about we go back to my crib?" Both guys and Frido burst out laughing.

I looked at Frido. "What are they talking about?" I already knew the answer to the question, but I prayed that he would give me another. Frido stared at me but didn't say anything while the guys behind him laughed and looked me up and down. "What the fuck are they talking about, Frido? Did you show them that video?" As I said that, the two guys broke out laughing again.

"Yo, ma," the Puerto Rican said. "Can I hit that?"

"You asshole!" I yelled, glaring at Frido. "You fucking asshole! How the fuck could you do that shit to me? I can't believe you showed these motherfuckers that video!"

"Not just us, mami," the black guy said.

I looked at him. "Fuck you!" I spat.

The black guy shrugged his shoulders. "A'ight." He and his friend laughed and gave each other pounds.

I looked at Frido through slit eyes. I was boiling with anger and embarrassment. I couldn't believe he had disrespected me like that. "I thought I was supposed to be your fucking girl, maricon. I thought you said you were falling in love. You gave me this fucking necklace!" I grabbed the F pendant and squeezed it in my hands. "What the fuck was all this about? How could you disrespect me like that?" My eyes welled with tears as Frido raised an eyebrow and looked at me like I was crazy.

"Chill, ma," he said, putting a hand up. "You disrespecting me right now."

"I don't give a fuck!" I snapped. "You fucking disrespected me!"

"Who the hell are you?" a female voice said from behind me.

I turned around to see who the voice belonged to. It was another Latina with curly brown hair down to her shoulders. I took a second to size her up. She was wearing an army green tank top with matching army green khakis, and black, strappy sandals. "I hope you're not talking to my man like that, bitch!" she said, coming toward me. *Her man?* I was about to go off on her when something that I hadn't noticed before caught my eye and made me catch my breath. Around her neck was the very same necklace I had on. *What the—?*

"I can't believe you played me like that," I said, taking off my necklace and throwing it at him.

Frido easily caught it and stuffed it into his pocket. "Thanks, ma. I can give this to someone else now."

"Asshole!"

He looked at me and shrugged his shoulders. "You're old news, ma," he said with a cocky-ass smirk.

I squinted my eyes. "Old news?"

"Yeah, bitch," the female behind me said. "Old news. Frido don't want your tired ass."

I spun around. "Why don't you mind your own fucking business, bitch?" I snapped at her. She was standing just a few inches away from me.

"Frido is my fucking business," she spat back at me. "So why don't you leave before you get hurt?"

"Hurt by who? Your ass?"

Pointing her index finger at my face, the bitch said, "Bitch, you don't know who you're fucking with. I ain't the one. I will beat your ass right where you stand."

"Get your finger outta my face, bitch!" I snapped.

"Make me!"

I glared at the bitch for a few long seconds, my hands itching to lay into her. I couldn't believe this shit was happening. I couldn't believe I was so stupid and had fallen for all of Frido's shit. I believed everything that motherfucker told me, and now here I was looking like a fool while this bitch, wearing the same necklace as me, called Frido her man and disrespected my ass. I was boiling inside with so much anger that I didn't even realize my arm had swung out until I punched the bitch in her face.

"You bitch!" she screamed. Even though I'd hit her with a solid punch, she rebounded quickly, lunged toward me, and hit me in my jaw. Although it hurt like hell, I reached out and grabbed her by her hair.

"I'm gonna kill you, bitch!" I yelled, pulling her hair with one hand and slapping her with the other. Not to be outdone, she grabbed a handful of my hair, too, and hit me on the back of my head. We fell to the ground, clawing, slapping, punching and pulling. She was a much tougher fight than I thought she'd be. A few times I cried out from the blows and scratches she delivered. Of course I made sure she cried out too.

We were two cats battling on the concrete while everyone around us cheered and carried on. For every piece of flesh that my nails managed to scrape away from her face, the bitch's nails did the same. I pulled hair; she pulled hair. I punched; she punched. I kicked; she kicked. I don't know what was fueling her attack, but I know for me, each blow represented a piece of my dignity that Frido had taken away from me. He'd put that tape out there for who knows how many people to see. Piece of shit. I fought harder as my rage increased. The bitch and I went at it until people started pulling us apart.

"Let me go!" I yelled, trying to push someone's arms from around me.

"I'm gonna kill you, bitch!" the bitch screamed. I was still struggling to get loose when she broke free from the hands around her, rushed me, and hit me viciously in my mouth.

"Oh, shit!" I heard someone yell out as blood flooded from my busted lip. The bitch would have hit me again, but she was pulled away before she could. I was hurting from her last blow, but I still fought to get loose. I didn't want the bitch to get the last hit. I tried as hard as I could to get free, but I couldn't. Over and over the bitch and I demanded to be set free.

"Chill out!" the person holding me yelled.

"Fuck you and let me go!"

This happened for another couple of seconds until gunshots rang out in the air. People scattered like ants all around me, while others dropped to the ground and covered their heads. Whoever had been holding on to me had let me go and was gone with everyone else. I was so busy struggling that I had no idea how weak I was. With no one to hold me, I fell to the ground. I lay there dazed and bleeding. My head hurt from the blows the bitch had given me and my scalp hurt where my hair had been yanked.

"You should have bounced, ma," Frido said, standing over me. "Now you got that pretty face all fucked up."

I lifted my head slowly and looked up at him through blurred vision. "Why?" I asked in a whisper.

Frido gave me the smile that had gotten me hooked. It was ugly as hell now. "You were just a part of the game, ma. Now this part of the game's over."

"Fuck you," I spat as tears fell from my eyes.

Frido smiled again. "Nah, ma. I had enough." As sirens sang out in the distance, Frido chuckled and then walked away.

I wanted to get up and chase him down and give him what I gave the bitch, but I was too hurt to move. While people rolled out before the cops came, I laid my head down on the ground and cried. I'd been played to the tenth degree.

# 12

My mother was hysterical when she came to pick me up from the hospital where the cops had taken me. I didn't blame her, because I looked like shit. I had stitches in my lip, stitches above my eye, and stitches in my scalp. Along with my lip, my right eye was swollen, and because my eyeball had been scratched, I had a patch over it. I had scratches on my face and neck and my side and arms were bruised. Somehow my button nose came through untouched.

My mother hounded me for all kinds of details, but I wouldn't give her anything more than the bare minimum: I had a disagreement with the bitch and we fought. Eventually she realized that I wasn't in the mood to talk and she left me alone. When we got home, Shanice and Stevie were sitting outside on my doorstep. Word about the fight had gotten around. When Shanice saw me, her eyes opened wide and she broke out in tears. Stevie looked at me. His eyes were black and his hands balled into tight fists. "You alright?" he asked.

I nodded. "Yeah, I'm cool."

"I don't believe in hitting chicks, but I promise, I'm gonna fuck that bitch up."

I stared at Stevie and saw the dead seriousness in his eyes. I shook my head. "Don't worry about it," I said. "It's done."

Stevie scowled. His golden skin was turning red with anger. "I ain't letting her get away with this shit."

"I said it's done, Stevie." I stared hard at him. He was breathing heavily and his nostrils were flared. "It's done," I said one more time.

Stevie watched me for a couple of seconds and then his hands opened up and his shoulders slumped. "Come here," he said, grabbing my arms and pulling me into him. Rubbing my back, he asked, "You sure you alright?"

"Yeah, I'm fine."

"Alright. You know I still wanna get with you, right?" Stevie chuckled.

I pushed away from him and punched him playfully in his arm and laughed. We all went inside and after I called my job and lied and said I was in a car accident during lunch, Stevie and Shanice sat with me while my mother fixed me some food that I knew I wasn't gonna be able to eat. Stevie sat on the floor while Shanice sat beside me on my bed and held onto my hand. She didn't say much. I think my looks really freaked her out. They didn't ask me for any details about the fight, but I gave them anyway. I changed the story around a little, though.

Told them that the bitch and I were fighting over Frido. I never mentioned the things Frido did to me. I was sure that sooner or later they'd find out about the video, and that shit really hurt me. It was like being raped for everyone to see. I lay my head on Shanice's shoulder and cried silently.

Stevie and Shanice stayed for a little over an hour and then left so that I could get some rest. I hugged them and thanked them for being there for me. Stevie kissed me on my forehead and before he left, he said something that surprised the hell out of me. He leaned close to my ear and whispered, "I love you, Angel." I looked at him. He never called me Angel. We stared at each other, and as unbelievable as it was, there was definitely a spark.

When they left, my mother came in my room and lay on the bed with me. She didn't ask me any questions. She just held onto me until I fell asleep. Some time in the middle of the night I was awakened by a tapping sound. I painfully lifted my head and looked to the window. I was two stories up and if there was a tapping at my window, that meant that someone was throwing rocks at it. There was only one person who did that. I smiled and got out of bed slowly and made my way downstairs. When I opened the door, Ray looked at me and sighed. "Jesus, ma," he whispered. I didn't say anything. After making sure the front door was unlocked, I stepped outside, closed the door, and we sat down on my front steps. We didn't speak for a few minutes. We just sat and listened to the nighttime sounds of the borough.

"How you feeling?" Ray finally asked me after a while.

I shrugged my shoulders. "I'm alright."

"Yeah, I know you a'ight. Now tell me the truth."

I exhaled. "I feel like shit," I said honestly. "My head hurts, my mouth hurts, and my eye hurts."

"Tell me that you fucked her up as bad as she got you."

I nodded my head. "Yeah, I did."

"A'ight."

We got silent again. It was a little awkward. That was the first time we'd gone so long without speaking. I listened to the sounds of sirens in the distance and the zooming of motorcycles as they flew down the street. Looking down at my bare feet, I said, "So why didn't you come with Stevie and Shanice?"

Ray didn't answer right away. He just stared out at the street. Finally, he said, "I felt too guilty to come."

I looked at him. "Guilty? Why?"

"I should've been there for you. If I had been there then this shit wouldn't have happened to you."

I smiled. "Don't blame yourself," I said softly. "I should've listened to you from the start. You were right about Frido hurting me."

"Did he hit you, too?"

"No."

"Oh, okay."

"But he did worse."

"What do you mean?"

I took a deep breath and held it as I thought again about how I allowed myself to be disrespected. When I exhaled slowly, teardrops leaked from my eyes. "You're gonna find out about it sooner or later," I said.

"Find out about what?"

I frowned and leaned my head against Ray's shoulder. And then I told him all about my weekend and what had happened afterwards. When I finished my story, Ray eased me off of him and stood up. Looking out to the street, he said, "That nigga's a dead man."

I looked up at him. "Don't worry about it, Ray," I said, not liking the change in his body language or the anger in his voice.

"'Don't worry about it'?" he asked, looking down at me. "The nigga's putting that video out there for ma'fucka's to see, and you say don't worry about it?"

"It's already out there," I said solemnly. "There's not much that I can do." Ray clenched his fists at his side. Even though it was dark, I could still see his muscles tensing. "What's done is done. I got played. It's as simple as that."

"Nah, it ain't that simple, Angel," Ray said. "It ain't that fucking simple at all. That ma'fucka's gonna pay for this. He's gonna pay for everything that's happened to you."

I stood and grabbed his arm. "Relax, Ray. You're scaring me."

"You ain't gotta be scared," he said, pulling his arm free. "Frido's the one who got shit to be scared about."

I grabbed his arm again. "Ray, Frido's dangerous. He don't give a fuck about anyone or anything but himself. Don't go looking for trouble."

Pulling free, Ray said, "I don't give a fuck how dangerous that nigga is, Angel. He's fucking dead."

"Dead how, Ray? Frido is strapped and he won't hesitate to pull that trigger."

"He could pull his trigger all he wants!" Ray said loudly. "Believe me, I'll be pulling mine."

"Pulling yours?" I looked at Ray intensely. "What are you talking about?" I was really scared now. Ray didn't answer me. "What the fuck are you talking about, Raymond?" I asked again.

Ray shook his head. "I gotta go," he said.

I grabbed his arm. "Go? Where are you going? Ray, what did you mean, you'll be pulling yours?" Ray pulled away from me again.

"I gotta go, Angel!"

"Go where?" I yelled. "Where the fuck are you going? Answer me, goddamn it!"

"I'm going to handle Frido," Ray said.

"Handle him how?"

"With this," Ray said, pulling a .45 from his waistline.

I looked at the gun in his hand. "Where did you get that, Ray?"

"I've had it. I bought this shit after my brother was killed."

*Jesus.* I shook my head. "Give me the gun, Ray," I pleaded.

"Hell, no!"

"Don't do this, Ray. Please! Give me the fucking gun!"

"That ma'fucka's gonna pay, Angel."

"Please, Ray!" As I yelled out, my front door opened and my mother stepped out.

"What's going on out here? Angel, why are you out here? Ray. Oh my God! Ray, what are you doing with that gun?"

"Ray, please!" I pleaded again. "Don't do this."

Ray looked from my mother to me. He was not the Ray I knew. "I gotta go, ma."

I grabbed his arm but he pulled away again. "Ray!" I yelled as he turned and headed down the block. I looked at my mother. Her mouth was hanging open as she watched Ray running away. "Mom!" I yelled. I turned and watched Ray disappear. "Ray!"

# 13

I rushed upstairs and called Stevie and told him what had happened. I was panicking so bad that I had to repeat myself a couple of times. I couldn't believe this was happening. I didn't think things could get any worse than they had already been. Ray had a gun. Jesus! I called Shanice afterward and told her about Ray. Within twenty minutes she was at my house. My mother called Ray's house and spoke to his mother and told her what happened. When she was done, I took the phone and dialed Ray's cell over and over, but he never answered. Damn it! Where the fuck was he? I paced around my house frantically. I would have been out looking for him, but my mother wasn't having it, so I had no choice but to wait for word from Stevie, who was out looking everywhere and anywhere he could for Ray. He had a gun. And he'd had it since his brother was killed. Damn. I never knew.

It was almost five in the morning before Stevie finally showed up at my house. I'd been standing outside with Shanice. I probably would have been pulling my hair out, but my scalp was too damned tender, so I bit my nails instead. Stevie looked at me and shook his head. "I couldn't find him anywhere."

"What do you mean you couldn't find him?" I yelled. "How hard did you fucking look?"

"Angel, I went to every spot I could think of. And then I went to every spot I couldn't think of."

"Shit, Stevie, look some more. He has a fucking gun."

"I know, Angel, but damn, this is fucking New York City."

"So? You gotta find him."

"I know," Stevie said, his voice softening. "But I don't know where else to look."

"Damn!" I folded my arms across my chest. This was the worst.

"What about his old hangout spot over in Queens?" Shanice asked.

"I went there, too, but he wasn't anywhere around. I didn't really expect him to be there, anyway. For real, the only place Ray'll be is wherever that nigga Frido is. Angel, where did Frido hang out at?"

I shrugged. "I don't know. The only place he really goes to that I know of is the basketball courts."

"You don't remember where he lives?" Shanice asked.

"No."

"Damn," Stevie said. "I don't know what to do then."

"Try his cell again," Shanice suggested.

I sucked my teeth. "What's the use? I've called his phone about a thousand times already and he hasn't answered. He's not gonna answer if I call again."

"What about his mom?"

"She hasn't heard from him either," I said.

"Damn," Shanice whispered. The rest of the day crept by with the same result: no one could find Ray. After trying everything we could, which included calling hospitals and police stations, Stevie and Shanice went home to get some rest.

As for me, I was going on my second sleepless night. I just couldn't relax. I was in my house stressing over Ray's disappearance. *Where the fuck could he be? Is he dead already? Did he kill Frido?* I was ragged with worry. My mother tried to console me, hoping that I'd get some rest, but nothing she did or said could bring me any comfort. Eventually she gave up and went to bed. I paced back and forth around my room, hoping to hear a tapping at my window, but that never happened. I called Ray's cell over and over, but he never answered. *Please, God, let Ray be alright.*

I was sitting on my bed, flipping aimlessly through the channels on my TV when the phone rang. I grabbed it and hit the talk button. "Hello?"

"Angel." It was Ray. I looked at the clock; it was twelve-thirty in the morning.

"Ray, where the fuck are you? Are you alright?"

"Yeah, I'm cool."

"Please tell me you didn't kill Frido."

"Nah."

I sighed. "Good."

"But I'm about to."

I caught my breath. "What?"

"I'm at the basketball court. Frido's here too."

"Ray," I said, getting out of bed. "Don't do anything stupid, alright?"

"I won't."

"Good. Just come over to my house."

"After I shoot this ma'fucka, I will."

I frowned. "I thought you weren't gonna do anything stupid, Ray."

"Killing Frido isn't stupid, Angel. He's a fucking waste of existence. A bitch-ass drug dealer who doesn't deserve to breathe."

"That's not for you to decide, Ray."

"It is for me to decide. It was for me to decide the day the drug game took my little brother away from me. Indirectly, Frido's responsible for Rashaad's death. And he's responsible for what happened to you. Now he's gotta pay. His life for my brother's life. His life for your dignity. I'm gonna kill that ma'fucka."

*Click.*

"Ray?" I called out. "Ray, are you there?" My response was a dial tone. "Damn."

He was at the courts.

He was gonna kill Frido.

I moved as fast as I could to put my sneakers on. I thought about calling Stevie and Shanice but decided against it. I figured the more people around to cause confusion the more likely something bad would happen. After putting on my New York Giants cap and grabbing some money to buy tokens for the train, I left my house. I wasn't even trying to tell my mother that I was out to try to prevent a tragedy.

# 14

I had luck on my side because the train was just arriving when I stepped onto the platform. Thankfully, the train was practically empty, so I didn't have to deal with anyone staring at me. I tried to be as calm as I could, but it was hard. My palms were wet and cold with nervousness. Damn. All this shit was my fault. I closed my eyes and said a silent prayer to keep Ray from being hurt or pulling that trigger. I didn't want him to end up dead or on lockdown. Because I hadn't gotten any sleep, I had to fight with my body to stay awake. I didn't know what I was going to do or find when I got there, but I needed to be as alert as I could.

After switching trains a couple times, I finally made it into the city, and as fast as my sore and tired body could, I made my way to the courts. It was now nearing one in the morning but the humidity was still high. My heart beat harder with every step I took as I got closer. My mouth became dryer, my hands sweatier, my breathing quicker. I was a block away when I heard a gunshot and people yelling out.

Shit.

*Please don't let that be coming from the courts,* I thought. I quickened my step and rushed as fast as I could to the basketball courts. I met what I feared the most when I got there. Some people scattered around, while others stood and watched in silence. Frido stood above Ray in the middle of the lighted courts with his .45 pointed down at Ray's head. I looked at Ray and gasped. Blood was oozing slowly from his chest, and his gun lay off to his side. For a second I couldn't move. I just stood frozen, thinking only two things: Ray was about to die, and it was gonna be my fault. I stood that way for a few more seconds and then opened my mouth. I didn't know what I was going to say until "No!" came flying out. "Frido, don't!"

As I walked toward them, Frido looked up at me. "What's up, ma?" he said with a sinister smile. "You're not looking so good."

I was about to curse him out, but I caught myself and bit down on my tongue. "Frido, put the gun down!"

Frido shook his head. "Sorry, ma, but your boy came and paid me the ultimate disrespect by trying to throw down. Then he was stupid enough to try to shoot my ass. My gun ain't going down until it's smoking and this nigga's brains are spread on the court for decoration."

"Please, Frido," I said, taking slow, cautious steps toward them. I was about ten feet from them now. My knees were shaking as my heart skipped beats. "Please, Frido," I begged again. "Don't do this! You don't have to do this."

"Go . . . away . . . Angel!" Ray yelled out. "This matfucka . . ." he paused and coughed painfully a few times. "This . . . ma'fucka's . . . mine."

Was he crazy? He was seconds away from being another sad statistic and he was still talking big shit. I looked at him, ready to ask him what his problem was, and that's when I saw something that broke my heart. For all of his big talk, Ray was looking at me with wide, frightened eyes. I exhaled softly and then looked at Frido. "Please, Frido," I begged once again. "Please don't do this shit. Killing him's not gonna prove a fucking thing. Everyone knows who you are and gives you the fucking respect you demand. Ray's my friend and he was just pissed about what happened to me."

"I don't give a shit how pissed off this nigga was," Frido yelled. "He came after the wrong motherfucker. I'm Frido, bitch!" he yelled, kicking Ray in his midsection. "You don't fuck with me. Nobody fucks with me! Say good-bye to this nigga, ma. His time's up."

I took a few more steps forward. "No!" I screamed out as tears exploded from my eyes. "God dammit, you pussy, leave him alone!"

Frido shook his head. "Pussy? You know what, bitch? I'm tired of your fucking mouth." Frido raised his arm and pointed his gun at me. "Maybe I should shut you up right here and now."

I took a deep breath and held it in as Frido's arm tensed up. I was going to die. Not Ray. I could practically feel his finger contracting to pull the trigger. But before that could happen, Ray screamed, "Angeeeeel!" As he called out my name, he swung out with his foot and kicked Frido's legs from underneath him, sending him crashing to the ground. As Frido's back hit the concrete, I watched stunned as his .45 flew out of his hands and skidded toward me, coming to a stop against the side of my sneaker. I didn't move at first. I just stared at the gun. Ray had saved my life.

"You punk-ass motherfucker!" Frido hollered out. I looked up. He was punching Ray in his face and midsection over and over while Ray struggled unsuccessfully to get him off. "I'm gonna kill you, bitch!" Frido yelled, his attack growing fiercer.

"Ray!" I yelled. Then I looked down at Frido's gun and stared at it. It demanded my attention.

"Angel!" I heard Ray call out.

I looked up. Frido was relentless with his intent to kill Ray. He was now banging his head over and over on the ground.

The .45 whispered out to me again.

I looked down.

Then up.

Then down again.

And then I picked up the gun.

I don't remember ever pulling the trigger. I just remember hearing a loud bang, Frido falling, people screaming, and then eventually hands around me and the gun being pulled away. "Ray!" I yelled out as police officers wrestled me down to the ground and slapped handcuffs on my wrists. "Ray!" I yelled again as they dragged me away and shoved me into the back of their car. "Just let me see Ray!" I yelled, crying hysterically. "Just let me see Ray!" But I never got the chance as they drove off.

# Epilogue

**R**ay survived the gunshot to his chest, while Frido died instantly from one to his head. I'm not a pro with a gun. I just got lucky. It wasn't my intent to kill Frido. I just wanted to save Ray's life. But I'm not gonna front. After what I'd been through I was glad that my first and only time shooting a gun had been so on point.

If Ray hadn't kicked Frido's legs from underneath him, I wouldn't have been around to enjoy the life I was currently living. Before all of this shit, life for me was just about partying and living free. But when you have shit happen to you like what I had, it makes you stop and reevaluate the way you're living.

One major change that happened was that I fell in love. And you'd never guess who I fell in love with. Stevie. Believe me, falling in love with Stevie was the last thing I ever expected to do. When we all used to go out, he was so busy being a dog that even though I thought he was cute, I never bothered to see past his ways. But after Frido's death, Stevie changed big time. Instead of hanging out and chasing ass, he started to come by my place. For a while all we ever did was chill at my house, or go to the movies sometimes. We became really good friends and eventually one thing led to another and we ended up having sex.

That wouldn't have been a big deal except that after the first time we did it, he held me in his arms and admitted to me that he'd always been in love with me. He said that when he thought of settling down, it was with me. That blew me away, and at first I was a little skeptical about him saying that. After all, Frido had said the same kind of thing to me.

It didn't take long to see that Stevie was serious about his feelings, though, and after a few weeks of beating around the bush, we made it official and started dating. A few months after that, I found out I was pregnant. When I gave Stevie the news he did something that blew me away—he proposed. Without even thinking, I said yes. Right now Stevie's at school finishing up his degree in business. He's already got a job lined up in Virginia. We don't have a date set yet. It's weird, but being with Stevie has really made me happy. Ray broke out laughing when I told him about hooking up with Stevie. He said he had a feeling that we'd hook up eventually. I don't know where the hell he got that idea. It wasn't like I was ever sending out any signals.

My relationship with Ray's as tight as ever. I can't tell you how much I apologized to him for everything that happened. Being the sweetheart that he was, Ray shrugged his shoulders and acted like what he did was no big deal. But we all know it was. I wish he could be around to hang out with Stevie and me. Unfortunately, he'd been locked up for a year for gun possession. I thought I was gonna have to go to jail too, for killing Frido, but charges were never filed against me because what I did was considered a justifiable homicide, since I saved Ray's life. The cops might not have said anything, but I know they weren't unhappy to see Frido gone for good.

I might not be locked up, but I still go to the prison and visit Ray every week. Ray's my family, and I make sure he knows that. We're gonna throw him a big-ass party when he gets out. Hopefully Shanice will be able to make it. She moved to Florida to be with some Dominican guy she met at a club. I speak to her every week, too. She sounds happy, and that makes me happy. I miss my girl, though. I don't know if I could ever be as close again to another female as I was with her.

But you never know. Like I said, my life's different now. I'm different. The crowd I hang around with is different. I guess I have Frido to thank for that. He may have played me, but at least I didn't lose the game.